I0729301

The Courageous Adventurer

Timothy Patrick Means
Book Two
Pirates Born of Iron & Blood

Mad Dog Publications

To the readers who love adventure and the spirit of living a pirate's life. To the ladies who imagine a handsome pirate captain who could steal more than treasure. We all dream of living without restrictions or laws, but a pirate's life was hazardous, and you could find yourself hanging at the end of a rope.

INTRODUCTION

IN JUNE, IN THE YEAR of our Lord 1712, Thomas Banish, a boatswain mate, sailed aboard the HMS *Defiance*. As his ship rounded the Antilles, it was battered by a tropical hurricane and was struck by a rogue wave, causing him to be thrown overboard into the turbulent sea. Nonetheless, a lifeboat broke loose to his good fortune, and he could crawl aboard to ride out the rest of the storm inside the small craft. Four days later, he washed up on a deserted island. Now marooned out in the middle of the Pacific, he waited weeks for his rescue, but none ever came. He only had the chance to take the small boat back out to the shark-infested waters where, hopefully, he would be rescued by a passing ship bound for a safe port.

After gathering some supplies of coconuts and bananas, Thomas rowed past the reef, using parts of downed palm trees that he had chiseled into a paddle and wedges of coral as a blade.

During his days at sea he was exposed to the elements. The tropical sun baked his skin during the day and night; he practically froze from having no blanket to keep himself warm. Soon the coconuts and bananas he had collected were running out. He tried to catch fish using a fishing line and a hook on his person, but his attempts were unfruitful without suitable bait.

The long days floating atop the choppy waves allowed him time to reflect upon his life and all his wrong choices, leaving him feeling destitute. He could do nothing but wait for the angel of death to relieve him of his misery.

His thirst was unbearable, and he often imagined cupping his hands into the salty blue water to relieve his thirst. Still, he knew the results of such an action and the horrifying death that would soon follow. During his time as a sailor he had experienced what it means to be aboard a sinking ship—having been cast adrift in a small lifeboat, struggling to survive with other shipmates who had succumbed to the temptation of drinking the salty mixture. The madness overtook them after they drank their fill; they crawled out of the boat to disappear forever beneath the waves.

One day, in his delusional state, something happened. Thomas was sure he was dreaming. He fantasized about being rescued by Spanish-speaking fishermen. In and out of a conscious state, he imagined himself taken to a Spanish harbor. This dream felt surreal, even being bashed upon his head, and the echoes of laughter from the coward striking him in his face seemed genuine.

Sometime later he awoke inside a dark and musky dungeon. As he focused on his surroundings, he was suddenly aware of the throbbing pain in his head. He discovered a big bump at the back of his skull and blood that coated his blonde curly hair. *What have I done to deserve this*? he asked himself.

One day while overhearing the guards talking among themselves, he realized that he was imprisoned in the Spanish port named Trinidad. It didn't take long to comprehend why he received the punitive treatment since they were at war with the British. The truth was he had survived death to end up a prisoner of the Spanish who rescued him.

Each day in this horrid place left him saddened to know he would die within its walls. Giving up any hope for freedom, he accepted his fate. That is until one day when something unexpected happened, and he had his first encounter with a notorious "Iron Born Pirate." He sat alone in the darkness pondering his fate with no options left.

In an attempt to save his life, Thomas was granted

his freedom from the hellish prison. However, both of them were on the run for their lives. In the British Navy, harboring a pirate was a capital offense. The penalty would be death by hanging. The pirate with him would fare far worst. The only option would be to search for his pirate brothers, but he could pay with his life at the end of a saber in their clutches, being the enemy.

All these thoughts invaded his mind as he sailed out to the open sea to an unknown destination. Inside the boat with him, the young pirate remained unconscious, unable to comprehend the dangers they faced from a world out to destroy the existence of all Iron Born Pirates.

CHAPTER 1

THE IRON BORN CARELESSLY MADE enemies of other pirates sailing the Caribbean waters by their guile and cunning practices. Months had passed, and the Iron Born Pirate crew had many encounters with merchants and pirates alike; the result was plunder and booty for all sailing under the black flag. Still, one truth rang out: The continuous damage to the wooden hulls and superstructure was a constant nuisance that required repairs to be completed in haste. Redbone left few options in choosing a suitable harbor to stay in while the repairs were completed on his two ships.

Now the *Hell's Fury* was safely anchored in a shallow inlet. It had been a while since the crew members had been entertained. As they invaded the small township, soon rum was overflowing, and the women were never lonely of a partner for the night. However, there was never a shortage of eager volunteers wanting to join the brotherhood rather than facing death at the end of a sword and choosing St. Kitts as his resting spot.

As the days slowly passed, the repairs on the two ships began in earnest. The fact that both men and ships rust in the harbor if they remain too long made Redbone anxious to get underway. Besides this, it was a fact they were sitting ducks. Throughout Spanish Maine, a price was offered to capture all Iron Born Pirates. Keeping a wary eye on the people of St. Kitts, Redbone, always suspicious, watched for any sign of danger.

One day, as days usually began, there was a roll call of all buccaneers. Currently numbering close to a hundred and fifty men, it could be easy for an argument to break out occasionally. The quarrel was often over a love interest or a sour loser at dice. In no time the pirates' full pockets were running low, and for some unable to afford the company of a working girl, they busied themselves onboard the ship.

Mauricio Barros observed a merchant ship that appeared in the harbor and set anchor nearby. Repairing the sailcloth on the quarterdeck, he accidentally jabbed his thumb for the second time. He quickly became frustrated with the sewing needle and sucked away the tiny trickle of blood. He watched the crew on board and studied the captain and junior sailors. They were still too far away to tell, but somehow the captain looked familiar.

From what he could tell, the merchant captain was of Spanish or Portuguese descent. His olive skin was unmistakable, much like his own. Forgetting about the newcomers, Mauricio concentrated on repairing the stiff cloth and accidentally poked his thumb a third time. As luck would have it, Mr. Schmidt happened to stroll by. Although few words between them were ever spoken, he was likable enough, and Mauricio had no reservations when he looked up and spoke.

"Excuse me, Mr. Schmidt, do you have a minute, *señor*?"

"Certainly. Mauricio, is it?"

"*Si*, that is correct."

"Well, Mauricio, tell me what I can do for you."

"I was wondering if you could tell me when we're to depart. I have noticed that the repairs to our ship are almost complete."

"True, but Redbone decides when the tides are favorable to depart. I don't imagine it will be much longer. From what I know, he's waiting to hear from a Dutch governor who has offered a sizable reward for our assistance. It seems that on the tiny island of Bonaire, the Dutch West India Company is being attacked by a consortium of French pirates. Redbone, up for the fight, has been stifled until he understands what's required of us, Iron Born."

"Oh, I see—yes, never engage in a fight unless you've had time to access your opponent's strength."

"You see, Mauricio, you're catching on, indeed. Look over at the merchant's vessel docking at the pier. This boat is the one we've been waiting for; it's easily discernable by the Portuguese flag flying off its stern. Hopefully, Redbone's letter is on board! I intended to visit that vessel when you stopped me."

"Excuse me, Mr. Schmidt, would you mind if I escort you to the boat? The captain is of Spanish ancestry; perhaps you'll need an interpreter?"

"Doubtful—my Spanish is impeccable but, yes, indeed, by all means, join me if you wish."

Soon the two were off, walking down the gangway toward the merchant ship. Along the way few words were spoken between them. Mauricio began asking questions about Mr. Schmidt's life, upbringing, and, most importantly, how he became a pirate, eager to learn about the life of his first mate.

A reserved man, the giant pirate only divulged a few groans and grunts but nothing to explain his choices in life. Although when the conversation changed to Schmidt's mother, surprisingly, a crack in the man's armor seemed to open slightly, and he described his childhood in the Netherlands where his father was a doctor. According to Schmidt, the man was stern and heartless. Education was paramount. However, Schmidt was an exemplary pupil and a gifted mathematician. Occasionally, he received a bad grade from his headmaster—not because of Schmidt's lack of knowledge but because of his daydreaming of becoming a famous buccaneer engaged in swordplay.

Schmidt's mother, a saint among women, understood her son most and constantly encouraged him to become a doctor like his father. Nevertheless, there were seven children, with four boys who could fulfill their father's wishes. For Schmidt, it was not to be. He had different desires. Because of his size, few picked fights with him, but the ones who did were in for a match as the two titans would square off, with bare knuckles, and go at each other as if their lives depended on it. Sadly, the outcome of such a display of violence would be met with a leather strap when his father got home. Again, most often his mother came to the rescue! A lesson taught early—never give up, never surrender.

Just as they approached the merchant ship, Schmidt confessed his regret for seeing his mother and the look in her eyes when he came home bloody from such a brawl. Still, as he grew older, he and Redbone first met at a time like this. Back in Port Royal, in fact—at a tavern. He was enjoying the company of a pretty lady, having dinner, when an argument broke out about the price of gunpowder somewhere not far. In those days Redbone made a living where he could, and since gunpowder was in high demand, Redbone could charge whatever he wished.

Redbone faced not one but four pirates by himself at the time. The odds were stacked in the pirate captain's favor. Regrettably, this pirate captain wasn't thrilled with the price and called Redbone a liar and a cheat. To this day Schmidt could not say why he intervened, but there it was. He described himself standing up and knocking the first man he saw to the ground with a punch to his face, then took the other, gripped him by the neck, and landed a crushing blow to the man's jaw, sending him to the floor unconscious. For his part, he did all he could for the stranger.

Afterward when Schmidt returned to his table, the lady he was with saw him playing his part in these acts of violence, which was too much for the lady so she walked away in haste. Nothing to be done, Schmidt refilled his glass and watched the show. Redbone was brilliant and quickly outmaneuvered his opponents, killing the captain by running his sword through his belly. Seeing himself alone to face Redbone, the other man turned and ran for his life.

Behind Redbone were spontaneous clapping from Schmidt and an invitation to join him for a drink. The friendship was bonded as tight as steel. From then on the two had become inseparable.

"Oh, look, we're here," said Redbone.

Seeing a man securing a rope on the mooring line, Schmidt stopped and said, *"Necesito hablar con tu captain,"* translated in English, "I need to speak to your captain."

"Hello, can I help you?" came a voice behind them.

"Good morning, Capitán. My name is Mr. Schmidt, the first mate aboard the *Hell's Fury*. I believe you have a correspondence for me?"

"Mr. Schmidt, you say. Hum—sorry no, perhaps something for your Capitán Redbone?"

"Yes, of course, my captain, I meant. Tell me, señor, is there a message for Redbone aboard your ship?"

"Well, no, I'm afraid, something more."

"More, what do you mean by more?"

"There is a man I've brought, a Danish man from the island of Bonaire, to see Redbone. It must be something important for the Dutch governor to send an attaché."

"Please tell me, where is the man now? I'm anxious to speak with him."

"I'm afraid he's still recovering from seasickness. You see, the crossing was quite treacherous, and we encountered a bad storm. Now I'm sure he'll recover soon; be patient, and as soon as he's better I will send him to see your captain."

"Are you sure I could not persuade you to let me see him?"

"No, I'm sorry, but no. The man is still my responsibility. As I have told you, he's sick. I'm sure he'll be over it soon. I'm so sorry, but you must excuse me. I still have to make arrangements with the authorities and unload my cargo."

"Excellent. Thank you, señor, for your time; please, have a pleasant day until we meet again." After a simple bow, the first mate walked away.

As he and Mauricio returned to the *Hell's Fury*, Mr. Schmidt remarked, "It's a good thing I have a bit of patience or else that merchant captain could have found himself looking foolish with a lump on his head. I'm not the sort of man who accepts the word no too often—today he caught me in a good mood."

"Yes, I'm afraid my cousin Diamantino is quite—how should I say?—obstinate. Even growing up, he would not bend or give in to other opinions."

"Your cousin, you say? I find that a bit humorous, to say the least; nevertheless, we shall give your cousin Diamantino time to get the representative well. It wouldn't do to have the man sick in front of Redbone. No, oh no, indeed. Meanwhile, I will ask you to stay busy with your cousin and inform me when the attaché is ready to meet Redbone. Look, as I said before, it looks to be a pleasant day."

"That is true, Señor Schmidt, but one never knows when the weather will change."

"No, Mr. Barros, one cannot predict the weather. At any moment the clouds overhead will change—much like alliances."

Hum, Mauricio thought, *a strange thing to say*, then he watched Schmidt go up the gangway to the pirate ship. After turning back, he looked again at his cousin busy unloading their cargo and wondered if there was a hidden meaning in the first mate's comment.

CHAPTER 2

Days later came the news that Redbone was waiting to hear. The Dutch attaché had recovered from his sea crossing ordeal and was anxious to meet with Redbone to discuss terms. To Redbone, being handsomely rewarded for his services would pay his crew for their efforts and clear the debt owed to the workers repairing his ship from their last skirmish.

A meeting was set at six o'clock that evening. The Iron Born crew understood the importance of this meeting, and all anxiously waited for the Dutchmen to arrive.

Mauricio, new to the pirate brotherhood, decided to visit his favorite tavern instead. His work at repairing the sails was finished. He set out alone toward the small port city. If his presence was needed back at the ship, he informed Mr. Schmidt where he could be found. Being thrifty with his money, he always had enough in his pockets to quench his thirst.

When he appeared inside the tavern, there, of all people, was his cousin Diamantino waving for him to join his party. There was something about his cousin that got to him: the way he acted as though he were better than him, most often while growing up together. He and Diamantino often got into fights. Mauricio hesitated to sit at their table but looked about to see what places were available. Unfortunately, seeing no other place to sit, he grudgingly sat down next to Diamantino, who patted him on his back, welcoming him.

"Tell me, Cousin, what are you drinking?"

"Few choices, I'm afraid, the usual—rum will do."

"Wench, come here and pour my cousin Mauricio a rum. Will you please, m'lady?"

"Right away," came the sharp response.

Unexpectedly, laughter broke out from Diamantino, and he shouted, "Whatever are you thinking, Mauricio? A pirate—you? I've never heard of anything so foolish in all my life. What is it with the Barros? First, you abandon your post in Cartagena to become a pirate! Then your little sister Mariana runs off to Trinidad to become a prostitute. I swear it's like my dear poppa has always said: My brother, Fausto, your father, must have fallen on his head when he was born and raised brainless children!"

"Please listen, Cousin; I do not appreciate you talking about my father, Fausto, in this way. Please reframe your words before I take offense!"

"Oh, Cousin, do not be offended; why, your father is one of my dearest uncles. Sadly, though, his children turned out as they did. The family blames your mother for her lack of motherly discipline. As I have said, you are family. Drink up; the evening is young."

Mauricio took a long swig. "What news do you have of my mother? How is she? I haven't spoken to her in months. I tried to explain everything in my last letter to her and Poppa. Still, I wasn't sure how she would take the news of me becoming a pirate. She must understand that I had little choice at the end of a sword. Damn you for speaking about my sister Mariana as you did. Tell me about her; what have you heard?"

"Oh—well, we all know she was a little loose growing up, your little tramp sister, but when your mother found out, why it was just too much for her, I'm afraid."

"Cousin or no cousin, señor, your words are harsh and insulting. Leave your thoughts and opinions to yourself, and tell me about my mother, Diamantino, or else I shall lose my temper and bash you about your head and shoulders."

"Calm down, Cousin, we're family. Besides, look around the table; you are outnumbered. Now calm yourself or else I will not give you your letter."

"Letter—what's this about a letter?"

"Your mother has written you!"

"Okay, fine, Diamantino, I shall remain calm; you have my word. Now, señor, please give me my letter."

"I don't have it at the moment, I'm afraid. It's back in my cabin."

Mauricio took a long breath and emptied his mug of rum. He looked at his cousin and said, "Tell me, Diamantino, when are you returning to your ship?"

"The night is young, and we must get caught up on what's been happening in our lives. As children we were in constant clashes; now we are men, and there is a lot to tell. But for now, let us have another rum."

"Why not? It does not look like I'm leaving too soon, does it?"

HOURS LATER, WHAT ANIMOSITY THEY felt for each other was soon forgotten, much like the amount of alcohol they consumed. Walking back to the pier seemed most difficult as they could only sway back and forth with each step they took, supporting one another. In the end they finally made it to Diamantino's ship. There, the offer came to have another drink. At the time it was a wasted offering. Mauricio was so far gone that he'd not be able to appreciate it. But for now, why refuse or argue? Diamantino struggled with a match to light the lamp inside the captain's cabin. Once he did, he stepped back, swaying.

"Now where did I put that letter? Oh, wait—I know, inside my leather pouch." After picking it off his bunk, Diamantino unlatched the strap and added, "Did I tell you your mother was crying when she handed me this letter? I suppose she had few choices on how to save your sister. That's why she implored you to go to Trinidad and bring Mariana home."

"Tell me, Cousin, how is it that you know so much about what my mother had written me? That is, unless you have read her letter. Tell me, did you do such a thing?"

"Mauricio, again, you are family! We are family. What affects you will certainly affect me in some way. Like I told you, your father is my favorite uncle. Yes, yes, of course, I read your mother's letter. If for no other reason than to save your family from certain damnation."

Shaking his head, Mauricio thought of his cousin's words and laughed. Again, why argue or make a scene? After opening the letter, Mauricio slowly read the contents. As expected, his mother's tears stained the paper as she must have been distraught when she wrote it. Inside the letter, his mother begged him to save Mariana, explaining that it was not her fault the stable boy could not marry her. It was his father's decision. Ever since she ran away, the family regretted their choice. Now what mattered most was to save Mariana at all costs. He was her only hope left her. From his mother's hands, she was asking him to swear to God he'd save his sister. She had little time left. According to the doctors, she was growing ill. The letter ended with these words: "Please, son, you must bring Mariana home to us before it's too late."

After closing the letter, Mauricio sensed the effects of the alcohol seem to fade somewhat and immediately felt the heavy burden upon his shoulders.

"As I said, Cousin, if your parents had been more understanding, perhaps your sister Mariana would have never run away. But as she is a whore, who'd ever marry her? She'd have to be married to bring honor back to the family. No, I'm sorry, you have a decision to make!"

Looking back at his cousin, he responded, "Yes, it is true but you, señor, have your nose stuck so far up the Barros family's arse that you are not exempt from helping me. Connected by blood as you have boasted all night, you will provide me help to save my sister. Tell me, Cousin, how soon are you to sail?"

"Hum, yes, my dear poppa would become angry if he ever discovered our family needed help and I refused. I would never want to see the disappointment in his eyes. Yes—of course—okay, my ship was loaded with its cargo this morning, the very reason me and my crew were celebrating our good fortune back at the tavern. Thinking about it now with all stores loaded in the hull, nothing is keeping us from leaving St. Kitts on the morning tide."

"Tell me, where are your sailing charts?"

"Why? What is it you have in mind?"

"Already regret for my decision to become an Iron Born Pirate is present within me. You have no idea of the brutality of my captain. If I chose to abandon my post with these Iron Born Pirates, it would not be a slap on the hand as you'd expect from the Spanish military. No, Cousin, this man they call Redbone is the devil incarnate. For now, I don't know what would happen to the men helping me or myself."

"This regret you are experiencing could only be expected to come from a fool."

"A fool, man, yes—fine, a fool that was given the choice of life or death. Read your Bible. When the devil tempted Job, did not Satan ask God what man wouldn't give to save his life? He would give away any he had to live. Tell me, then, is it a fool to want to save your life? You judge so damn easily as if you are perfect in every way. You, Cousin, must understand that both I and Mariana had little choices when we decided to change our lives. It is not simply black and white as you make it to be. No, for us, there seemed to be no way out of our predicaments."

"You always have a choice when choosing honor above all else."

"You have read for yourself my mother's letter. How can a son refuse her wishes? Perhaps for the first time or even a long time, I feel desperate, almost like a caged wild beast. Now I must divert to an act that I never expected to realize—betrayal!"

"Yes, I can see where that decision is not one to take likely."

"Hear me, and make me this promise: If I do not survive this decision, you will tell my mother that I have tried my best to fulfill her wishes, even to death!"

After seeing the pirate ship preparing to disembark, Diamantino went into action and pulled out his sailing charts.

"Now listen to me, Mauricio, if your ship is sailing for Bonaire, then on the way you will be passing by the island of Tobago. You must convince your captain to let you have a boat and visit your family because your mother is ill or some such excuse for leaving your ship. There, I will meet you in Tobago a week from now. Once you are safe aboard my ship, I will bring you to Trinidad. Then you can save your sister if she agrees to come with you. That, my friend, might take some convincing. Regrettably, from what you've told me about your pirate captain, he will refuse your request, thinking of jeopardizing his men. No, I'm afraid you will have to steal a boat somehow and escape."

"Listen for a moment, Diamantino. What if I stay aboard your ship and we leave together, forgetting about meeting in Tobago, and you can take me directly to Trinidad?"

"No, absolutely not. Do not forget we've spent a night drinking together; it will be a small task to find out whose company we've been keeping, and the pirates will be hunting us down in time. I'm afraid if I heard they'd keep my cargo and kill my crew, no telling what you'd suffer."

Suddenly, a knock was heard on the door.

"Yes, who is it?"

"Captain, there is someone on deck to see you. It's a giant man asking for your cousin Mauricio."

"Please, tell the man we'll be there shortly."

Turning to Mauricio, he said, "You see, as expected, your pirate companions are looking for you. Go to them but don't say anything about Tobago. We will depart within the hour. My ship is faster than your larger ship and will arrive there a day or two before you. For your part, you must be diligent and stay aware of your heading and navigation. Constantly be aware of your compass position. Ask the navigator what your location is, such as that. In no time we'll meet. For now, let us meet your pirate friend. Hopefully, he's not in a bad mood; I'd hate to disappoint that fellow."

"Yes, Mr. Schmidt, the giant! For my part, the man is pleasant enough when he's giving orders. But when he realizes that I have abandoned my post to save my sister, the fury that man could bring to bear would be dreadful, I'm afraid."

After leaving Diamantino's cabin, he and Mauricio appeared on deck, both still somewhat drunk from the night before.

Mauricio, seeing his first mate, yelled out, "Señor Schmidt, I'm so glad to see you have come here to your cousin's boat to exhort me home."

"Hum—indeed, no, but I bring good news. Redbone has met with the Dutch attaché, and on the morrow's tide we set sail for Bonaire."

"That is good news; we have been rusting our timbers waiting for word too long. I am anxious to get underway, believe me." Mauricio turned around. "Cousin, it has been a pleasure; too long have we lived our lives apart, without words spoken. If ever we see each other again, it shall be a fine day."

"Goodbye, Mauricio. I hope your mother survives her illness."

"Are you ready, Señor Schmidt?"

"Aye, let us shove off, shall we?"

On the way back to the ship, the two men could speak frankly with one another again.

Unexpectedly, Schmidt turned to Mauricio and said, "I'm sorry to hear about your mother."

"Yes, me, too; I didn't know she was sick until I got the letter from Diamantino. Listen, Señor Schmidt, I realize we are not part of a social club or other nonsense. But I must ask, what are the chances of Redbone dropping me off in Trinidad? Part of my dying mother's wishes was for me to rescue my sister from a house of ill repute."

"Hum, strange request, indeed. Mauricio, ever since you have joined the brotherhood, you have taken orders without argument or delay. I am certainly a fine buccaneer, but I must ask, do you not understand that we are the hunted? Ever since Trinidad, we have faced mortal danger, not only from our fellow pirates but also the French and Spanish alike. If caught outside the brotherhood, you will face certain death at the end of a rope or worst. This is a decision that all of us must face, to abandon our families to search for treasure and fame. To me, the answer is clear. Redbone would never allow you to travel to Trinidad. Don't forget, the Spanish control it, and to risk everything so a man could save his prostitute sister is nothing short of ridiculous!"

"Mr. Schmidt, may I say, Señor, that you are a man

of conviction. You are faithful to our captain in ways that make one believe that he has a grip on your soul or worse. Your devotion is greatly appreciated, and if no one else sees you in any other light, they are missing the point. I have taken the vow. I now bear the marks of the brotherhood scarred in my body. Those words were spoken to pledge me to the cause. You, sir, see black and white—no other shade of color. To you, there is Redbone, our captain, the *Hell's Fury*, our ship, and the marks on our wrist. Nothing else matters. I want to say, for my part, I see you as a man I could call a friend one day. If ever the day comes and we meet on opposite sides of the plank, then know this: It has been a pleasure to know you."

"Mauricio, you have a quirky side, as if you were dropped on your head as a child or something. I'm proud to call you my Iron Born brother—apart from that, I pray that day never arrives when I see you on the opposite end of a plank. You would not survive the ordeal, believe me. Now hurry, let us get to the ship; we have preparations to get done before we depart. Have you noticed your cousin's ship sailing out of the harbor?"

After turning to watch Diamantino's ship sailing out to open water, Mauricio thought, *Until we meet in Tobago, Cousin.*

Unexpectedly, out of charter, Schmidt said, "Saying goodbye is bittersweet."

"Schmidt, it seems I've heard that before."

"Yes, perhaps you have—a play or some such poetry display. Now, if you excuse me, there is work to be done."

"Señor Schmidt, I meant what I said."

"So did I, Señor."

Those were the last words spoken between them. Over the following days at sea, Mauricio was true to his word. He kept inquiring about their locations on the map to the navigator under the ruse of becoming a pilot himself. Then the day arrived when they were to pass Tobago during the night. Already having taken provisions with him, he arranged to unlatch the longboat and prepped to shove it over the side.

As expected, off in the distance the island

appeared. One chance to escape the *Hell's Fury* clean so Mauricio did not hesitate. When at last he was floating in the water, he watched for any sign that his company was discovered missing. Seeing nothing out of the ordinary, he grabbed ahold of the oars and pulled hard.

At some distance away the island looked dark and menacing. Gratefully, a small lantern appeared swaying side to side, some ways off. He immediately knew that Diamantino had kept his word and was waiting. *Now. No time to waste.* He paddled hard to get to the merchant ship. Still, he regretted his choice to knock the men on guard atop their heads; he wasn't a man without feelings. He hoped they would be alright, but these were desperate times.

What he had done by deserting would never be forgotten. When he announced to Schmidt about appearing on the opposite side of the plank, he knew exactly what he was saying. To face the giant alone would be something most regrettable. No one knew what lay ahead on this journey. What other perils would he face since abandoning his ship? Alone to face his decision, he understood one truth above the rest: Blood is thicker than water!

Hopefully, he wasn't too late to save his sister. *Mariana, what have you done, little sister? Why choose this life for yourself? Indeed, you had other options*, he thought.

Chapter 3

Inside his prison, dimly burning oil lamps gave off little light in the dark space. A window with iron bars provided some needed fresh air. Sitting on a bed of straw that smelled severely of the previous tenants who no doubt used it as a place to urinate, Thomas pondered what was to become of him. Suddenly, he overheard a commotion outside his prison cell near the prison entrance. There, he noticed a young man struggling with two guards mistreating him. One guard pulled upon his long dark hair while another punched him hard in the stomach.

The way he was dressed gave the appearance of a wealthy man of commerce but more refined than an ordinary merchant. He looked to be in his mid-twenties; there was something strange in the way he could not defend himself from the guard's brutal punishments, as though he was hurt.

Without waging any defense, he took each blow to his body without a fight. Unexpectedly, the larger of the two guards struck him on the jaw, and he fell, unconscious, to the floor. Thomas saw the evidence for him not offering any resistance as he lay there. Dripping blood emptied onto his coat from some wound he had suffered.

The guards found the man's condition; both were amusing, and laughter erupted. Afterward, they opened Thomas's cell, discarding him onto the smelly bed of straw. After regarding the cowardly pair with contempt, Thomas suddenly received a kick to his body, which was a promise of more retaliation if he dared to object, at which point he happily remained quiet.

The guards closed the iron door and locked it tight. Thomas quickly raced to the poor soul to see how he was faring. Now that the young man was without his faculties, he could closely examine his wound. After looking down at the stained jacket, he quickly unbuttoned it and discarded it nearby, with only his white shirt stuffed inside his trousers. Thomas undid it to lift it free. His flesh was exposed; now the single knife cut to his abdomen was visible.

Thomas quickly realized he had to stop the bleeding or the young man would die. Looking inside the small cell, he searched for something he could use to aid the man's wound. But then again, Thomas had been taught to adapt. Gratefully, having some fishing line upon his person, he removed his right shoe and pushed on the heel, causing it to open. Inside the small compartment were small metal hooks, a sewing needle, and a few gold coins.

One never knew if they ever needed to bribe their way out of a fix such as this. But he felt that currently, his release was second to saving a life, and that could wait.

What was worrying to Thomas? Could the man even survive, especially after losing such a significant amount of blood that continued to empty outwardly upon his coat?

Thomas ran toward the iron cell door, calling out and taking only enough money to bribe the guards. At first he was ignored, but then he yelled out persistently that he had an urgent matter that he must discuss while flashing a coin in his hand. The guard's immediate response was to force him to be quiet, threatening him with a beating. However, seeing the flashing coin expelled that rejoinder.

Wisely, the guard chose to listen to his proposition. The language barrier still buffeted any quick response, but happily, he had a bucket of fresh water and white linen within the hour. They were both happy with the exchange at the cost of only one coin.

It was a blessing from the good Lord above that the man had no organs punctured from his knife wound. If he had, he would have bled out; no amount of fishing line would be able to stop the bleeding. He threaded the fishing line through its small opening, took his small needle, and closed his wound. Once he finished, he began to search for other injuries. After removing his shirt entirely, he discovered a terrifying sight. Each man's wrists had a peculiar scar, like swords that crossed a goblet. Both his wrists looked seared, you could say cauterized in some way.

For Thomas who had heard stories about these pirates with marks on their wrists, the sight frightened him. He froze in place and didn't move, recalling tales of a group that sailed these waters, a gang of bloodthirsty and ruthless pirates. They called themselves Iron Born Pirates. A band of blood brothers could never leave their fellow pirates behind, no matter the cost.

He had heard tales of entire towns being destroyed because one of these Iron Born Pirates was killed in exchanges with the local authorities. Afterward, when finding their dead companion, they would bring the body back to their ship; after dressing the deceased in the most acceptable attire, they would send their comrade off with a lavish funeral. The cost was equal to a king's ransom. Honestly, they were brothers until the end.

Now here rested one of them, close to death. Inevitably, his companions would be looking for his body, this Pirate. Now, after seeing such a one close to death, all would pay the cost for his demise unless Thomas could save him from certain death.

This town needs to be warned of the impending danger, Thomas thought.

Stepping back, he was not one to rush headlong into any situation. These circumstances took a minor consideration. He had never experienced an encounter with one of these pirates, but it would undoubtedly be a battle to the death if he had. Now here of all places lay one of his nemeses, unconscious and dying. He must consider the question of what he should do next. This young man seemed to be a complete mystery of sorts. *Why was he here in Trinidad? What was he looking for?* Thomas asked himself.

Having considered all his options, he realized that

the Iron Bloods could be just as quickly generous to those that saved their own. In times past they were known to allow such an individual to become part of the pirate crew if they survived the ritual of becoming an Iron Blood. From stories he heard, if one chose to become a pirate, the inductee must survive the dance with the Bloody Hag, a device made of cold iron, smiling with an old hag's face.

Her body and shape were voluminous, with sizable breasts. On both sides of her body were two long slots above her hips. That place was reserved for swords that the pirate captain himself provided.

Having prepared themselves for possible death, the inductee would stick their wrist through the openings around her hips, with their palms facing upward at a designated time. Everything was adjustable to fit any particular man's height.

Then the pirate's first mate, a Mr. Schmidt, would chain the poor soul to the cold device. The man was fastened in such a way that gave the illusion he was embracing the witch himself. Afterward, the first mate provided goblets of rum to each crew member, not to be consumed until after the ceremony. Now it was too late to change their mind about becoming a pirate.

The pirate captain, Redbone, would then appear on the quarterdeck. A hush would come over the men as they stared at the master of the ceremony above them.

The captain would solemnly chant a saying: "Iron Blood, True Blood, begins ye tale of this wretched soul. Who will soon float above Heaven or Hell? If he is found worthy to bear ye marks, now swear your life for all these your shipmates, who watch you disembark. If yea not worthy and you die in the test, will you rest forever with Davy Jones?"

While the pirates continued chanting, the captain walked to the Bloody Hag, displaying two short swords to his crew. The swords glistened in the sun, their razor sharpness polished to perfection.

The crew would become excitedly loud, knowing what was soon to occur. Frenzy would quickly erupt throughout the ranks of men, seeing the swords that they were all familiar with, each having felt the sting of steel against their wrist.

The captain would pivot to face the inductee and turn to the two men holding ropes attached to the upper half of the Hag itself without saying a word. He would give the signal to start the ritual. Suddenly, the top half of the Hag's body would be taken up several inches into the air.

Two guide rods would keep the top of the iron witch on track.

Suddenly, as everyone watched, the dense upper half would come to a stop, resting precariously above the inductee. The captain would then shove each sword into the small slits on the sides of the hag's body. Each blade was set inside its proper location, with only the sword's sharp edge exposed beneath the flat iron body.

The pirate captain would examine his crew for one final time, searching for an objection to this man becoming a crew member. Having seen none, he would turn back and order the two men holding the ropes to let go. The heavy metal half would come crashing down with a loud clanging noise, cutting through the man's wrist in a single blow.

The man's blood would drain into two narrow troughs inside a golden vessel that sat on a golden scale. His blood would tip the scale, upsetting the balance of his life. His life was now in the balance, so to speak; he was helpless and could only watch as his blood filled the golden vessel. The captain would offer a toast to the poor soul as he began his journey to becoming an Iron Born crew member. The crew would drink to his success.

The captain, satisfied that the first part of the ceremony was complete, would walk back to withdraw the two swords, allowing the man's blood to pour openly from his wounds. After looking at the first mate, Redbone would order him to be unchained. Once he was released from the grip of the Bloody Hag, he would fall to the wooden deck, half dead from blood loss. Mr. Schmidt would then take a red-hot iron from the fire. The branding iron with the symbol of the two crossed swords and goblet in the middle was quickly shoved into both wrists, cauterizing the wounds and stopping any further blood loss.

If the man died in the process, he was considered unworthy of becoming an Iron Born. His body would be carelessly carried over to the railing and tossed overboard for the sharks to feed on. The goblets of rum issued to the crew would then be poured out into the sea. However, if he survived the ritual, every crew member would drink their fill of rum while toasting their new shipmate's long life.

The young man lying there had gone through the ritual and survived to tell the tale. *But who could have been so foolish to stab the poor bastard?* Thomas wondered. Unexpectedly, the man moved and began to cough. After feeling his forehead, Thomas discovered that he was burning up with fever. An infection could be setting in. If he didn't receive some medical attention soon, he would surely die where he lay.

These Spanish jails were the worst in treating prisoners from other counties. He wouldn't be there if not for the misfortune of falling overboard. Knowing what he must do, Thomas suddenly stood to his feet and called out to one of the guards in English. The one guard he so easily bribed from earlier wasn't in sight. Regrettably, the biggest and most arrogant guard stood not far off. Of all the people he had to communicate with, he had to negotiate with the one who enjoyed inflicting pain on every poor soul stuck in this hellhole of a prison.

Thomas waved to the guard that he must come over to him. Soon he saw the towering figure approach. The guard cursed something in Spanish that he couldn't understand. Ignoring his comment that no doubt translated in English meant, "You're in for a beating!" Thomas quickly asked if he spoke any English. Surprisingly, the guard's answer to his question was a few English words he could barely understand.

"I need to see someone of authority at once!" Thomas ordered.

The guard just laughed at him, as if understanding his request, and began to walk away, repeating his words like a joke he had heard.

Before he had gotten far, Thomas shouted out, "Apparently, you do not understand the danger you find yourself, my friend, nor the townspeople, for if you had, you would not be laughing so joyfully but instead would be soiling your trousers, you fool!"

Thomas was doubtful that the guard understood what he had said, but he obviously comprehended the word "fool" well enough. The guard turned back and walked toward the cell door. Now it seemed that Thomas was to receive a lesson on proper manners!

When the guard reached for his keys to unlock the cell door, Thomas shouted, "Look, see the man before you worsening!"

The guard looked down at the young man with little concern, still not understanding Thomas's distress.

"He's an Iron Born Pirate! Look upon his wrist; you will see the marks of the swords and goblets," Thomas shouted.

"*¡No! ¿Como podía ser? Piratas de Hierro,*" which translated means "No! How could it be? Iron Blood Pirates." The guard shouted as he realized what treachery he had done to the man and what fate would await him once his crewmates arrived.

Thomas stood back, smiling, then suddenly saw the guard's arrogant and proud demeanor change. Fear unabated gripped him sorely as he slowly opened the cell door. After looking inside, he could see what Thomas was saying was true.

Again, saying something in his native language, "*Tengo que advertir al magistrado a la vez!*" which must amount to, "I have to warn the governor at once!" the man ran out of the cell and locked the iron gate. He turned away, yelling loudly, "*Piratas, piratas,*" leaving the dark musky dungeon behind.

Thomas could still hear him shouting a considerable distance away as he ran throughout the town of Trinidad.

Alone, Thomas turned to the sick man lying there and said, "Well, my friend, it looks like we're both going to acquire our freedoms very soon, I'm thinking. Once their governor verifies what I have said is true, no doubt we together will be set free from this wrenched cell."

While waiting he had time to attend to the young

pirate. It was apparent he needed medicine, but for now, all Thomas could do was see what happened next.

After standing on his feet, he stared out the prison bars. A harsh reality struck him as he realized there was a chance that both this Iron Born and he could be murdered, then thrown into the sea. It was a possibility that couldn't be ignored. For the first time Thomas felt apprehensive about his decision to tell the guard about the pirate. Perhaps he should have shut his mouth, but that wasn't like him.

WITHIN THE VERY HOUR A chorus of pounding drums and marching feet was heard approaching. Soon within sight came a group of armed guards that appeared inside the dungeon. Everyone came to an abrupt halt; they all turned to face one another with their muskets and bayonets crossing their heads.

While they stood to attention, suddenly walking in the middle appeared a flamboyant man dressed in a blue silk jacket and matching trousers with white stockings, including a black powdered wig. He proudly approached the iron bars to look inside the small cell.

"Hello!" Thomas replied. After asking the man if he spoke English, he waited for a response.

"Yes! I do, señor. I'm the local governor for this humble town; my name is Edwardo Santos Félix Escobar. Is it true what I have heard that you have an Iron Born Pirate in your cell?" he asked, with fear gripping his every word.

"I'm surprised you, being the justice in this town, didn't know this already. Look at the man's wrist; if your men had been more alert, they would've noticed it immediately. Instead, they have mistreated him in their foolish devotion to rid your town of any unwelcome guest. Perhaps your town has made the biggest error in your miserable lives. Yes, to answer your question."

"This cannot be!" the governor replied abruptly.

"Why, here lies the truth before you. Look for yourself," Thomas answered.

After looking downward, the troubled governor

stared intently at the reason for his discomfort in the form of two disfigured markings upon the man's wrist.

Thomas smugly replied, "Now you're facing a dilemma, are you not?"

"I know of these pirates; they are bloodthirsty and cunning," the governor replied.

"I might suggest an answer to your dilemma, if it pleases your honor. What if you provide me with a small boat filled with provisions and medicine for his wound? I shall take this wretched soul far away from town, provided you make it worth my while," Thomas suggested.

Surprised by his candid remark, the governor looked at him and asked, "What cost would be worth your efforts?"

"Oh, perhaps a small measure of gold for my troubles is all I be asking."

The governor turned around to face his men who hadn't broken ranks. Then after turning back again, he responded, "Would one hundred gold doubloons be satisfactory?"

Thomas smiled and said, "Yes! I believe that would be to my liking. May I suggest you release us from this dark hole at once before his pirate companions arrive here looking for the wretched soul?"

With a quick flashing of the governor's hand to his guards, one of them reached for his keys to unlock the iron door.

After turning to the still unconscious young pirate, Thomas said aloud, "What is uncertain is why he was ever here. What was the reason he had for visiting your small port?"

"I do not pretend to know or care; you shall have all you requested within the hour. I want you and this pirate scum out of Trinidad immediately!" the governor yelled.

After turning back around, he walked past his guards and left the dungeon behind him. Two dungeon guards later appeared and promptly opened the cell door. After walking past Thomas, they picked up the still unconscious pirate to carry him out into the sunlight, free of his prison cell.

Thomas quickly followed. As they approached the small pier with a small boat tied up at the docks, the two guards stepped inside without a word and deposited the pirate across the keel. Once they had finished, they stepped out onto the pier and waited for their next orders.

Thomas asked one of the guards where he could wash up before setting sail. He stood firm without moving, smelling of dungeon piss and much like a rotten carcass.

The guards looked at one another, not comprehending what was said and unsure how to answer.

"Bathroom, bath. *Baño, necesito un baño. Tomar un baño.* I need to bathe," Thomas announced. Then after glancing into the empty boat, he exclaimed, "I don't see any gold in the boat!"

Both guards, still not comprehending his meaning, gave him empty stares.

"Look, I don't see any gold. *No veo ningún oro.* Do you?" Thomas asked.

No one said anything that he could understand. They merely stared at him as if he was from another world. Luckily, the guard he had some success communicating with earlier approached with a canister of fresh water.

Thomas looked at him and said, "*Necesito un baño, huelo agrio.* I need to bath; I smell sour!"

In his broken English, the captain of the guards replied, "All of your supplies are coming!"

"Good, I'm pleased; now tell me where I can bathe myself. I mean *tomar un baño.*"

Again, the other guards looked at one another with surprise.

The captain that knew a little English shook his head. Suddenly, his eyes lit up as he announced, "Marie's."

"You can take me?" Thomas asked.

He understood the question! A bright smile appeared on his face. After giving orders to the other two guards, he motioned for Thomas to follow him toward the city.

"Good, thank you. I won't need all of you," Thomas

ordered.

The guards needed to watch over the pirate inside the boat. It was a dangerous game he was playing. If anything happened to this pirate, there would be no bargaining with his companions. They would not only destroy this town but Thomas as well!

The guard that promised to take him to Marie's turned to him and politely introduced himself as "Alejandro"; then he turned back to the other guards and gave an order that caused both men to come to attention. Although a quick dip in the ocean would take care of most of the smelly odor, Thomas felt he deserved a little comfort, perhaps with a lovely woman, before setting sail. But would time allow such a luxury?

At once they both ran to Marie's. The smell was divine, and Thomas realized he hadn't eaten since the day began. There would be little time for play, maybe just a glass of rum with a bath. Still, it would be worth it, if nothing else, to rid himself of this odor he'd had to endure. They soon passed a bakery, ran through the cobblestone streets, and turned a corner.

They ran through the town with no time to eat until they rounded a corner. At the end of the block sat a two-story building, brightly painted a rose color. At the front entrance of the building stood two voluptuous women inviting each passing pedestrian to come inside, enticing them to be entertained. Hanging out of the windows were ladies calling down to the men walking on the street below, slightly dressed in various colors.

As they approached the entrance to the building, each of the prostitutes stepped aside, eyeing Thomas and his companion hungrily. Alejandro seemed to know where he was going; since he was a regular at this establishment, he stepped inside as if he owned the place.

Ignoring the enticing group of working girls, Alejandro approached the madam of the house, who watched them enter the building. She looked to be close to thirty in age. Her jet- black hair was tied in a bun, with her voluminous body filling a flowery dress. Her bright brown eyes and charming smile would be a welcome sight for any would-be sailor.

Excitedly, Alejandro explained the scenario to her in his native Spanish tongue, but a few words were as quickly unmistakable in any language: "Iron Born Pirate."

Without hesitation the madam of the house, whom Alejandro called Abella by name, called one of the attractive young girls "Mariana." Abella gave instructions to the young girl that Thomas could barely understand. When they stopped talking, they turned and looked at him with a fleeting glance.

As they continued conversing, Thomas eyed the attractive young Mariana carefully. While she listened to instructions, he noticed her slim young body covered in black lace and her long brunette hair braided with a silver coin bohemian headpiece. Her soft complexion, beautiful wide brown eyes, and smile would be more than he could ever hope for in a woman if she decided to show it.

After their communication was over, she approached him with determination. Thomas smiled, trying to say something ingenious as she approached. Ignoring him, she grabbed his hand and dragged him upstairs into her private parlor.

Inside the room, the girl closed the door behind them; she ordered Thomas to disrobe from his smelly clothes using hand gestures. He then noticed a bathtub in the corner of the room partly filled with clean water.

One thing became apparent as he slowly unbuttoned the large brass button from his naval shirt. Seemingly, he wasn't moving swiftly enough; out of utter frustration, the young girl slapped his fingers away and promptly ripped his shirt off his body. Next was his blue trousers. Almost feeling modest about the whole affair of taking off his clothes, he again wasn't quick enough as the young girl willingly took control to remove his entire garments from his body until there was nothing left. He stood there naked.

More hand motions and exploitative words that sounded like he was being cursed aloud told Thomas to get inside the bath quickly. No arguments. He did as directed and placed his foot into the lukewarm water before immersing his entire body in the tube.

The young prostitute stepped out into the hall. She

yelled out something to someone that wasn't visible from his location. A moment later a young Spanish boy appeared, running toward him with the hot water kettle. He quickly dumped the entire kettle of boiling water into the tub without hesitation. Then, as speedily as he arrived, he disappeared out of the room in a hurry, only to return minutes later with another kettle full of steaming hot water.

Then Mariana carelessly dumped some herbal fragrance inside the water, then dropped a soap bar between his legs. She placed her hands above her hips and said something in Spanish that Thomas took to mean, "Clean your worthless smelly carcass."

Suddenly, another prostitute came into the room carrying a silver tray. A salami stick, some cheese, and a loaf of bread were on top. Beside her, another girl appeared carrying a glass decanter filled with fancy liquor and a small crystal glass. He watched as she filled the glass, then handed it to Thomas, smiling.

"Now you're talking," Thomas exclaimed. Feeling somewhat happy with his new turn of events, he quickly downed the entire glass of its contents. Then he handed it back to the girl. After taking his cup, she flirtatiously smiled, filling it full. After motioning for the other harlot to rip off a piece of bread and a few cheese slices, she quickly handed him all he wanted; after eating his fill, his spirit was renewed. The prostitute holding the food tray quietly set it down on a small table near the tub and left the room.

The simple virtues in this life can be had when one's circumstances have changed suddenly to the positive. Such was Thomas at that moment when it all seemed as though everything was going his way. Looking at his situation, he developed a whole new outlook on life.

Mariana, the young prostitute who brought him to her room, stood back, watching him act like a pampered king. After a loud belch and feeling satisfied, Thomas eyed Mariana, knowing all that was needed was a specific womanly dessert. Unfortunately, his world was rocked by bells clanging throughout the city and distant voices screaming in Spanish, "*Piratas.*" This warning could only mean one thing: The Iron Born Pirates have arrived to claim their fallen comrade.

A look of fear on the young girl's faces suddenly gripped them as Mariana's expression changed. She looked at Thomas as if searching for answers. He stood up naked in the tub, claiming he needed some clothes.

Mariana quickly nodded her head in understanding, hurrying over to her Armoire. She began to rummage through the drawers until she gathered a complete wardrobe of civilian men's clothes and promptly returned.

Thomas hurried to get dressed; he knew there was no time to lose. He raced downstairs as fast as he could. Throughout the brothel the prostitutes were crying, holding on to one another in fear, as the news of approaching *piratas* reached the town, signaling everyone that they would soon be invaded.

WHEN THOMAS ARRIVED AT THE bar, Alejandro stood, eagerly awaiting his arrival. Together they ran from the establishment in a hurry, ignoring Abella, the house's madam, who was busily calming her working girls.

They exited the front door and ran down the narrow streets toward the harbor. When they arrived at the small pier, a small detachment of military soldiers stood at attention. Amid the small group, the governor excitedly looked around for any sign of where Thomas had gone.

After returning to the small boat, Alejandro, first and foremost, quickly saluted the governor, explaining where they had gone.

When the governor saw Thomas standing behind, he hastily ignored Alejandro and addressed him only by saying: "Here is your gold. Now you must leave at once."

Anxiously looking inside the small boat, Thomas noticed the young pirate was still asleep. Near him sat a small wooden chest next to the tiller. Thomas stepped inside the small craft and untied the mooring ropes without wasting time. After taking an oar, he shoved it hard against the wooden pier, casting the small boat adrift toward open water. He untied the rope to the mainsail and unfurled the canvas. An offshore breeze quickly engulfed the sail. Soon the tiny craft was leaving the harbor, headed for open water.

He saw white sails approaching a few miles offshore, still some distance away. It would again take some time before they could reach the tiny Spanish port. At first he hoped to intercept the approaching ship. However, with no real plan of action other than to deliver the still-unconscious pirate to his shipmates, he had expected more time to consider his options. This new turn of events left him with few choices to save the small port and himself. He would have to rely on the pirates' gratitude for finding their shipmate alive.

He reluctantly steered the small craft toward the approaching sails. He glanced at the small port he left behind, unsure if he would ever return. But if fate spared him this day, it would be a place that he hoped to visit again.

The small craft gained speed and soon cut through the waves at ten comfortable knots. The small boat rocked back and forth as he sailed onward against the pounding waves. The water splashed against the gunwales, causing the salt spray to fill his nostrils as the wind buffeted his departure. At that moment, being a sailor, he never felt more alive than when he was at sea. Glancing at the approaching ship, he thought he could see the pirate flag proudly displayed off the transom. If he lapsed in his judgment to meet these Iron Born Pirates and fear overtook him, he would not find the courage to fulfill his destiny.

Eyeing the boat's interior, he saw the provisions that the governor had provided. A small wooden chest set alone was unmistakable. Thomas excitedly wanted to see his reward for doing such a noble deed as saving the small town, if only for the last time. After taking a piece of rope, he tied the rudder in place. He lifted the big chest and sat it on his lap, reaching forward. It had three iron bands over the lid. In the middle was a clasp with a black lock that held the top closed. Looking around, Thomas didn't see a key anywhere. *That's great; how am I supposed to open it? That accursed governor*, he thought.

Feeling disgusted with this new predicament, he set the chest back in the hull and covered it with a white piece of canvas, returning to the rudder. After untying the rope, he again steered toward the floating ship. Looking behind, the town of Trinidad grew smaller and smaller as the approaching sails appeared taller. After studying the vessel, its outline became more pronounced. Cannons in two distinct positions protruded outward from their open hatches. They were unquestionable, poised for battle.

Noticeably, he could see tiny figures running about the decks, barely visible to the naked eye. Thomas surmised that he was already spotted, approaching their direction. He knew that he couldn't possibly pose a threat to any of them. Still, he thought it best to hoist a white flag of truce, but where on earth would he find one large enough to be seen a long distance away or even a pole to hang it on? Yes, the mainsail was there, but the white flag on top of the mast could be confused with being part of the sail itself.

Studying the young pirate, he realized his lip looked bruised from the guard's mistreatment in the light of day. After further examination his wound appeared secured; all the stitches remained.

Following the coastline, he occasionally passed by a small group of shanty houses where the poor lived, off the sandy beaches. The residents were mainly men cleaning fish or drying meat upon a bed of poles. Occasionally, women could be seen inside their huts, cooking upon stoves made from stones. It seemed a much simpler, happier life than he had lived.

He saw many strange things in the places he had visited on his travels, such as people that eat monkey brains for dessert. In some remote spots, cannibals eating human flesh were the most bizarre. There were places where one could fish whenever one wished and be in the company of a lovely lady filling a glass of rum that never went dry. If he survived this latest adventure, he promised himself that he would return to some small village such as these and live out his days, telling heroic stories to small children.

The ship was getting closer, separated by at least five miles. This pirate ship's course remained fixated in the direction of the defenseless town. A single purpose, no doubt, to take back their comrade. Maintaining his course, Thomas soon closed the gap between them.

As he meticulously studied the English naval ship, something seemed familiar about the wooden vessel—in the way the mainsail was set taller than the ship's forecastle, and the bowsprit netting just beneath her fore sail reminded him of another boat that he had seen before.

I wish I had a spyglass aboard the tiny skiff, he thought. Perhaps there was one inside the gunnysack that Governor Edwardo sent him. After tying off the rudder again, he lifted the white canvas bag near him. Reaching inside, he discovered packaged meat, bread, and cheese. To his amazement there was a spyglass wrapped around several nautical charts. "Bless you, Governor," he exclaimed.

After taking the spyglass to his eye, he looked ahead toward the approaching ship. He realized that it wasn't a pirate ship, but instead, it was the HMS *Dolphin* of the British Royal Navy.

"This is quite a predicament, isn't it, my young friend?" Thomas said aloud, staring down at the unconscious pirate. "Well, I know the captain of the *Dolphin* quite well; he wouldn't hesitate to aid me in my plight. But then again, being caught out of uniform, I could face court-martial. Assuredly, being seen with an Iron Born Pirate, you, sir, would hang from the gallows." Still no response. Thomas laughed aloud, seeing his situation as quite humorous.

Without hesitation Thomas set down the spyglass, changing his course, heading east, away from the ship, and back toward the open sea. It would not be difficult for a faster ship to overtake him in this small craft, but they would go about unabated if they had no reason to investigate this little boat.

Scrambling about the boat, he looked for a hat or something to disguise his Caucasian features. Now, assuredly, one of the British officers would be informing the captain of the small craft; no matter how insignificant, they would be eyeing him carefully for any sign of a threat.

He noticed the boat was leaking slightly, after looking down at his feet. Water swished back and forth with each rocking wave. The boat's bilge was black greasy water where the two sides met at the keel. Quickly, he reached down to rub the hard planks of wood. He gathered the black tar-like slime in his hands.

He saw a straw hat partly stuffed under a dirty canvas, undoubtedly left behind by the previous owner. Quickly, he grabbed ahold of it and set it on his head to hide his sandy blond hair. With his hands black from the smelly goo, he quickly began to rub it over his entire face and arms. Convinced that his disguise would work, he remained steadfast and didn't look back.

He had no idea what waypoint he should plot. But at this moment none of that mattered; getting away from the approaching ships was what counted most. As the small vessel turned opposite, an offshore breeze filled the sails. After looking over his shoulder, he noticed the other ship's course and direction. As expected, he posed no real threat, looking the part of a local fisherman.

This one chance to get away meant everything. He couldn't waste it and did everything to put as much distance between himself and the HMS *Dolphin* as possible. The more distance he traveled over the rolling waves, the smaller the ship became. As he crested each rising wave in his attempt to escape, even the land behind him soon began to fade.

A compass. I need a compass, he thought. Indeed, the governor would have supplied him with one. Again, after tying the rudder in place, he checked inside the bag; as he hoped was a brass compass and charts of the local area. He scrutinized it. Off the Trinidad coast sat a series of small islands on the map. He quickly steered toward the largest one. If he were seeking shelter, it would be the obvious choice. Immediately, he navigated toward it. According to the chart, a group of smaller islands was located east of this more massive island named Caiman Brak.

As he rode a big wave to its height, he looked one

last time behind him—all he could see were only small white sails as they drew closer to Trinidad. The island now ahead of him was easily accessible. He knew that he would bypass every island on the map as he charted a new course for his escape.

Diplomacy was the order of the day. It was always a grand pompous affair when the British Navy arrived at a foreign port. For now, the distraction of preparing the British ship to anchor at the port would aid him in his plight to escape.

The small boat approached the island ahead; the water changed color. Instead of a deep aqua blue, it appeared like a crystal pale blue color, completely transparent.

The ocean bottom slowly rose upward as he got closer to land. Not wanting to run aground, he maintained a safe distance from the coral bottom that would rip open the small boat's hull.

Changing direction slightly, he maneuvered the boat to pass away from the island's sandy beaches, still maintaining a safe distance from the coral beneath. The wind had changed direction, being affected by the island's landmass.

He had to adjust to the new conditions by changing his sail. As he sailed on, the blue water sparkled above the surface, reflecting off the tropical sun like millions of tiny diamonds.

Usually, the tropical heat was unbearable, but thankfully, upon the open water, it was barely noticeable. The salt spray created by the boat slapping against the waves couldn't be avoided, and soon Thomas found himself partially drenched. He paid it no mind, as it made him feel alive and uncaring about his current condition. As he turned eastward while passing the island, he could see another small fishing village ahead of him, much like he did on the mainland.

Small, half-naked children ran to the beach as he passed by and excitedly began waving, bidding for his attention. Thomas returned the gesture briefly as the coral beneath him started to look uncomfortably close. Again, steering the small boat away, he soon passed the small village, and it slowly disappeared out of sight as the children continued playing in the surf.

As he rounded the island looking toward the east, another isle appeared over the horizon that seemed to be eight or ten miles away. He steered directly for it without hesitation, knowing he was still in danger of capture. A silvery-looking fish suddenly broke the water's surface off his port bow. Thomas knew as a sailor that there could be many reasons for this behavior, but he hoped that his knowledge of these events didn't mean that the fish was avoiding being eaten by large reef sharks.

Near where the fish appeared, on the surface, was a black tip dorsal fin cutting through the water. *They're not far from our boat*, was what he feared most. The tigers of the sea were always hungry. "Easy as she goes!" Thomas whispered to himself, grabbing the rudder tightly. He maintained his course. He knew that if he ran aground at this moment, it would be the end for him and his unconscious companion.

"If only my family could see me now," he whispered. Suddenly, his heart sank as he realized for the first time that he had never considered his loved ones back home in England. He left his dear mother and sister Kathy there while he was away seeing the world. It was a solitary life that he chose, returning to the sea shortly after the loss of his wife, Ann. The fever took her just four years ago.

Now considering his predicament, he understood that by running away to save this stranger, he had prostituted himself to piracy. *A pirate*, he thought. "No, I could never join that hearty bunch of cutthroats, although I might be hanged for harboring one such as this."

AS THE SUN BEGAN TO set, he had just approached the lush island covered with green growth. It was a place that reminded him of an earlier time in his life when he was just a lad. After becoming a British sailor, he was soon stationed upon the HMS *Devonshire*. One day, while on patrol, its steering rudder had broken. He and a fellow sailor were chosen to complete the repair. They anchored off an island such as this.

At the time they were just south of Borneo Island. He and the other sailor were inexperienced in things that could eat you alive.

Hugh Hansberry was actually from his hometown, just a year older than himself. With a sudden shout from the quartermaster, a single rope was tied about their waist, and both were ordered into the crystal water. They were let down near the stern of the ship. At first all went according to plan. Hugh undid the brass bar that held the top piece of the rudder in place. He managed to grasp the replacement piece as best he could while paddling the water.

The swollen board was stubborn and would not budge. Hugh had to pound on it using a heavy hammer until it became loose. Unfortunately, he attracted the attention of an unwanted guest. The unexpected attack was fierce and deadly. The shark appeared from beneath the ship and, in one single bite, ripped open Hugh's stomach, and his entrails poured out into the water, turning everything around a deep red color.

Remembering the look of terror in Hugh's eyes, Thomas shivered suddenly. The scream that followed was ear-piercing. His lifeline was jerked upward, and he found himself back aboard the ship without warning. Recollecting that horrific day, he thought of how Hugh had hung onto the last moments of his life. His eyes had rolled upward as he whispered the last call to his mother and died.

It was his first encounter with sharks, the sea devils. After looking over his port side, Thomas yelled, "You'll not eat me today, ye bastards of Davey Jones." Ahead of him, another small island came into view. Not even a beach was visible, meaning it was inhabitable. The green growth looked as if it invaded every inch of volcanic soil. *What soil? It was a rock that erupted out of the depth of the sea and nothing more,* he thought.

Quite unexpectedly, Thomas heard moans coming from the pirate. He hadn't time to investigate or to check on the man. The two were running for their very lives. Once again, the ocean bottom began to draw upward, much too close. Thomas instinctively steered the small boat away from the lonely isle, thinking about the British ship approaching the small town he left behind. He wondered what reception they would receive; he had no idea and couldn't bother himself with that concern.

He saw a pair of white cranes taking flight when he looked back toward the island. He watched them glide just about the water toward some unknown direction. It seemed natural for the birds to fly away from all their troubles to him. *If I was a bird, how marvelous that would be. At a time such as this, when all else is wrong with my life, I could fly away and leave everything behind,* he thought.

SEVERAL HOURS HAD PASSED SINCE he had left the town of Trinidad. At any moment the British ship should be entering the port. He estimated that he had already traveled over twenty nautical miles. It should be far enough that his small sail would be lost in the swelling seas. The fact that the brigand stirred from his unconscious state was a positive sign. At the time there was no way to check on his fever as the small boat began to get tossed about over the bouncing waves. He was now looking beyond, toward the next island that seemed further than before. The sun was beginning to set, and soon he would only have the stars to guide him and nothing else.

Without warning a muffled echo of cannon fire erupted a considerable distance away, toward the direction of Trinidad. Thomas turned to see what he feared most, the British naval fleet declaring war on the Spanish. He continued to stare back toward the mainland for any sign of smoke that he was sure he would be able to see.

His heart sank, suddenly thinking of the damage that one cannonball could hurl down on the defenseless that sounded like a bombardment being fired at the town. Thomas quickly understood it to mean one thing: death.

Chapter 4

A silent assembly stood on the decks of the pirate ship *Hell's Fury*, waiting for their illustrious captain, Matthew Redbone. The crew stood silently atop the decks as the ship rocked. The sounds of creaking timbers from the superstructure were all that was heard.

Mr. Schmidt, the bloodthirsty first mate, stood with a scowl looking over the crew. His large stature was a figure that wasn't to be agitated. He had a long scar that ran across his right cheek, resulting from an attack by a highwayman in which the man paid with his life. He eyed the crew for disrespectful arrogance as they prepared for the sacred ritual of inducting a new member into the Iron Born brotherhood.

From deep within the ship's bowels came two pirates escorting a man. Drums suddenly began to pound out a rhythm beat as the recruit was led to the famous Iron Blood Pirates' Bloody Hag. Mr. Jack Newberry, who looked to be in his early twenties, surveyed the audience before him. Some faces looked outward with an expression of dread for the approaching enactment, while others shone fire in their eyes that blazed with excitement, knowing that soon they would be seeing his blood running from his body.

A single cast-iron pot was mounted atop an iron pedestal near the railing, with one pirate stoking the coals inside. The two red-hot irons stood at the ready. The lone pirate looked up, adverted from his task, to catch a passing glimpse of Mr. Newberry, for whom the irons were prepared.

The drums stopped; an eerie hush fell over the

crowd. The only sounds heard on board came from the splashing waves hitting against the wooden hull and the heavy wooden masts, whose weight creaked slightly in their keeps. The sails above the yardarms moved somewhat from the gentle breeze, their riggings holding fast.

Walking up the wooden steps, Mr. Newberry was led to the upper deck. When they arrived at the quarterdeck, the Bloody Hag stood. Her face displayed a grin as if she was laughing at him for being so foolish. Jack stood alone before the monstrous creation to be tested and began having doubts.

Mr. Schmidt, the first mate, then walked over and tightly grabbed hold of Jack's arm. Escorting him to the device, he shoved his arm inside, positioning it with his palm facing upward. Afterward, Mr. Newberry looked over at the first mate, searching for the slightest sign of compassion. None was given as the man shoved Newberry's other arm inside. Now Jack stood as if he was hugging the ugly creature of death. Subsequently, he was chained tightly to the emotionless device and waited.

Without warning the captain appeared on the quarterdeck, whispering between the men, then came to an abrupt hush as they stared at the master of ceremony walking above them. Redbone himself began to solemnly chant the saying, "Iron Blood, True Blood, begins ye tale of this wretched soul. Who will soon float above Heaven or Hell? If he is found worthy to bear the marks, now swear your life for all these your shipmates, who watch you disembark. If ye not worthy and you die in the test, will ye rest forever with Davy Jones?"

At that precise moment two hearty swashbucklers grabbed hold of ropes and hoisted up the top half of the Bloody Hag. A crewman stood ready and watched eagerly for when the heavy iron would pass the first notch. Afterward, he inserted two iron pins in place.

The captain slowly walked over toward the beasty creation. He withdrew two small razor-sharp swords, inserting each blade into its correct slot; the captain stepped away inside the iron maiden.

Mr. Newberry began praying for mercy for his sins

as he watched the metal piece rise above his head. The pin was quickly removed, and then, gazing back at Redbone, he saw the man raise his right arm. Suddenly, the crew's chanting arose to a fiery pitch, shouting aloud the sacred words of the oath of becoming the Iron Blood Pirate.

Without warning Redbone's arm fell to his side, and simultaneously, both men holding the ropes released their grip. Immediately, the heavy maiden came crashing downward upon Mr. Newberry, who suddenly felt the cold steel slice into his wrist.

The sting of the blades hurt like hell. He wasn't anticipating this deep, burning pain. Instead, he had illusions of not feeling any pain at all, perhaps the romantic misconceptions of youth. But there it was, this deep pounding hurt, as his nerves within his wrist were cut asunder. He then was introduced to more of the same when their captain looked upon the two pirates, who motioned for them to prepare the lines and hoist the other half of the iron creation back up.

Now the deed was done. The two blades that dug deeply into his wrist were suddenly jerked away, leaving him to feel the warm flowing sensation of his blood pouring outward upon his skin. Suddenly, the two pirates pulled the top half back, securing it back in place. Afterward, the ropes hung freely to the side of the device as the two men walked away, their part playing out in this death dance.

Jack's view was hindered by the sizable laughing figure ahead of him who wore a sickening smile, as if to say, *Look, you fool, you're about to die.* All at once Jack began to feel flush and light-headed. His blood poured into a large brass basin set atop a scale weighed down by brass weights in another tray.

What happened next came as a bit of a surprise. As Jack stood chained to the cold iron, dying, Redbone, the captain, unexpectedly called out to a crewman to bring the rum. Turning his head, he saw a young man hurrying toward the captain. Just as the boy approached, Redbone grabbed a goblet from his hand.

He smiled, walked over, and said, "Aye—Mr. Newberry, sir, drink up, lad; it shall hasten ye flow of your blood to end your suffering."

At this point in the ceremony he felt thirsty, but how the captain knew this was a mystery that he couldn't answer. Leaning his head toward the shiny cup, he began to gulp the elixir down his parched throat. The alcohol was beneficial. Immediately, he felt the effects, relaxing his body and easing his pain as he continued to bleed out. It could be considered a form of mercy, but he didn't argue.

The chanting continued as the men around him refused to cease singing their song. He felt light-headed and waggish. He knew that death was getting closer; somehow the thought of it was no longer frightful. He quickly made peace with God, asking for this misery to end. He wouldn't fight death to stay alive. He had made his peace, feeling proud that he never took a life; somehow this seemed important to him.

The world around him began to change; he no longer felt his body drifting in and out of consciousness. At one point only moments earlier, he felt nauseous at the thought of his blood being poured out. For whatever reason, this made him sick to his stomach. Soon, however, that feeling was gone, replaced with something more pleasurable. The anxiety and stress faded from memory. Even the chanting voices didn't seem so loud as before. Now they sounded muffled. The rocking motion of the ship was barely noticeable as well. Instead, the world around him swirled gently as strange forces controlled it.

He knew now that it wouldn't be long. However, a flashing memory appeared as he remembered his dear mother back home. He wanted to be buried near her and forever rest in peace next to her grave, but a disturbing reality befell him. According to the custom, he remembered that his body would never see home again if he died during the ritual. Instead, his corpse would be tossed overboard, no more than shark food to be discarded.

Suddenly, without warning, Captain Redbone yelled out a command, loud enough to wake the dead: "Ye has fulfilled his share of the bargain. Release him from thee bonds."

At that moment two men raced toward him to

unchain him from the iron maiden. Once released he collapsed upon the deck, unable to stand. He was lying helplessly upon the wooden planks, his eyes barely open to see the world around him. However, suddenly, he heard heavy steps approaching, someone in his blurry vision he guessed to be Mr. Schmidt by the man's size.

At that moment the stranger grabbed ahold of his bleeding wrist; without warning Jack felt a hot, burning pain indescribable as a red-hot branding iron pressed deep into his wound. His screams overpowered any other sounds aboard the ship, as if the last bit of strength within him was spent in repudiating the invading iron.

When the other arm was lifted, he had no strength or voice but only the tears of the last resistance against the man who insulted him in this cruel manner. While lying there he heard muffled voices saying a toast to his journey: "He's still alive; death has not taken the man." He understood the eventual end of the ceremony had come at last. He survived the encounter with the Bloody Hag, as the crew was offered a goblet of rum to see him off.

Two stout men came near him to hoist his body off the deck. They brought him to the doctor's cabin. There, Mr. Newberry was placed upon a bed of straw. He prayed as he closed his eyes and traveled to some unknown place more pleasant than his earthly home, not permanently.

Afterward, still standing near the Bloody Hag, Captain Redbone turned to his first mate and said, "Arrrr, the lad lives, would he not, Mr. Schmidt?"

"Yes, I believe so, Captain. Jack has a strong will, sir."

"Aye, that be good news. The brotherhood needs stout young members that show fierceness and inner strength."

"Yes, sir, will that be all?"

"No, I'm afraid not, Mr. Schmidt, sir. Come to my cabin; I have a matter I want to discuss with you alone."

"Yes, Captain, as you wish."

Then an unexpected interruption by the Dutch attaché, Wolfert Hoff, who unexpectedly appeared and said, "Splendid display of pirate loyalty—why I was astounded to see the pirate ritual for myself."

"Arrrr tell me, you fancy a try at the Bloody Hag—do ye?"

"No, indeed, captain—believe me, I have stories, but none compare to seeing the actual event played out before your eyes. It's nothing short of amazing, Although the sight of blood makes me queasy."

"Aye—blood is the business ye be in, sir, if we don't find ourselves spilling our blood, then it be someone else's ye be spilling. But tell me how ye are feeling. Seems much better; the color has returned to yer face."

"Oh yes, Captain, nothing that a glass of rum won't cure. So, tell me, Captain Redbone, how soon before we reach Bonaire?"

"According to ye charts, if ye continue to have favorable winds, should be there in a week or so aye imagine—why, do ye have someplace to be?"

"Oh, it's my seasickness, I'm afraid. I can't seem to adjust to the movement of the rolling seas."

"Arrrr, a land lover ye must be, man. Now enough of this complaining. I have a ship to run, if ye will excuse me, sir."

"Yes, certainly. Captain, I wanted you to know how pleased the governor will be when he hears of the treatment and hospitality you and your crew have shown me while aboard your pirate ship—what did you call it? I can't seem to remember; please forgive me."

"Arrrr, man, ye test my patience, ye do. Allow me to say this once and for all: The very timbers ye be standing on and what keeps you from drowning be the deck of the *Hell's Fury*. No finer ship sailing these waters!"

"Yes, that's it, the *Hell's Fury*. Tell me, Captain, how did you come to call her by that name?"

"It be simple, Wolfert Hoff. Those seeing ye black flag flying off her transom will soon discover the blasting of cannons and the rising smoke of their doom, as if to say they suddenly found themselves in the place we call Hell, sir—thereby thee name, *Hell's Fury*."

"Oh, I see."

"Good day, sir." Walking away, Redbone was

becoming annoyed by babysitting this Dutch governor's representative. Still, as a hefty price for their services, the Iron Born would soon be rewarded if only he didn't slit the man's throat and throw him overboard.

A short time later after arriving at the Captain's cabin, both men stepped inside. Redbone strolled over to a wooden table at the back of the room. Next to it stood an ornate gold lampstand. Several charts lay open with a compass and sextant in a box now open. He took a match from a brass container resembling a dragon and lit its candle. He then walked over to open a window to the outside, allowing fresh air to remove the room's stuffiness. Turning to his first mate, he said, "Arrrr, Schmidt, have a seat there."

"Yes, Captain."

Afterward, Redbone walked over to a small crystal canister and poured two glasses of cognac. He handed a glass to Mr. Schmidt and began removing his embellished coat. Then he laid it across an oversized wooden chair. Now exposed was his small arsenal of pistols strapped across his chest, his gold-handled sword flashed in the sun that filtered into the cabin as he moved about the room.

After lifting his glass he took a long drink, then sat down. Turning to his first mate, Redbone said, "Aye, there be the matter of Mauricio Barros, the pirate who has abandoned his post and stole a lifeboat to visit his sister in Trinidad?"

Now feeling a little anxious, Mr. Schmidt said, "Captain, sir, I didn't exactly give him permission to leave." Then he added, "Mauricio spoke of a need to fulfill a promise to his sick mother when he mentioned it to me. I refused him, sir."

"Aye, see," Redbone sneered.

"We're pirates, damn it all to hell. I reminded Mauricio of that fact and told him any visits to any Spanish port of Trinidad would put us in danger. Explaining that ever since Tortuga, fellow pirates are sailing these waters in search of us."

"Arrr, rightly so, Mr. Schmidt. We'll put the matter to rest, but you, the first mate, shall be responsible for delivering punishment when we find our Mr. Mauricio Barros. Ye, most of all, should realize what the penalty for abandoning ye post shall be," the captain said pointedly.

"Yes, sir, the taking of his leg. It's that plain, that simple, sir!"

"Ye be correct. I keep a tight ship. When one of our brothers leaves us deserted, he shall pay for this disgrace with something of his own body, the mere object that allowed him to escape—his leg, of course."

"I understand your meaning, Captain," Mr. Schmidt replied sourly. "Sir, there is still the matter of the crewman caught stealing a knife from his shipmates. It's a matter that requires your attention back out on the deck, sir."

"Aye, of course, give me a minute, and I will join thee shortly on the quarterdeck."

"As you wish, Captain," Mr. Schmidt replied, then finished his glass and walked out of the captain's quarters, taking his place on the main deck among the men waiting for the captain to reappear.

After taking a final drink from his glass of cognac, Redbone sat down, examining the navigation charts of the Spanish Main. *This has been a challenging voyage thus far—no real booty to speak of, just cargoes of oil and tobacco*, he thought. *To set things right, a Spanish galleon is needed to bring the men happiness, filled to her timbers with jewels and gold bullion.*

After looking over the charts, he tried to position themselves near the shipping lanes in the hope of coming across a fattened goose with a golden egg. Their devotion depended on counting their gold doubloons or soured on nothing for their seagoing voyage except a few eight pieces! Then again, the Spanish and English warships buffeted their attempts at plunder.

Yes, they possessed a formidable fighting force of two ships—a three-mast Brigantine and a Barque with her shallow draft—plus her accompaniment of eight cannons. But he realized that compared to the fighting strength of an HMS man-of-war with her sixty-plus guns, it would be a battle to the end.

After rising from his chair, he put on his decorative

overcoat, leaving his cabin to deal with the problems aboard his pirate ship, as the captain was customary.

When he reappeared out onto the deck, all the company of men was eagerly awaiting him onboard; only God commanded more respect than he.

"Arrrr—bring forth the accused," Redbone demanded in his deep voice. He stood high above everyone atop the quarterdeck to show strength and resolve.

Suddenly, there appeared two pirates escorting a young man in irons. They walked in front of Redbone and came to a complete stop. The young man looked at the captain, appearing angry while awaiting judgment.

Looking down at young Jimmy Cain, Redbone addressed him with grave concern, knowing that the penalty for thievery is the loss of a hand. *Surely, he must realize what he has done*, he thought. Still, it seemed like yesterday when he was fished out of the water. He had been adrift for days; he was the only shipwreck survivor, ninety miles from land. A fire broke out on board, and soon fire engulfed the entire ship; sadly, it sank. He and some other sailors survived their encounter by getting inside a small lifeboat.

While they drifted upon the open sea, the other two men had suffered under the blazing tropical sun, with no water to drink, and soon perished. He alone was found alive. Jimmy Cain eagerly took the test to become one of the crew. *He is fearless, but is he that foolish to steal from one of his shipmates?*

Redbone asked the accuser to be brought forth as a hush fell over the ship. Mr. Albert Steinway, the crewman who repaired sails, stepped forward across from Jimmy; he refused to look at the youth but instead held his head low.

"Aye, tell thee your story Mr. Steinway," the captain called out. "Ye have accused this here young Jimmy of stealing your pearl-handled knife, have ye not?"

"Yes, sir, Captain," Mr. Steinway replied. "He stole it for sure, sir. That be true enough, that young pup."

"Aye, then nothing else to say to thee—Mr. Schmidt, bring me the block and the ax. We shall remove his left hand for thievery, we shall. Make haste, sir," the captain shouted, then added, "We wouldn't want to prevent the boy from being able to defend himself now, shall we?"

Looking down at the youth, Redbone asked a simple, pertinent question: "Arrrr, Jimmy, ye are right-handed, are ye not?"

Young Jimmy then yelled, "It wasn't me. I'm not a thief, sir!"

"What, ye say—ye be not a thief, ye say? What then are thee—a liar as well?" the captain shouted. As he leaned forward against the rail, Redbone looked down at the lad sternly and asked, "Do ye know the punishment for lying to your captain?"

"No, sir, it wasn't me, sir. The truth be told, sir, Mr. Steinway is in love with a pretty young whore in Tortuga that I bedded on our last visit to the port. I had no way of knowing he had feelings for the young lady."

"Arrrr—what is that you say? Love is it then?" the captain questioned.

"All of this is over a girl named Esmeralda, a French harlot back at Tortuga," Jimmy said.

"Ye harlot, you say, man?" Redbone answered.

"Yes, it's true enough, Captain. It was our last night in port. Mr. Steinway was occupied with duties aboard the ship. I was free to visit the young lady. While I was in the throes of passion, Mr. Steinway burst through the door. A fight broke out between us that was ended by a quick punch to Mr. Steinway's jaw. Sadly, he promised to get even with me, sir."

"Aye, tell it quick, Mr. Steinway!" the captain shouted. "Is the boy a thief or not?" was the captain's angry response to the accuser.

"Well, Captain, sir, maybe I was a bit mistaken on who took my knife, sir; that is to say, sir, that it seemed to me that young Jimmy there did admire it, so it seemed natural that he would have taken it, sir."

A scowl appeared on the captain's face as he walked down the stairs leading to the main deck. Redbone stopped mere inches from Steinway as he roared, "Men of the true blood brotherhood, what are we? Are ye not brothers of our own spilled blood, which we all took an oath to become true mates to the end of our lives. Still, some feel that a cheap whore is worth more than ye own blood, brother?"

Steinway's knees began to knock together; any smartness fell from his expression, as he had never seen his captain's rage. Not expecting a physical response from Redbone, the punch across his jaw knocked Mr. Steinway to the deck.

Mr. Schmidt was quickly ordered to release Jimmy. Instead, he was called to take Mr. Steinway and place him in irons to make him dance the bow waltz for the next hour, under full sail.

"Afterward, he shall bear the mark of the liar's tongue," the captain shouted out as a warning to every member of his crew.

"Aye, aye, sir!" Mr. Schmidt responded.

Before he knew what was happening, Mr. Steinway's wrists and ankles were shackled with metal bracelets. Each band had a large steel ring welded outside, with a long rope tied to it. He was then dragged to the ship's forecastle and hoisted overboard under the bowsprit. He was straddled across the vessel's figurehead, a painted witch with a green face and protruding jaw, which was now pressing against his back.

Being fastened tight with several ropes, he hung in this precarious position with his arms and legs wide open and half his body positioned just below the waterline.

In times past some unfortunate souls couldn't survive this ritual; when their ropes had come undone, they were merely left to bang against the ship's hull until they succumbed to the pounding waves and drowned. Eventually, their ropes were cut free; they became shark food that floated away.

This trial to test a man's metal was used in such cases as this, especially when someone was accusing his fellow blood brother of being a thief, in which he would lose his hand for the offense. All of this because Mr. Steinway fell in love with a whore. This betrayal was inexcusable in the sight of the captain and his crew.

After seeing Albert secured in place, the captain

ordered, "Set sail."

Once the ship lugged forward and gained speed, Redbone felt it was the appropriate time. He then took the hourglass and turned it upside down. As the sand slowly poured down through the narrow opening, so did the life of Mr. Albert Steinway. The ship took on speed within moments, moving forward across the waves. At first he could quickly breathe, but the boat's weight pushed him forward, in and out of the troughs of pounding waves. He soon found himself taking longer breaths of air, which were becoming increasingly difficult.

The weight of the water across his body was something he didn't expect. Yes, he had seen this ritual performed on other crew members, but somehow he never expected to find himself here. Rethinking his love for the young whore back in port, he regretted his decision to lie about young Jimmy.

It was purely out of jealousy. After seeing Jimmy atop his love, making her scream as she was, he felt compelled to do something about it. Not the smartest thing that he had ever done, but still, he couldn't help himself.

The last crashing dip into the waves took too long to reach the other side. Besides this, the ship's rocking was happening at an alarming rate. Try as Albert might, he couldn't resist the pounding waves. As he struggled to take a breath, each attempt was becoming strenuous. His own body was quickly tiring, and having the wooden figurehead pressed into his back ached him sorely. He prayed for the ship's rising into the next trough, which was a short experience. The passing minutes seemed like a lifetime, and he doubted if he could continue this horrible experience.

One thing becoming frighteningly clear was how his head was free to bounce about, slammed against the ship's keel. His legs held tight by the ropes hadn't moved, but his arms felt looser than before. This fact hadn't aided him in the least.

From his angle, each time the ship dipped under the waves, he strained to look above the water for the welcoming light of day, filling his lungs as often as he could. Truthfully, he was growing increasingly tired, and each time the ship crashed into the waves, he felt his strength fade, barely able to resist the onslaught. He became tired of not letting the saltwater enter his lungs, which he knew would mean certain death. He was gasping with every breath he took. He already knew the hard reality: He was drowning slowly.

What self-worth Albert had in his miserable life would soon be taken from him. The promise of love from the young whore, whose empty promises to love him only, seemed meaningless as he faced his mortality.

His arms and legs pulled apart prevented him from bracing himself for each impact of the heavy water. He could barely feel his legs strung from the iron bracelets cutting deep into his flesh, his eyes were burning. His back and chest hurt him sorely.

As the wooden ship was tossed about the roaring seas, he realized he had a front-row seat to his doom. *Why had I acted so foolishly?* he continually asked himself. Perhaps if he were not so damned weak, he would not have fallen so deeply in love with the pretty young thing named Esmeralda.

It was becoming darker, and he had no more strength to resist. Even the ship's movements seemed insensible as he again would take another breath before the vessel dipped under the waves. His miserable life, what there was of it, didn't turn out as he had hoped. With high expectations of being an Iron Born Pirate, he soon forgot his pledge to his fellow pirates. Instead, he was ready to offer young Jimmy the loss of his hand. No, he deserved to die; this final truth he accepted bitterly.

The last careening dips of the ship into the powerful waves seemed less intrusive than the previous trips into the black water. Although Albert seemed able to exhale some water, he knew it wasn't enough and began coughing up saltwater instead.

Everything around him began to grow dark, his breathing more difficult. He kept his eyes closed to the outside world, hoping not to see the grim reaper of death coming for him. He had already said his goodbyes to his life, looking toward the next. His body seemed strange and foreign to him as he felt lifted into another world. The last thing he remembered was hearing the ship's bells as he collapsed upon the deck, completely exhausted and feeling nothing from then on; his world was growing black.

Unexpectedly, he found the words within himself and yelled out in a desperate fight against death itself, "You shall not have me, oh angel of death."

But then, surprisingly, the captain's words were heard saying aloud, "The liar's tongue, Mr. Schmidt."

"Aye, sir!" was the first mate's muffled response.

Then as he laid there in and out of consciousness, Mr. Steinway heard approaching heavy footsteps, a heavy thud afterward. Near him was a heavy cast-iron pot with red-hot coals burning inside. He felt the heat near his head, then, knowing what was about to happen, he saw, to his horror, a pair of muscular legs standing near the pot.

He cried out, "No, no!"

Suddenly, he felt large fingers opening his mouth widely—a pair of tongs gripping his tongue. Then came the most excruciating pain he had experienced in his life, as a red-hot knife sliced his tongue asunder, cutting away large amounts of flesh until his tongue reached a point. Then the tip was split in two as if he were a snake licking the air. His screams of pain shattered the quietness of the ship as each pirate aboard the *Hell's Fury* measured the futility of betraying a fellow Iron Born brother.

Afterward, Mr. Steinway was taken to his hammock and carelessly thrown inside. While he rocked side to side with the ship's motion, he prayed that this whole affair was nothing more than a nightmare, complete with the smell of burning flesh that invaded his nostrils, as the pain he felt was unimaginable.

One last time he tried to call out the name of the pretty young whore, Esmeralda, knowing that she would never hear his words that beckoned her to come—to kiss her upon her lips again—but his request would soon fall silent, and drifted away. However, the result of his Godless jealousy was burningly apparent, his new companion for the rest of his life, as the blistering, searing pain and coughing up of seawater would attest.

Chapter 5

Appearing on the quarterdeck of His Majesty's battleship, the HMS *Dolphin*, a seasoned British lieutenant came to an abrupt halt in front of the ship's captain. After saluting his commander, he said, "Sir, the boarding party has been alerted; they are standing by waiting for your orders."

"Thank you, Mr. Hockings," Captain Harrington replied. Then, looking back at his men, he said, "Supply muskets to every boarding party member, along with a double supply of shots."

"Yes, sir," the lieutenant answered. Afterward, another salute and the young man was off.

All the sails were secured as the wooden vessel slowly drifted toward the long pier, which had become suddenly deserted of any locals. Still, there was no opposition or greetings from the townspeople.

Quickly, crew members tethered the ropes to the dock, and a gangway was soon placed.

Standing on the pier, the men quickly gathered at the base of the gangway. Their proper uniforms had polished buttons, their muskets pointed upward.

One soldier leaned over and whispered to his mate. "What now, Mr. Billings? Are we in for a battle, I suppose?" Martin, the young cadet, asked the sailor next to him.

"Depends on these foreigners. Damn, I should have never left England and dear Rachel," the man said with regret.

"Oh, don't worry your head, Tom Billings; she'll be fine, if we get ourselves free of any confrontations with these unpredictable Spanish," Martin assured his friend.

While everyone stood sharply at attention, the captain appeared at the gangways and slowly descended onto the pier. He was dressed in a dark blue coat, white trousers with matching white stockings, and black shoes, secured atop with brass buckles. He wore a white powder wig under his naval captain's hat on his head. His shiny brass buttons, with medals pinned across his chest displaying his bravery in battles fought, glistened in the sunlight. His sword was fastened to his body by a black belt and a shiny brass buckle. He looked distinguished as an officer representing the Royal Navy when attending foreign dignitaries.

As the captain stepped onto the wooden pier, the small company of soldiers drew out their heaving chests and threw their shoulders backward, forming a rigid stance. The captain eyed his men carefully, looking for any imperfection, while arriving at the head of the column. He felt proud of his men and how they performed their duties on this voyage, far from home. With his men filed in ranks behind him, his lieutenant gave the order to advance as they followed behind, approaching the port town of Trinidad.

Unexpectedly, the sound of music was heard approaching. Assessing the situation, Harrington ordered his men to form ranks. Surmising no threat from an adversary who played music, he ordered his men to stand at ease while they approached. The tune the band played seemed happy and gay, almost like a tune that one would play at a park setting back in merry old England.

A small group of musicians came into view, behind them a detachment of Spanish soldiers dressed in greenish uniforms. A carriage with two white stallions followed at the rear. Inside the wagon were a man and a woman. The man was dressed much like himself, except his dress was a more flamboyant attire and more colorful with a white powdered wig and blue silk shirt. The woman wore a white hairpiece, which was quite long, and a blue silk dress with a matching lace hat and a small umbrella that she twirled above her head in her clothing.

None of the British soldiers broke ranks. They

remained at attention with eyes staring forward at each other. Harrington reached down for the hilt of his sword as if feeling the steel blade comforted him somehow. Their ship drifted in on the afternoon tide, but having to leave in a hurry would be another matter altogether.

The wagon slowly approached and came to an abrupt halt. The band arrived, then stopped abruptly only twenty feet away. Separating into two groups, each band member stood shoulder to shoulder while playing their instruments, directing their stares to the approaching horse-drawn carriage. Two servants raced to the small door as a red carpet was unveiled at the foot of the carriage, and with the help of the two servants, the two nobles reverently appeared.

Straightaway, Harrington was somewhat amused seeing the two nobles, as the man was dressed in beautiful silks of the brightest colors and decadence, which one would expect from such aristocrats. His plump wife, who struggled to walk upright in her small shoes, was dressed in all white lace fabrics and was aided, leaving the coach by one of the servants who carried a silken umbrella above her head.

"Good afternoon, Capitán. My name is Edwardo Santos Félix Escobar. I'm the local governor for these Spanish territories. The fine lady beside me is my lovely wife, Countess Maria Consuela Anita Escobar."

After bowing respectively, the lady curtseyed, afterward sticking out her hand for the captain to kiss.

"How do you do, Madam?" Harrington responded as he bowed his head in respect; taking her hand, he gently kissed it on the lace glove.

"I am fine, Capitán, thank you for asking," she said pleasantly.

Edwardo was one to cut to the chase and quickly asked: "Capitán, what brings you to our fine city on this lovely day?"

"Quite frankly pirates, sir. We've been on the search for the dreaded band of cutthroats known as the Iron Born Pirates. Perhaps you've heard of them?"

"Oh, yes, everyone's heard of the Iron Born, Blood Pirates, but they have not been seen in these waters, which I'm aware of," Edwardo replied. "Perhaps this is nothing more than vicious rumors set about by my Spanish constituents, made to confuse and nothing more."

"Perhaps you're right," Harrington answered. "However, I would accept such a statement if not because one of our British merchant ships was attacked not more than fifty miles south by those vicious, bloodthirsty dogs. One survivor lived long enough to tell the tale of who attacked them, sir. I will not rest until I see everyone hanging from the gallows."

"It is disturbing news," Edwardo retorted, "but as you can see, there are no pirates here; if, indeed, there were, I would see their destruction. For now, let us show you our hospitality by inviting you to be our guest for dinner this evening."

"I would like to thank you for your offer, sir. May I add that your English is excellent," Harrington commented.

"Well, thank you for the compliment. In my youth I attended one of your universities back in England and have fallen in love with your culture, señor."

"Come, Capitán; you can ride with us to the governor's house. Your men will be shown the same hospitality as yourself; you have my word."

After boarding the carriage, Harrington announced, "I regret to inform you that we will not be able to stay long. We will only be in your lovely city for a short time; soon we will be off again once we resupply our ship. There is the matter of the pirates that sail these waters harassing trade between our two countries."

"When it comes time for you to leave, we will be happy to supply your provisions for your journey, to aid you in your search for the pirate scum," the governor responded.

Harrington was soon escorted back to the waiting carriage, and the conversation between the captain and his host soon changed to other topics involving the king's court back in England, including the latest fashion craze the ladies were wearing to the latest dance. All of this, of course, was quite boring to a British naval officer. But still, his host seemed eager to hear any news about England; Harrington was more than happy to oblige.

THE FOLLOWING DAY, SOMETIME DURING breakfast, a Spanish officer appeared saluting the governor; he handed him an official parchment. After asking forgiveness for the interruption, Edwardo quickly read the document. Then he looked up and said, "Well, Capitán, it seems that your prey, these Iron Born Pirates, have been reported invading a small fishing village near Santo Domingo, where they raped and pillaged the residents."

"They must be stopped at once!" Harrington replied with a slam of his fist on the table.

"These *piratas* are elusive. We have sent out mighty warships to find them, but they seem to outwit our attempts in every way, then disappear without a trace."

Then turning to his guest, Harrington announced, "We shall set sail upon the morning tide to hunt them down, sir; you have my word."

It was the third day of his visit, and Harrington was eager to return to his search for the bloodthirsty pirates. Though his host's hospitality had no end, it almost seemed to him that Edwardo was hiding something. He couldn't tell what it was, but he knew how to read people and their expressions.

On their last night together while discussing their government's trade policies, Harrington's first officer, Mr. Breckenridge, asked to speak to him privately. After leaving the dining table for the moment, the two men stepped outside onto the balcony for some privacy.

Mr. Breckenridge seemed somewhat out of sorts, pacing about as if scrutinizing the reason for his visit. Being straightforward, Harrington ordered the man to get to the point and explain his motive for the interruption.

"Captain Harrington, sir, I have recently heard the news from a Mr. Hampshire, the boatswain mate, who had recently visited a local brothel. As he was entertained by a lovely young woman in her boudoir, he saw a British sailor's uniform neatly tucked away in her armoire. When he inquired about to whom the uniform belonged, she quickly closed the cabinet doors, and he was abruptly asked to leave the establishment without any explanation."

Harrington stood silently, gathering his thoughts on this new revelation as he pondered its meaning. Suddenly, turning to face his first officer, Harrington replied, "Obviously, Mr. Breckenridge, this town of Trinidad holds secrets it's not willing to share. I could tell the governor is eager for our departure and will soon be glad to see us set sail."

"Sir, all the men are eager to get underway, to put this port behind us."

"Understood! Are all the stores and supplies completed as I asked?"

"Yes, sir, we loaded the last bit of cargo yesterday; the ship is ready to sail, waiting for your order."

"Very well, Mr. Breckenridge, we sail at the morning tide so prepare the men. What of the British sailor's uniform and the man who wore it?"

"I shall inquire more deeply into this new light of evidence when I return to my host. If one of our naval crew is being held against their will, sir, it is our duty to free such a man. That will be all for now; I shall see you shortly aboard the ship."

"Thank you, Captain!"

After stepping back, Breckenridge saluted his commander and returned to the HMS *Dolphin*.

Harrington returned to the dining hall and apologized to his host for the brief interruption.

Edwardo responded, "I hope there are no problems with your ship or men, Capitán."

"Quite the contrary, Your Excellency. No, it was reported that one of my men stumbled across a British royal uniform in a local brothel house or what appeared to be a British sailor's uniform."

"I see," Edwardo replied, then after standing to his feet, he picked up his wine and took a sip. Contemplating his words carefully, Escobar said, "I'm sorry but sadly, you have been misled, Capitán. You see these sorts of things happen all the time. Foreign sailors often come to our little port to barter with the local ladies of pleasure. A lady entertaining a traveler wearing clothing resembling a British uniform was undoubtedly seen. This event is something that's of no importance that you should not worry yourself over, señor."

"Still, you see my distress for such a matter. If it is, indeed, a British uniform, my immediate response would be, how did it get here?" Harrington replied, baiting his host to watch his response.

"It would be easily explainable if, indeed, there was a severe storm that blew across our inland waterways, causing one of your ships to seek shelter in our harbor. I can assure you, Capitán, this has not happened."

"Damn it, man, there has to be a reason for the man to be out of uniform. Such a man would find himself court-martialed, no matter what pleasurable service he sought. A British royal sailor would never give up something so valuable unless it were a matter of life and death."

After seeing the two men about to wage war, the countess suddenly broke out in laughter, reliving the news of the latest fashion back in England as her way of relieving the stress. An awkward silence fell into the room as no one spoke but stared at one another, looking for a weakness in each other's composure. Edwardo quickly broke out in laughter, easing the tension in the situation.

Remaining steadfast and firm, Captain Harrington suddenly stood to his feet and announced, "It is getting late. To my regret, I must return to my ship to prepare for an early morning departure."

Edwardo and the countess expressed disappointment at seeing their guests leave, begging him to reconsider and stay a little longer. They added that the evening was still young with so many stories yet to share.

"Duty calls," the captain explained.

After walking over to the countess, he kissed her hand as he bowed, promising to return someday. Edwardo called to a servant, ordering him to bring around the carriage immediately. He returned to his room to gather his belongings and arranged them to be delivered to the house. The captain was escorted to the door, then out to a waiting carriage. Before Harrington climbed inside the wagon to leave, he turned to the governor and repeated the importance of knowing the sailor's whereabouts.

Edwardo smiled and wished Harrington a safe journey. Again, he repeated his statement that there was no such person in their small town; for if there were, undoubtedly, he would know of their existence.

After getting inside the carriage, Harrington gave a final tilt of his hat as the carriage man snapped his leather whip above the horse's head, and the transport was off. Harrington recognized that Edwardo had information he wasn't sharing; he was already devising a plan to retrieve such a garment once he returned to his ship.

As soon as the British captain had left, Edwardo hurried to his office and called to his servant. When a youth appeared, he bowed before the governor. The governor suggested that he might be found escorting two soldiers to the prison for desertion. He was handed a letter to retrieve Pablo Garcia, the *captain* of the royal guards.

After the short carriage ride back to his ship, Harrington understood this mystery about the missing British sailor couldn't go unanswered. When he arrived at the dock, he stepped out of the carriage and walked up to the gangplank. There to greet him was the master of arms announcing his presence to the crew.

Captain Harrington addressed the officer in charge and said, "I wish to speak to Mr. Humphries at once; have him come to my quarters immediately."

A young sailor appeared at the captain's quarters within several minutes, knocking on the door.

"Come in," said the stern voice through the door.

The royal marine saluted the captain and said, "Sir, you wished to speak to me, sir."

"Mr. Humphries, I have an assignment that I need you to complete. It could be dangerous and rewarding simultaneously, but it must be completed before we set sail in the morning tide."

"Of course, sir," the man responded.

Then, standing at attention, he listened to the plan

explained in detail. Harrington ordered him to investigate a brothel named Marie's, where it was reported that a British uniform had been discovered. If it was at all possible, he was to retrieve the naval uniform and return to the ship before they set sail in the morning. Harrington knew that whomever the uniform belonged to could easily be identified by the sailor's name sewn inside the shirt. The hope was to find the man, not his dead body.

Harrington addressed the marine more casually by saying, "Tom, I chose you because of your work recovering the French sword back in New Providence; this is important to me."

Understanding his orders, he stepped backward, saluted his commander, and said, "Of course, Captain, consider it done, sir."

Tom went below decks to prepare himself for the mission, leaving the captain's quarters. He changed into black clothing with a set of leather boots made of deerskin that he had repurchased from a trader in the Americas. As the last bit of cargo was being loaded aboard the ship, he crawled down the mooring line past the stacked crates onto the small pier.

He knew the approximate location of where Marie's was located from reports of sailors visiting the establishment. He had only visited it once, a few days ago. This mission was essential to his captain; he would complete it as if it were no other.

He hoped to bargain with the madam for the garment and not be forced to use violence unless it couldn't be helped. That type of business he wished to avoid at all cost. Courtesy for the right price would be on his way back to the ship; no one would be the wiser. A working girl would give out many favors for the mighty dollar; this was merely business and nothing more.

With his hooded disguise, he could've easily been mistaken for an ordinary street beggar or perhaps a fisherman returning home from a hard day out to sea. His mother was Spanish, and his ability to speak the local language made him famous among his sailor friends, especially when it came to him bartering with the working girls.

As he snuck down the cobblestone streets, they seemed deserted except for the occasional drunk that stumbled past him, singing a song out of tune. While patrolling the area a constable carrying a nightstick looked on as he walked past; his appearance remained covered except for his eyes visibly staring back at them.

The walk to the house of reputation wasn't that far; he soon arrived at the entrance of Marie's. Standing outside the door were two men talking and having a smoke. Ignoring them altogether, he walked past without even a passing glance. One of the men said something funny in his native language about his dress. Understanding what he said, Tom let out a loud, nervous laugh as he continued inside past the doors, enjoying the man's humor.

IT WAS PAST MIDNIGHT WHEN he arrived inside the parlor room. The place looked deserted, with no one around. After closing the door behind him, he continued walking toward the decorative bar just ahead. Unexpectedly, he heard voices approach; looking for cover, he ran over to hide behind barrels of rum stacked in a corner. He was quickly dropping to his knees. He did his best to conceal himself. As he listened he heard a woman's voice speaking assertively.

"Carlos! I do not care what His Highness Edwardo has ordered you to carry out; you simply cannot have that British uniform unless you pay for it. Nothing within these walls is free, not the girls, not the alcohol. You must pay the price like anyone else, do you understand me?! Besides, I don't have it with me; it was given to a smuggler."

"Please listen to me, Abella," the man argued. "If you do not give me that British uniform, I am instructed to take it by force."

"Carlos, you can try, but you shall not get very far," Abella answered.

A distinct sound of a weapon being cocked was heard upstairs above him at that very instant. Carlos knew as a soldier the sound of a pistol's hammers being pulled back into place. He lifted his eyes into the dark shadows and saw two gun barrels pointed downward at him by some unknown accomplices of Abella.

"Have it your way then. But mark my words: It shall not be easy for you or your girls when I return," said Carlos, who then left Marie's, slamming the door behind him.

Abella looked miserable as she weighed in her rebellious performance toward Edwardo, the governor, staring down at the floor.

A large man came into the room, carrying two wineskins. "Abella, here is the wine you ordered," the man said as he laid the large wineskins on the bar.

"Thank you, Feliciano. You have always been there for me when I needed your help."

"What is it, Abella, that's bothering you? I can always tell when something is not right."

Another man's voice was heard coming down the stairs. "Oh, Edwardo wants something that he cannot have, and he doesn't want to pay Abella for it," Nicolás said, shoving his two pistols into their holsters.

"Don't give it to him," Feliciano argued.

"I wish it were that simple," she explained. "However, it's locked away in a special place, just in case I had company this evening wanting to take it!"

"Certainly," Feliciano said, then watched as Abella walked upstairs to her room.

"How about pouring a drink for you, *amigo*?" Nicolás asked.

"No, I was told by Abella that you are cut off; your drinking is costing us too much," Feliciano explained.

"Fine, I'm going to return home to my fat wife. There, I can have a drink and be entertained simultaneously."

Upon hearing this, Feliciano shrugged his shoulders and laughed aloud.

"Tell Abella in the morning that I'm around if she needs me to do something involving my pistols. But she will have to pay me for it; nothing is free," Nicolás said.

Tom remained motionless, hidden in the dark shadows and watching every move the big man made in securing the house. After locking the front door, he checked each window, ensuring they were locked. After he finished he returned to his room at the back of the stairs, softly closing the door.

After several suspenseful moments, everything grew quiet inside the old building. Tom's options were few; he reasoned within himself on what to do next. Perhaps if he offered this Abella some treasure, she would give up the uniform freely without any argument, or he could quickly take it from her and return to the ship without any mishap. But if she screamed, he had few options left. One certainty was upon him, for the morning was just a few hours away: The ship would sail without him if he didn't complete his task in time.

The madam's room was located just at the top of the stairs. He listened to her footsteps and the creaking of the bedroom door opening; it was evident to him where her room was located. But was the uniform in her room or hidden somewhere else? He had no way of knowing. This mystery left him in a quandary of sorts.

SOME TIME HAD PASSED, AND he felt it was now safe to reveal himself. After crawling outward from his hiding place, he took small steps toward the stairs. The first step on the wooden platforms creaked as he placed weight on the small board. It couldn't be helped; he took the next step slowly.

At the top of the stairs was a dark hallway. Tom crept down the hall, passing bedrooms where the ladies of pleasure were asleep. In particular, while passing by one bedroom the sounds of a creaking bed were heard, no doubt a lady and her client at work. He continued the short distance, stopping outside Abella's door, and stood quietly as a mouse for a moment. Not hearing any sounds from within the room, he turned the knob slowly. He first noticed a small window overlooking the bay, with a large four-poster bed in the middle of the room.

As he crept into the room, he heard the sound of a pistol being cocked without warning.

"*Pare onde está intruso,*" the feminine voice called

out in Spanish, translated, "Stop where you are, intruder!"

"Yes, Madam," Tom replied without question in English.

"You're English?" the woman's voice was heard asking.

"Yes, please forgive my rudeness," Tom answered while bowing respectfully.

"I'm not accustomed to having strangers enter my boudoir unless I've invited them. You, sir, I don't recall inviting. Tell me, thief, what brings you here?" Abella asked.

"Let me assure you, Madam; I'm no thief. I have a reason for being in your room to offer you a reward for something of no importance or significance. It's a British uniform that you might have in your possession."

"How did you know about that, stranger?" Abella asked, being surprised that he knew of such a thing.

"Please allow me to introduce myself. My name is Tom Billings. I'm a royal marine on His Majesty's battleship, the *Dolphin*. I'm here to make you an offer for this small trivial item. A mere piece of fabric, so to speak."

"Whatever could you mean, señor?"

"Now let me offer my apologies once more for this intrusion. But there is a universal language that I believe we all speak: gold doubloons," Tom announced.

"Man, now you're speaking my language," Abella replied with a funny laugh. Then she reached over and adjusted the wick on the lamp. Suddenly, a light shone brightly into the room.

Now Tom could see a voluptuous-looking woman, with long, thick, black hair, sitting upright in her bed with a small gun pointing at his heart. "It's alright, Feliciano, this intruder and I are about to discuss some business; you can go back to bed now. Thank you, my friend."

At that moment Tom turned around; there, he saw a large man named Feliciano standing as if ready to pounce upon him, holding a large knife in his hand. Gratefully, he walked away silently.

"How much gold are we talking about, señor?" Abella asked, disrupting Tom's wary eye upon the large man walking away into the darkness.

I didn't even know he was there, ready to strike me down, Tom thought. Then turning his attention back toward the lady, he said, "I suppose twenty gold doubloons."

"Let's make it fifty, señor, and not play games with one another. It's too late for that. Have we got ourselves a deal?" Abella asked with a sinister laugh.

"Done, Madam!" Tom announced but then explained that he had to return to his ship with the uniform and that he would return shortly with her payment before the morning tide or else he would be left behind.

"Sir, do you take me for a complete fool?" If even she did trust him, what if he didn't pay? Then she would end up on the dirty end of the stick and he would come out smelling like a rose.

"Time is of the essence," Tom announced, noting that he must be on his way back to the ship as soon as possible. "If I may ask, what do you propose?"

"I shall get dressed, follow you back to your ship, and give that British uniform to your captain myself, thereby assuring my payment in full," Abella replied.

"Be it as you say, let us be off; few precious hours are left before daybreak."

"Yes, of course," she agreed.

After throwing the bedsheets away from her body, she rose out of bed, wearing a silken red nightgown with her large breasts displayed. The sight instantly captured Tom's attention; having been at sea for a long time, he felt aroused by what he saw.

After stepping behind a small curtain, she begged his patience as she got dressed. The fancy gown was soon thrown over the curtain, and a nearby dress was removed; a few minutes later she looked radiant.

Reaching into a large wooden armoire, she opened a secret side door to remove the uniform. Gripping it tightly under her arm, she grabbed her purse and announced, "I know a quick way to reach the harbor. Follow me."

When they arrived downstairs, she went to the back of the house, unlocked a back door, and they walked out into an alley. They followed it around several small buildings until they reached a clearing on the docks. There, across the wooden pier was the HMS *Dolphin* tied up. But as Tom was about to step forward from the shadows, Abella grabbed his arm and whispered, "Wait a moment, two guards are patrolling the docks. Let us wait until they pass."

"Why?" he asked, surprised by her hesitation.

"It's simple. If Edwardo, the governor, knew I was betraying him for some measly gold pieces, he would undoubtedly throw me and my girls into prison until we rotted. Let us wait, please," she begged him.

"Of course," Tom replied, then stood back into the shadows, keeping perfectly still.

Soon approaching laughter was heard as they hid in the shadows. Tom listened to male voices laughing about something humorous, not knowing what they meant by the remark; he could only guess that it involved a visit with a lady of pleasure.

Abella snickered, silently understanding the meaning of their laughter, but remained still as they passed a few feet away and continued around the corner of another building.

"Now is the time," she whispered.

After slipping off her shoes, she ran toward the tall ship in her stockings. Tom followed closely behind on her heels the whole way.

When they reached the gangway leading up into the boat and began ascending the wooden structure, a voice called out, "Stop; who goes there?" The sentry pointed a musket in their direction.

"It is I, Tom Billings. Get the captain at once," he ordered the sentry.

"Tom, what are you doing? You could have gotten your fool head blown off," the man announced. Then noticing the woman behind Tom, the sentry yelled, "Hey, who's that you have with you?"

"She is my guest. Now hurry and get the captain."

"Yes, of course," the sailor replied, running off toward the back of the ship.

While waiting Abella smiled and announced that

she had never been aboard a British warship; she didn't realize they were so large.

"Yes, well, remember we were such a large distance from home. These ships have to withstand the combative seas they cross and still be strong enough for battle engagements," Tom explained.

"Tell me, Tom Billings, do you have someone special back home that waits for your return?" she asked.

"No, why do you ask?" he replied, surprised by her question.

"All women that offer comfort to those lonely men far from their homeland wonder about such things; it's only natural," she remarked.

"What is it, Tom?" a man's voice spoke out.

Turning to see Captain Harrington approach, Tom said, "Captain, let me introduce you to Abella, the lady who owns the naval uniform; she has agreed to sell it to us for a price," he explained.

"A price, indeed," Harrington replied. He looked disgusted with the arrangement. "Let me first see what I'm purchasing."

"Certainly, sir," Tom replied. After taking the uniform from Abella, he handed it to his captain.

After examining the uniform's collar, a single name appeared sown inside: "Thomas Banish." Harrington then turned to Abella and said, "Where is the man?"

Both Tom and Abella looked stunned and unsure how to answer. However, Tom explained in Spanish what the captain had asked, not sure what to say.

Abella replied, "I have no idea where the shirt's owner has gone. At one point he was being entertained by one of my girls. Next, there was news of pirates arriving in town, and everyone scattered for their lives. Perhaps the man you seek ran into the hills to hide?"

After hearing Abella's account, Harrington looked disheartened and said, "See the quartermaster pays the women what she wants." He returned to his cabin, gripping the uniform tightly in his hands.

However, no one knew that she left out the part of the Iron Born Pirate, which Alejandro had told her about, for a good reason. She knew that if the British captain began to search for the sailor there in Trinidad and caused a ruckus, the governor could look at it as an insult, and perhaps war could break out over such a trivial thing as a missing man.

Tom seemed surprised by his sudden change in demeanor, turned to Abella, and said, "Let us go see the quartermaster then."

"Yes," she agreed, then followed him to a small officer's quarters located beneath the captain's stateroom near the stairs.

With a knock on the little wooden door, Tom called out, "Mr. Hamish, are you awake, sir?"

A rustling behind the door, and soon the door squeaked open to a small officer's cabin. "Yes, what is it?"

"The captain ordered me to pay this lady the sum of fifty gold doubloons."

"The captain?" the man repeated, still tired from being woken up.

"Yes, I was ordered to pay this lady the sum of fifty gold doubloons at once," Tom repeated.

"If the captain wants it, so be it."

He closed the door, then returned a short time later with the payment in a cloth bag. After Tom handed it to Abella, she eagerly counted each coin until satisfied that it was all there.

THE MORNING LIGHT BEGAN TO appear; it was time to depart. A warm southern breeze blew unexpectedly, causing Abella's cologne fragrance to fill the air with an aromatic scent of roses. Instantly, Tom was reminded of how sweet women could smell compared to men; he sighed aloud.

Catching his awkwardness, Abella laughed slightly, knowing the effects of her womanhood upon a man who's gone without a lady's attention far too long.

Slowly, Tom escorted Abella back to the gangway as a voice echoed from the officer on deck to prepare the ship to leave port. Several sailors appeared at their stations, loosening the ropes and mooring lines.

The forces of nature had caused the morning tide

to arrive, and while his shipmates hurried about preparing to leave the small harbor, Tom felt a loss within him, wanting to stay in port longer. Abella's smile only begged him to stay, but regrettably, he could not.

Arriving at the gangway, he stood silent and could not say goodbye. A simple farewell should go without a hitch, but it didn't. She had something that he missed, and he wasn't so eager to let it go.

After walking over to him, Abella planted a soft wet kiss upon his cheek, asking him to look her up next time he was in port.

"I definitely will. I promise," Tom replied.

As he watched her leave, she had only taken two steps before stopping to turn back around.

Reaching into her small beaded purse, Abella withdrew a small silk handkerchief and handed it to him. Her perfume engulfed the little fabric. Tom gripped it tightly, thanking her as he watched her go to leave again. After stopping suddenly, she glanced upward for one final look at the man with whom she had a fascinating encounter. She returned to the small alley and disappeared into the shadows.

Tom sighed once more and walked back to his quarters aboard the ship. The dawn of the new day appeared. He occasionally lifted the scented silk handkerchief near his nose and breathed in her scent, which he hoped would never fade.

Abella arrived at her house a short time later and was about to walk through the door but she noticed something odd and out of place. There were traces of blood on the street tiles outside the building that dripped out from under the doorway. She reached for the handle and started to step inside. But without warning she heard a man's voice.

"Edwardo is angry with you, Abella."

Suddenly, a pair of hands gripped her, jerking her away. Although she didn't know whose blood it was on the tiles, she realized it must belong to her servant, Feliciano, whom she suspected was now dead.

CHAPTER 6

The sun setting over the distant islands was picture-perfect. In the appearing darkness, it would only take a quadrant or sextant to navigate by the stars, something that Thomas didn't have in his possession.

Unexpectedly, the young pirate began to stir. His legs began to kick at the sail fabric that covered his sweating body; he moaned as if in pain, calling out a woman's name that sounded familiar. No doubt, he was fighting off the infection that was trying to set in.

Thomas tied the tiller and leaned over to get the water jug. After opening the flask, he forced the young pirate to drink a little down. Afterward, lifting his shirt, Thomas checked his wound for infection and saw that it hadn't worsened, but was still looking sore and red around his stitches.

After settling back down and untying the rudder, he looked up and admired the remaining colors of the sunset with its pale orange hues and glanced at the compass one final time. He maintained a heading due northwest. On his current course, they would eventually reach a peaceful settlement on the island of Jamaica. There, he would reassess his situation to devise a plan to bring this young pirate to his brothers of iron.

He would then gain passage aboard a British ship bound for home. Of course, he was out of uniform. This situation would take some explaining to the admiralty. But still, it would be worth it to be home again.

In this tropical heat it was easy to get an infection from prevalent diseases due to the insect population in temperate climates. An open wound, especially one from a cutting knife, could quickly become infected, and a man could die because of it. Thomas wondered how he'd received it. Perhaps a jealous husband or dealings over money resulted in a heated argument. Whatever the reason, he seemed to be regaining consciousness. The young man called out "Mariana" several times in his native Portuguese, then fell silent again.

Thomas steered to position the sail's pole to the western horizon. The tropical winds continued to fill his sails as the small boat sped over the waves of the Caribbean waters. The boat bounced upon the waves driven by the warm trade winds blowing southwest. Now the growing darkness displayed the stars in the night sky that were becoming more visible by the hour until they completely lit up the lonely dark.

His pirate guest grew quiet and motionless. He lay asleep for many hours while Thomas steered the boat to safety. He felt tired, as it had been a long day. The passing hours of boredom and flopping atop the peaking waves were tedious.

Thomas closed his eyes, allowing the gentle rocking of the small boat to rock him to sleep. When he awoke the beginning light of a new day just appeared on the horizon. Now out to sea, all remnants of land had disappeared, and what remained was the vast ocean that laid before him. After reaching into the sack, he withdrew some cheese and bread for breakfast. At the same time he was maintaining a steady course ahead.

Throughout the day his eyes grew tired, and his body began to pain him. Occasionally, he would tie off the tiller to change positions in an attempt to get comfortable or to relieve himself. He was mindful that if a passing wave rocked the small boat and he fell into the water, it would mean certain death for them both.

THE FOLLOWING EVENING AS THE sun set on the horizon, being all alone with nothing but time, Thomas's only companion, he thought of his life and how he had arrived at this position. Above all else, his father, a tailor by trade, wanted him to take over the family business.

Still, he refused, seeking a profession as a British naval officer, much like his brother-in-law, Captain Harrington, who commanded his ship, the HMS *Dolphin*. Sadly, becoming a captain of his boat never was realized.

A seafarer was something that he grew up desiring to be. To sail upon the open water, along with visits to every exotic port imaginable, was a mere dream that occupied all his time as a youth until he was finally accepted into the British naval academy. After graduation he was given orders to serve aboard the HMS *Defiance*. His character and sound manners were a product of his beloved mother, whom he hadn't seen since his first voyage. She knew that he loved the sea and sought to learn everything there was to understand about seamanship from a young age.

However, another love of his life was a young lassie named Miss Ann Hammersmith. She was born into a family of merchants that he met while in port many years ago. They fell deeply in love and were married over seven years ago. He had promised that once he found his fortune, he would leave his love of the sea to be hers for the rest of their lives.

After his last voyage to the Azores, he returned home to be with his sweet Ann. Then she announced that she was pregnant. At the time he had no way of knowing how this one announcement would change both their lives. Several months later Ann died while giving birth to the child she was carrying. Thomas hastily returned to his first love, the sea, as his way of coping with the losses. He chose to steer and navigate the ship on many lonely nights rather than sleep down below with other snoring sailors.

Now all alone, inside the tiny boat and exposed to the twinkling stars above, it was easy to allow the pain of his loss to become exposed—no explanations to anyone for the tears that flowed down his cheeks. Just the hurt and sorrow he allowed himself to release that he could not contain any longer. While he remembered his beautiful wife's face, he called her name aloud: "Ann, I love you, my darling," which he uttered softly.

"Who is Ann? Your wife?" a man's voice spoke out from the darkness.

"You're awake," Thomas said, plainly ignoring the question while rubbing his eyes as he looked into the darkness and saw the young pirate leaning on his elbows, staring at him.

"Hello," the voice replied.

"So, tell me, how are you feeling?" Thomas asked with concern. He gazed into the darkness, looking at the man he was addressing.

"Very sore, señor, thank you for asking. So please tell me, where are we exactly?" the pirate asked.

"Somewhere in the southern Caribbean Ocean; we're heading for Jamaica. I have friends there who will aid us to escape the predicament in which we find ourselves," Thomas explained.

"I tried to rescue my sister Mariana from the house of prostitution but was unsuccessful," the young man answered potently.

"Mariana, where have I heard that name before? Oh yes, the girl that worked in the brothel where I last bathed."

"I'm sorry to hear that," the young man replied. "I tried to free her from that life she has chosen, but sadly, she is unwilling to leave it behind. Our blessed mother, back in Portugal, begged me to bring Mariana back home. I'm sorry to say that I failed and was stabbed because of it."

"So, tell me, who was it that tried to take your life?" Thomas inquired.

"That dog, his name is Feliciano; he is a mean bastard. He will not have that opportunity again, I assure you, señor."

"Well, the first order of business is to get far away, someplace safe. Now tell me, are you hungry?"

"Yes, I am. But first let me introduce myself; my name is Mauricio Barros. I am ever grateful for your help, señor."

After leaning forward to shake hands, Thomas said, "My name is Thomas Banish. Glad to make your acquaintance."

From that point on, a new friendship began.

After returning to the hard bench, Thomas again

grabbed hold of the tiller and explained, "I intend to travel to Jamaica. However, I fear that if my fellow British seadogs were to capture us, then we would together hang on the gallows—I, myself, for harboring an enemy of His Majesty's Navy, and you, for—"

"Being an Iron Born Pirate. Yes, this I know already, señor."

A brief pause was heard, then Thomas added, "Well, let me say, for being yourself."

Mauricio answered back, "I, too, am fearful of being captured." He went on to explain that he had abandoned his post aboard his pirate ship in a failed attempt to save his only sister. "I am a wanted man on two fronts; it is a horrible situation to find oneself in, señor."

"Agreed," Thomas said, suggesting Mauricio look into the duffel bag so that he might find them some rum to quench their thirst.

After a few moments the young pirate pulled out a large bottle containing the liquor, to which both men enjoyed several long sips. The small vessel rocked about upon the rolling waves as they maintained their course toward safety.

SEVERAL HOURS HAD ELAPSED, AND again Mauricio fell back to sleep. Already it had been over two days since they left the Spanish port. At the end of another day Thomas maintained his heading, having calculated that they should reach Jamaica within six days, providing they didn't run into a British ship—not to mention the leak in their boat; if it got worst, they'd be sunk.

He later awoke with the sun reflecting brightly off the water. The hard bench was more than he could stand on his backside; he took ahold of the trim rope he had tied to the tiller and got comfortable, falling asleep quickly. He couldn't be sure of how long he slept, but when he opened his eyes, there, ahead of him, was nothing but a vast ocean all around.

The young pirate remained asleep as Thomas steered the small boat toward Jamaica. Soon Thomas felt hungry and needed to eat something fast. After tying off the tiller, he went to where the duffel bag was located and looked inside. He saw fruit, a portion of meat, and bread, with some cheese inside. After grabbing a banana, he returned to the rudder and sat on the hard bench. As he peeled the banana and took a bite, he saw, to his horror, white sails against the blue water heading in their direction. At once he realized that if it was a pirate band, they were defenseless to protect themselves; if it was a British ship, then they were doomed.

Looking over at the restful sleeping youth, he thought, *How could I, after saving his life, allow him to be hanged?* It was a dilemma that he hated finding himself in, but truthfully, he could never kill in cold blood; it was not his nature. Perhaps at this junction it would be better to slit the young man's throat instead of allowing him to hang at the end of a rope. Maybe it was better to do it now, while Mauricio slept peaceably and was unaware of the danger.

At that moment young Mauricio suddenly stirred from his slumber and looked up at him with a smile.

"Good morning, señor."

"Good morning, Mauricio—or at least I would hope it is—but unfortunately, we are soon to have visitors, and the outcome of their visit, I'm not sure exactly what it will be."

"What do you mean?"

"Look behind you, my friend; there, you shall see a three-masted vessel approaching, still too far away to measure friend or foe. I, being a realist, choose foe!" Thomas explained.

"This is horrible news to wake up to, Thomas! I am too young to die." After proclaiming this fact, Mauricio stood up in the small boat and looked about for a weapon to use; finding nothing suitable, he grabbed ahold of a wooden oar and said, "I will not surrender without a fight."

Seeing Mauricio's eagerness and knowing that a wooden paddle was useless in an actual fight, Thomas began laughing aloud, which now seemed out of place.

At first taken back by the laughter, Mauricio stood silently looking at the man who saved his life until he could no longer hold back his laughter and joined in, thinking of their predicament.

With nowhere to run and without a spyglass to see the pending danger, they maintained their course toward Jamaica. It became apparent that the approaching ship intended to investigate them, as it kept its heading toward their direction without turning.

Thomas looked about the small boat and announced, "That does not mean that we can't run for our very lives now, does it?"

Quickly, Mauricio looked about the boat for anything substantial they could toss overboard to lighten their load. Immediately scurrying about the craft, he looked underneath the canvas tarp for other useless items to throw overboard. They found a fishing net and a long rope attached to a heavy anchor; Mauricio heaved them all overboard. Then suddenly, seeing the small chest of gold underneath the wooden bench where Thomas sat, he asked, "What's in the small chest?"

Looking down at his feet, Thomas smiled and said, "It's my reward for keeping you alive in the form of one hundred gold doubloons."

"You were paid well for your troubles; maybe you're more of a pirate than you care to admit, señor."

"Well, none of that matters if we are overtaken by this approaching ship. Now let us give our pursuers a run, shall we?"

Having said this, Thomas changed directions, steering the small craft into the wind. Quickly, the wind filled the sail, and the boat gained speed, bouncing over the waves. Thomas had hoped for an island to appear to hide behind, but for now it was important to achieve a safe distance from the mysterious ship that seemed to dog their trail and navigate in their direction.

This unknown ship and its hounding pursuit of them seemed determined; they wanted to overtake them for whatever reason. The white sails continued to draw closer and closer no matter what direction Thomas plotted.

Miles and miles of open water lay ahead, with no protected harbor or bay to hide. Everything seemed hopeless. They were now the hunted; try as they may, the white sail grew closer and closer until suddenly they heard a loud thunderous boom from the approaching ship, then a white plume coming from their bow. Another sound of something substantial approached as it cut through the air, traveling helplessly toward them. Unexpectedly, a large splash erupted off their forward bow.

Both Thomas and Mauricio looked at each other in dismay as they realized that the ship had fired a cannonball at them as a warning shot. They would have been killed instantly if the large round had hit the small boat.

"Well, Thomas, my friend, it looks like they want to have a word with us, does it not? Maybe we should give up our chase to see what these cursed devils want with us?"

"Yes, maybe you're right!" Thomas agreed.

Suddenly, he changed course and pointed the boat in one direction, not altering his course any longer; he knew that it was futile to run. It wouldn't be long before the ship would come alongside. Surrendering, in his soul, without a fight didn't appeal to him. Thomas sat down, disgusted, and watched the white sails continue coming.

Soon the figurehead came into view underneath the forecastle of a voluptuous blonde woman; as the ship appeared, it was plain to see the sails being trimmed by the men crawling about the main yard booms, trimming all their sails at once.

Standing, Thomas grabbed ahold of the rope to his small mainsail and lowered it. The little boat slowed as it began to bounce about the waves, with no wind within its sail to give it momentum.

Suddenly, a man's voice called out from the ship in broken English, telling them to maintain their course. As they watched helplessly, a longboat was lowered; as they waited a small company of men began rowing toward their direction.

Thomas looked over at Mauricio and said, "Well, now we discover our fate."

In response, Mauricio agreed by shaking his head from side to side, suddenly grabbing ahold of the wooden oar close to him, and saying, "I will not go peaceably, señor."

Thomas looked about to see if there be anything to use for a weapon but then much too quickly discovered that it was too late to resist, as several members within the approaching longboat held up muskets and ordered them to raise their hands.

At that moment it was too late to put up a fight. Regrettably, Thomas did as he was ordered, but Mauricio never let go of his grip upon the oar until the men inside the longboat came alongside and grabbed ahold of their sailing boat.

A muscular olive-skinned man, looking to be close to thirty years of age, was wearing a long red scarf atop his head, with gold loops in his ears and a deep scar across his chin. He suddenly spoke in a Caribbean accent, "So what place you be heading now?"

Thomas looked at Mauricio and said, "We're traveling to Jamaica. We have friends there that we must see; it's important!"

"No, sorry, you have that all wrong, I'm afraid," the man replied. Then he turned to his men, ordering them to see if there was anything valuable inside the small boat. Just as Thomas was about to resist, one of the men shot a hole inside the vessel as the others pointed muskets at their heads.

Now faced with no recourse or action, Thomas and Mauricio could only watch as the pirates quickly ransacked the boat, finding the small chest of gold doubloons and the last bit of food and water to make their way. They took everything from them and returned to their longboat.

"Mr. Stark, sir, this is all we found of value," one of the men announced, handing over the small chest of gold to his leader.

Now the small band of cutthroats all laughed, seeing their predicament. Thomas and Mauricio could do nothing but watch, not knowing if they would die. Helplessly, they sat in their boat that was now taking on water.

Just as the pirates lifted their muskets to aim, knowing that he was about to die, Mauricio yelled out,

"Señor; please wait a moment. Please, I wish to parley with your captain."

"What is this, you say? You wish to parley with our captain?" Stark yelled out. Then busting out in laughter, he said, "Not possible, I'm afraid."

"Yes, I must speak to him at once or else when he finds out that you had someone of great importance in your possession, yet you didn't inform him of the news. I'm sure that he would not be happy. Perhaps he would feed you to the sharks instead," Mauricio proclaimed.

"You speak boldly, my friend, but I'm sad to say that your words do not affect your outcome on whether you live or die. Sadly, it is time for you to die, and I will feed your bodies to the sharks," Mr. Stark announced.

Lifting the muskets, the pirates again pointed their guns toward their heads and were about to fire when Thomas looked at Mauricio and yelled out, "He's an Iron Born Pirate!"

The expression on Mr. Stark's face blurted it all; he yelled out, "Don't shoot them—not yet, men—not until we talk to Captain Beaumont."

Relieved not to be dead, Thomas and Mauricio both took a long sigh, anticipating the end of their lives.

Then Mr. Stark said, "Listen to me, man, if you be playing us for a fool, I will make you suffer first before I feed you to the sharks, as I said I would do, man."

"No, it is no lie; I speak the very truth to you, sir, let me assure you." Turning to Mauricio, he said, "Will you please show them? Roll up your sleeves."

As everyone looked on with disbelief, Mauricio slowly rolled up both of his sleeves and displayed the marks from the Bloody Hag on his wrist, signifying him to be an Iron Born Pirate.

"Our captain will want to have a word with you, young man, but perhaps not you, Englishman!" Mr. Stark explained. "Either way, you're both coming to our ship. Our captain will decide your fate."

Having said this, they took both men into their boat, with orders from Mr. Stark to empty their muskets into the small boat's hull. Afterward, as they slowly paddled away, the little vessel sank beneath the waves.

While four men paddled the longboat toward their ship, the muskets were quickly reloaded and soon were ready to fire if their prisoners tried anything foolish.

Thomas had the most to fear amid the bloodthirsty cutthroats. He was English and was most hated among pirates that sailed these waters, but young Mauricio would be welcomed aboard without question, a brother to all pirates. Whatever their fate, it was to be decided as they approached the ship and watched from below the small boat as groups of buccaneers lined the decks, looking overboard at what their pirate brothers had captured in their net.

CHAPTER 7

"WHAT HAVE YOU DONE, ABELLA, to upset Edwardo, the governor?" the male voice said as he carelessly jerked her away.

She recognized the voice as Pablo Garcia, the *captain* of the royal guards, with whom she'd had dealings in the past—this despicable man had a particular weakness for abusing her girls.

Abella said, "Please, Pablo, let me explain."

"It is useless; you can explain it to the governor," he remarked.

Passing through the narrow streets, they suddenly came upon a small company of soldiers heading toward Marie's. Abella became fearfully concerned, thinking of her girls back at the brothel. She considered many of them like family. She realized they were in grave danger because she decided to sell that ridiculous British uniform for a few coins.

A sudden jerk from Pablo, and her bag of gold doubloons flew from her hands all over the cobblestone alley. After seeing the large sum of money lying on the ground, he greedily knelt to pick them up, cursing Abella for her stupidity.

Just as he was distracted, the small weapon that Abella had hidden inside her dress was suddenly positioned at the artery in his neck, promising it would quickly be sliced open if he didn't do as she commanded.

Pablo remained on his knees without moving a muscle and said, "I want you to realize what you're doing, Abella. Assaulting one of His Majesty's royal guards is a serious offense; you could hang on the gallows for your actions."

"Well, let me ask you, Pablo, just how long do you think I would live once I'm in the hands of Escobar, the governor? Let us go this way," Abella demanded while pressing the knife's blade deeper into Pablo's neck.

However, just then a young lady ran past; Abella immediately recognized her as Mariana, whom she liked best among all her working girls.

Hearing someone familiar calling her name, Mariana stopped to turn back around and saw two figures standing in the shadows in the narrow passageway.

Standing in the open, Mariana yelled, "I must go."

"Wait! Come with us," Abella answered. "I have a plan to get us safe, away from here. So if you value your life, follow us now!"

Then she turned away, hurrying down a narrow passageway where she directed Pablo to another small street, followed by Mariana who approached at a safe distance behind, worried that they were being followed.

Soon they came to a small house overlooking the bay; immediately, Abella began banging on the heavy wooden door. Moments later a man's voice responded, "I'm coming. I'm coming. Be patient."

Suddenly, the door creaked open, and a gray-haired man with a long, gray beard stood with a small lamp, peeking outside. However, before he had a chance to say anything, Abella burst inside his home, never letting go of her grip upon Pablo or the sharp blade pressed against his artery.

"What kind of trouble are you into now, Abella?" the man asked.

"I need a boat," she responded hastily.

"At this hour. Are you crazy?"

"Miguel, you're the only one I could come to in my moment of need. The governor is after me; I fear for my life. You must help me, please!"

"The last time I helped you I promised I would never help you again, especially since you are holding this royal guard at knifepoint. Are you mad for bringing him here?"

"Miguel, you know how ruthless Escobar, the

governor, can be. If you refuse to help me, I pray that you bury my remains atop a hill overlooking the bay. Please, I beg you. My only other option is to allow myself to be tortured, and afterward, my corpse will be displayed in an iron cage, hanging over the village square."

"What do you plan to do with your captive?" Miguel inquired, knowing he had no choice but to help his daughter in her escape.

"As cruel as this man is, I should slit his throat and let him die like the dog he is. Perhaps if we are captured tonight, it would be my pleasure before I die to erase the existence of this cruel bastard who finds pleasure in beating upon helpless women. But once we're all safe, perhaps I will release him," Abella explained.

A sigh was heard from Pablo, who remained fearful of the blade that continued to cut him slightly in the neck every time Abella moved.

"All right, Abella, I agree to help you. But I can only promise to take you someplace safe. You must do as I say, understood?"

"Yes, Miguel, whatever you say, we will do it," Abella said, looking at Mariana for assurance.

They both agreed to his demands.

After hurrying to the backroom, Miguel returned a few moments later carrying a change of men's clothes and some rope, ordering that both women change quickly. After taking out his knife, he cut a small length of rope for tying Pablo's hands behind his back. Then he grabbed a scarf and gagged the man so he couldn't speak. After turning Pablo back to face him, Miguel looked him directly into his eyes and said, "If you try to scream or escape, I promise you, señor, you will be the first to die, do you understand?"

A rapid nodding of his head meant that Pablo understood correctly.

At that moment Mariana walked over to Miguel, handed him a pistol, and said, "Perhaps you could use this, just in case our prisoner refuses to listen."

Surprised to see the pistol in the lady's possession, Miguel asked, "Where did you find this weapon?"

"I have a story to tell, but now is not the time. We

should hurry," Mariana stated.

"Yes, you're right. Before we go place these hats upon your heads and stuff your long hair inside. Pray that we do not run into any military soldiers. My boat is anchored off the beach not far from here."

Looking out the window, Abella said, "It will be morning soon; we must hurry."

Again, after taking a final glance around his home, Miguel grabbed hold of a duffel bag and quickly filled it full of all his earthly possessions needed for the journey, including a spyglass and compass. He handed Abella another pack and told her to stuff it full of food items he kept in a cupboard. After giving Mariana a wineskin and water jug, he grabbed ahold of the prisoner and said, "It is time that we leave."

After walking outside, they could see it was still dark, but soon it would be morning. Once Miguel locked his door, they hurried away toward the beach. With no time to waste, they crept through the small sleepy town. Often they would stop along the way while they heard soldiers calling one another as they performed a house-to-house search, looking for Pablo, their *captain.*

In the darkness, torches were seen running about the city, and on several occasions they narrowly missed being discovered by merely hiding within the shadows. In a desperate attempt to escape, Miguel took a path that many smugglers used by the sewers. It was not pleasant for any of the women, but if it kept them alive, they would happily oblige the smelly experience.

Traveling down a narrow pipe, they soon heard the crashing waves ahead. Crawling out of the smelly sewer, accessible to the outside, they soon passed by a rocky shoreline. Ahead of them lay a sandy beach. They ran toward the fishing fleet; the sand beneath their feet felt cool and refreshing. At that particular time the morning fog was clearing. Now visible on the beach were many small boats just ahead.

Miguel knew all the fishermen that prepared their boats for the morning catch and simply waved hello. It must have looked strange having one of the guards with them, but gratefully, everyone was far enough away that no one paid any attention—especially to the fact that the women were dressed as men in their fishing garb.

Immediately, Miguel ordered everyone to get inside his boat. Once inside he handed the pistol to Abella, ordering her to shoot Pablo if he did not obey. She nodded in agreement, pointing the deadly weapon at Pablo's heart.

Miguel freed the anchor from the sandy beach and lifted it, placing it inside the boat. He began to push hard against the bow, trying to free the small vessel from the grip of the sand. He wasn't accustomed to the weight of three persons inside the boat. As a result he strained at the bow. Regrettably, it wouldn't budge but remained in place. Then, a young man named Escondido, whom he had known since he was a youth, approached.

"Miguel, where are you going with so many fishermen this morning, my friend?"

"I'm taking a few lads to my favorite fishing place," Miguel explained as he continued his assault upon the stubborn boat.

The two women gazed toward the open sea, protecting their feminine features. Pablo sat helplessly, still gagged; he could not utter a word, knowing if he tried he would die in his attempt.

"Escondido, could you please help me with my boat?"

"Yes, certainly, Miguel." After looking inside the boat, he saw the desperate look upon Pablo's face, a gag in his mouth and his limbs tied up.

Escondido turned to Miguel and asked, "Is it not true that you have been fishing already?"

"No, tell me what you mean."

"It seems you've caught a big fish, perhaps a red snapper," he remarked with laughter.

Miguel, not sure what to say, just smiled and said, "Listen, my friend, speaking of fishing, I hear it's better in Puerto Cabello in New Granada! I'm sad that I can no longer fish in these waters. You can always find me there whatever happens, but tell no one!"

"Agreed, your secret is safe with me, Miguel. You taught me much about fishing over the years, saving me from certain starvation; I remember your kindness when I had nowhere else to go as a young boy. I'm forever indebted to you for your kindness. Have a safe journey until we meet again. Now let me give you a hand with your stubborn boat."

As the morning tide was coming in, both men began pushing hard against the boat's bow; it slowly began to move. The sand was releasing its grip; gradually, the vessel drifted into the water.

As Miguel felt it breaking free, he jumped inside and hurried to grab ahold of one of the oars and dug it deep into the sand, pushing hard and driving the boat free of the beach entirely. Out in the water the approaching waves splashed against the transom as it moved out to sea, getting Miguel utterly wet for his effort.

Meanwhile, Escondido continued pushing the boat free of the beach until he was standing up to his waist in the morning surf. The small fishing boat bounced atop the waves as Miguel struggled to turn the boat. With the boat pointed out to sea, Miguel grabbed ahold of the sail and unfurled it, releasing it entirely.

With an offshore breeze, which quickly filled the sail, the small boat moved farther away from the beach until, at last, Miguel was able to grab ahold of the tiller to chart a new course away from Trinidad and danger itself.

The morning sun illuminated the white sand and the visible blue water with its picturesque colors coming to life, reflecting off its gleaming surface. Miguel hurriedly ran about the small boat, securing the sail and returning to the rudder, where he steered them out to sea.

AFTER AN HOUR HAD ELAPSED, they were now a few miles offshore; from this distance everyone could see the commotion happening back in the city. They could see many guards in their red jackets, searching the small buildings for Abella's whereabouts. The two women remained quiet, not moving from their location but gazing out to the open water at freedom.

At that moment Miguel looked at Abella and shook his head in response as he again found himself having to rescue his only daughter from injudicious mistakes she had made in the past.

Knowing *captains* of sailing ships through trade and having made a few friends over the years, he felt confident they could get passage on a ship bound for Jamaica, where they would be free. This decision to abruptly leave his home, where his wife and son were buried, suddenly weighed heavily upon him, in both his mind and heart.

Abella's mother died giving birth to her many years ago, leaving him alone to raise her and her older brother, Félix. Félix, who became sick of smallpox, passed away at the age of seven; ever since it was just the two of them. Abella, always the rebellious daughter, brought him many a gray hair, but regardless, he loved her and would not stand to see her die horribly. He knew of the governor's reputation for cruelty and what betraying him meant to any living soul.

After tying off the rudder, Miguel reached over and checked the bindings holding Pablo's hands captive. However, not feeling it adequate to keep the man from escaping, he withdrew his knife and pointed it at him as his way of warning if he resisted his actions. After taking another small rope from under his wooden bench, he tied Pablo's legs together, just as a precaution. Now unable to move or put up a fight, Miguel felt safe in knowing that his prisoner would not escape. Then regrettably, he removed the gag from his mouth.

Abella at that moment turned to her father and asked, "Where are you taking us?"

He responded, "I know of a small port we can travel to, and perhaps I can arrange for passage to Jamaica or some other port of safety. You have brought this trouble to my doorstep, daughter; I'm not very happy with you!"

"Father, please, believe me, I had no choice in this matter. I know I would've died in Trinidad if I had not taken action against this bastard who raided Marie's. Please forgive me, Miguel, for I had no choice in this matter."

After hearing her friend's response, Mariana nodded in agreement. "It's true; we would have died back there."

Turning to her friend, Abella asked, "How was it that you escaped? I heard the screams of the other girls as they were being led away, captive, so how was it that you were the one that got away?"

"Abella, you know men and their weakness for the female form. When I lifted my skirt to adjust my pantaloons, the guard who held me by my arm turned for a peek. As he was distracted, I kicked him in his male parts and sent him to his knees. I then took his musket from his belt and knocked him unconscious to the ground."

"Men, they're all the same," Abella announced.

"I ran away as fast as possible, knowing I could be shot at any moment for trying to escape. Thankfully, the other guards were distracted from dealing with the girls. Oh, my heavens, the other girls, we must rescue them!" Mariana shouted.

"I'm afraid it's too late for them," Pablo announced.

Looking over at her father as if to beg him to return to Trinidad, Abella's eyes pleaded for an answer on what they should do.

Miguel, in turn, responded, "We can do nothing for them now if we want to live."

After grabbing ahold of Mariana's hand to console her young friend, Abella said, "I had a narrow escape from the hand of this scoundrel sitting near you. If I didn't take my only chance to get away, then I imagine that I, too, would find myself in the governor's dungeon of torture."

"Torture, why?" Mariana screamed.

"I'm hopeful that Escobar will realize that the ladies working at Marie's did not know where we had disappeared and will release them sometime this morning!"

Pablo looked at the women with disgust and said, "You all will die, I promise you. This act of treason is a horrible thing that you have done. As soon as I reach port I will notify my governor of your offenses against His Majesty's servant. I will see you all hang."

Miguel looked over at the man and said abruptly, "That is, señor, unless I slit your throat and feed you to the fishes. Now be silent; you bore me."

After standing up, Miguel leaned over, grabbed ahold of the gag, reinserted it back into Pablo's mouth, and tied it tightly, not wanting to hear more from the man.

For hours no one spoke as the last remaining sign of land faded from view. Miguel reached beneath the seat, pulled out a wineskin, and handed it to his daughter. She took a long, slow drink. Afterward, she gave it to Mariana, who eagerly drank her fill, then gave it back to Miguel, who quickly quenched his thirst, feeling refreshed.

Miguel, looking with disgust at Pablo, the prisoner who had broadcasted their demise, returned the wineskin under the bench, not caring if the man was thirsty or not.

After reaching for his compass, Miguel would randomly check his course. Occasionally, he turned around and glanced behind him to ensure they were not being followed. Now out to sea they sailed on a heading unknown to everyone except him.

HOURS HAD PASSED, AND SOON the large orange globe slowly faded into the horizon. Within the hour an array of brilliant stars suddenly shone around. It seemed like an eerie blackness with no moon to light their way. Seagulls often flew above them in the darkness looking for food until they eventually disappeared from view. All anyone could do was sit on the hard wooden benches, trying their best to get comfortable for the long journey ahead into the unknown.

In the starlight, Abella glanced over at Pablo, who had lain down in the small space between seats and was peacefully asleep. She remembered the man and her first encounter with him back at Marie's. There was a young prostitute she took on named Maria, just barely fourteen in age; she showed experience beyond her years in pleasing men.

One evening it seemed a natural fit when Pablo showed up asking for someone new, someone young. This new girl, Maria, ended up being Pablo's favorite. What he liked most was that this young girl knew how to fulfill his fantasies and desires with her young body. One night

Abella was awoken by the sound of a girl screaming. She and her manservant rushed into the room and found the girl tied up with her hands behind her back, bleeding from knife wounds that this heartless bastard applied to her face and body. Hearing her screaming somehow aroused him with some perverted sexual desire.

After seeing the young girl bleeding, she immediately ran to her aid. Even then she should have listened to her manservant Feliciano, who wanted to kill him and be rid of him. *I should have slit his throat like the dog he was*, Abella thought. Sadly, gold has a way of bending one's values in life, but this girl would never be the same; no man wanted her after he had carved up her face and body.

For Miguel, the passing hours through the night drifted by slowly. Sometime in the morning he could see land off in the distance. There, ahead of him, were the lanterns that shined brightly from the small pier ahead. Everyone inside the boat was asleep and resting peacefully for if they had been awake, they would be excited to see the small port ahead, knowing that the first leg of their journey was almost complete.

There were still many more miles ahead before they would be safe. Miguel felt that he had gotten them this far and would hopefully bring the small group to safety soon. Of course, none of this involved Pablo, the royal guard—that man was another matter altogether. Something had to be done about this problem. After reaching down upon his belt, he felt his knife and quickly considered slitting his throat and tossing him overboard. It would solve all their problems, but could he live with himself? Killing fish is nothing like murdering a man. Unfortunately, he had to experience that very fact early in his life.

Not being from Trinidad, he was raised in another city named Puerto Cabello in New Granada as a young boy. There were limited options in the way of making a living, and he became a soldier. However, this decision proved to be regrettable, but he had little choice in the matter as his father insisted it would make a man out of him.

On a similar journey aboard a Spanish ship to discover the new world, Miguel had found the harsh mistreatment and abuse of the local Indians who became nothing but enslaved people.

One early morning when the dawn of a new day was only a few hours away, he had been on guard duty at his post. Suddenly, after hearing a commotion coming near, he saw Santiago, his commander who was drunk with wine, staggering. He was dragging a young, half-naked Indian girl toward his tent on the edge of the camp.

Seeing the poor girl's dismay, he approached Santiago, suggesting he let the girl go. In response he received a smack across his jaw as Santiago yelled at him to return to his post and leave him to his business.

Santiago continued to drag the girl away, but Miguel pleaded for her release, knowing what would happen to her. At that point being furious, Santiago reached for the sword on his belt; after pulling it free, the man tried to kill Miguel.

In response Miguel was suddenly fighting for his life. He knew that Santiago was more muscular and would soon pierce his heart. After several minutes of competing with the man, his strength was dwindling, and little of it remained. At that point Miguel was sure that he would lose his life.

Unexpectedly, the Indian girl arose from the ground and began hitting Santiago, who somehow had managed to get on top of him while trying to stab him through.

Now annoyed by her attempts to remove him from Miguel, Santiago took his right hand and grabbed her by the hair, tugging it hard. She let out a scream as he held a handful of her hair.

This chance was his only opportunity as Miguel wrestled the sword out of his hand and managed to get one hand free and place it over Santiago's mouth. He instinctively took the sword and stuck him through his heart, falling backward and dead on the ground.

Panic struck him deeply as he wasn't sure what to do. Yes, he was justified in protecting himself, but would the general commander agree? However, he wasn't going to take that chance so he immediately grabbed hold of the man's body and began dragging it off toward the river. After pushing the body into the crocodile-infested water, Miguel knew they would soon erase any evidence left behind. After seeing him struggle with Santiago's body, the Indian girl raced to help him in his cause.

All this now seemed like a forgotten nightmare. Miguel later remembered that the Indian girl appeared one night while he was again on guard duty. She had with her a handmade gold bracelet, which she gave him, that he had kept hidden from his fellow soldiers, not wanting to explain the girl's fascination with him.

It took many years to get over that nightmarish experience. Looking over at Pablo who was so free to condemn everyone including Abella, his daughter, Miguel pondered what outcome would result from it.

Now only a short distance from the small port, he saw the small fishing boats anchored just offshore. What to do about Pablo, the unwelcomed guest, was a question that continued to plague his mind. How to deal with this matter was the real problem. The ship's *captain*, loyal to the crown, many of whom he knew personally, would take the killing of a royal guard as an insult. But he had little choice in the matter, and now he faced this dilemma that rendered him no easy answer. Having dealt with his type before, they always demanded respect from everyone by merely wearing the uniform of royalty. The man would not make it easy on them.

Looking up into heaven, Miguel said a silent prayer knowing that killing a man was wrong, but he had little choice now. He gathered the courage within himself, knowing what he was about to do. Silently as he could, he tied the tiller in place and managed to go forward without waking anyone. Within reach of him, just a few feet away, was the anchor of the boat tied onto a long rope that was stored in a small cabinet at the bow of the ship.

Looking past the sleeping women, he could see the wooden door ahead. After leaning over everyone, he opened the door and saw his anchor lying there; just inside he lifted the heavy anchor upward, grabbing ahold of the long rope attached. He then returned to the stern of the boat and sat the anchor down near his foot. He withdrew his knife to cut off a large piece of rope. After taking the end of the rope connected to the anchor, he made a hangman's noose and fastened the knot to tighten securely.

Without regard or hesitation he leaned over to where Pablo was asleep, placing the noose loosely around his neck. Gratefully, he seemed to be a heavy sleeper. Then he gently put the anchor over the side of the boat and let go of it, causing the immediate tightening around Pablo's neck.

With a horrid expression and his eyes looking up at him, the look on Pablo's face was instantly terrifying. Now knowing what his outcome was to be, the man began making choking sounds through his gag as the rope tightened around his neck, strangling him where he was. Without hesitation Miguel lifted his body over the side while he struggled, kicking at the ropes that held him bound. Without being able to defend himself, he made a small splash as he was tossed overboard into the dark water.

As Miguel stared at the helpless victim sinking beneath the waterline, he could see the panicked look on Pablo's face, which quickly disappeared into the murky depths. As he watched Pablo continued kicking and struggled to be free as he sank lower. Miguel stood there, watching as the bubbles drifted by; the black depths soon overtook any sign of the descending man. Miguel looked over to see Abella staring at him, hearing a small commotion. Having nothing to say, she closed her eyes as if to return to sleep or perhaps say a silent prayer for the man that meant to see them all dead.

Again, gazing behind, Miguel looked for any sign that Pablo was able to escape. After seeing no sign of him appearing on the surface of the water, he returned to the back, untied the rudder, and steered the boat toward the fishing port.

Their problems seemed to be behind them, and Miguel knew that even if Pablo could get himself free, there were many miles still to swim before he could reach the shore. Gripping the wooden handle, he again closed his eyes and said a silent prayer, asking forgiveness from God and knowing that he had taken another life and would go to his grave with more blood on his hands.

All remained quiet on the tiny vessel. The morning light of a new day would hopefully begin to erase the shadowy darkness of the night and the horrid act of killing. Somehow being alive to see a new horizon brought a positive outlook for Miguel and a hope that they all would survive this ordeal.

SOMETIME LATER, OFF IN THE distance, the small pier became visible. Miguel steered the small craft into the little inlet, and they soon arrived at the small dock. Standing on the wooden pier was an older man mending his fishing nets as he prepared to go fishing that morning.

Steering the boat to a spot near the end of the pier, Miguel grabbed ahold of a small rope and placed it around an iron cleat, tying the boat off. Abella was the first to look up from her resting spot and wonder at her father, unsure where they were.

In the light of day she could see the saddened expression on his face, knowing what he did for them. The decision to kill Pablo and erase his existence was already decided by his actions when he threatened to have them all arrested. He was not a man to be trusted; he could testify against them, bringing certain death to them all.

Suddenly, the man tending to his fishing nets walked over and greeted Miguel with a pleasant good morning.

Miguel nodded in response and returned the greeting, "Good morning, señor."

The stranger looked down at the two women dressed in men's garments and quickly scrutinized the situation, realizing they were in disguise for some unknown reason, which he did not understand but did not care about.

With the boat secured, Miguel exited the small craft, turned back to look at his daughter, and said, "You stay in the boat with your friend; I shall return shortly. If anyone asks why you're dressed like a man, tell them you cannot say."

After watching her father disappear into the town, Abella felt frightened and vulnerable sitting alone. She turned to her young friend as if to say something and noticed she was still asleep. Now alone with her thoughts, Abella wondered what would happen to them next. Sitting there, exposed, the woman had few places to hide. All of this, including the fact that she never learned how to sail, made her feel she was helpless to escape.

As Abella sat there helpless to do anything, she concluded that two hours had passed since her father had disappeared into town. She frantically worried and supposed that perhaps the royal guards had captured her father and held him hostage; they would soon pounce on them to put them all in irons.

As time passed other fishermen arrived and busied themselves preparing for the morning fishing trips. If any approached or got close, Abella would tilt her head, covering up her feminine features as she ignored their presence as they walked past them.

After considering the time wasted waiting for her father to appear, her decision to stay there any longer seemed like a catalyst for disaster. Finding herself in this situation, she began to question why she hadn't surrendered the uniform that had meant so much to everyone involved, especially the governor. It would have been nothing to give him what he wanted, but why didn't she? For now, she couldn't answer that question, but there was something within her that felt as though there was an ulterior motive for the governor wanting that British uniform.

Then the older fishermen who had greeted her father earlier walked over and offered her some water to drink. Abella looked up at the man, thanking him for his kindness. Being quite thirsty, she accepted the bottle and took a long drink. Afterward, Abella continued to worry about her father. She had no answers on what was taking him so long to return. She stared back toward town where he initially disappeared, hoping to see him soon.

The old fishermen then asked if she was hungry.

Before she could think of an answer, Mariana

awoke, hearing their voices conversing. She sat up in a panic, looking into the blinding daylight at some older man standing on the pier. Then, after looking at Abella as if searching for an answer, she quickly asked, "What happened to Miguel? Where are they?"

Abella replied, "It's all right, don't worry. My father has gone into the town to seek help. I'm sure he'll be back soon. Here, would you like some water to drink?"

After nodding her head in response, Mariana grabbed ahold of the pouch and began drinking it down. Afterward, she handed it back to Abella. Still, she felt nervous as the old fisherman stood there watching their every move.

Abella returned the water bottle to the man and thanked him for his kindness. She then returned her gaze toward town as she pondered what had happened to her father.

The old fisherman smiled and returned to his nets.

A short time later Abella sighed with relief at seeing her father approaching. He was accompanied by another man whom she had never seen before. As the men got closer to the boat, Abella heard them joking about an event from their past in which the stranger blamed her father for starting a fight over a beautiful woman. Seeing them laughing together as if they were old friends brought a feeling of liberation from her fears, thinking they were out of danger.

As they appeared next to the boat, her father looked at his friend and said, "Let me introduce my daughter, Abella, and her friend, Mariana, whom I told you about. As I explained to you, there were some unfortunate circumstances that they have found themselves. That's why I asked you to allow them passage aboard your ship, the *Morning Star*."

"Yes, of course, Miguel. Do not worry yourself, my old friend, for we have known each other for many years and had on more than one occasion found ourselves behind bars for some of the craziness we have done."

"This is sad but true," Miguel announced.

A robust laugh erupted from the stranger, who looked inside the boat at the pair of women and said,

"Ladies, let me introduce myself; my name is Francisco Melendez. I am the *captain* of the two-masted ship called the *Morning Star*. The day after tomorrow we shall set sail for Jamaica, where I have many friends who will shelter you. You must be hungry now; please follow me back to the town. I know the owner of an inn who will shelter you for the night."

Upon hearing the news that they were going to travel to Jamaica, both Abella and Mariana felt thrilled and somewhat relieved, believing that perhaps this nightmare would have a happy ending after all. What her father and this *captain* had in the way of friendship, she did not know. But truthfully, she didn't trust men in general and felt suspicious, not knowing this stranger.

As Abella exited the small craft, she presented a fake smile outwardly as if everything was normal, and both she and Mariana walked behind Miguel and his friend back toward town. On the way Mariana suddenly realized that Pablo had disappeared.

"Where is Pablo, the royal guard?" Mariana whispered to her friend.

"He is sleeping with the fishes," Abella coldly responded.

"Oh, I see," Mariana said as she made the sign of the cross across her chest and continued following behind.

On the way to their unknown destination, Abella listened to her father reliving old memories as if he were a young man once again. He seemed happier than she ever remembered, while she and Mariana felt bare and unprotected in their disguises like men and remained staring at the ground as they followed closely behind.

Walking through the cobblestone streets, it was still morning, and most businesses were just beginning to open. As they passed a bakery, the aroma of bread cooking filled the narrow passageways, making everyone hungry for a taste of delicious cinnamon-filled pastries.

Continuing their way, other businesses such as silversmiths and cobblers opened their creaking doors and windows. When they saw their small company walking past, they looked on with wonder, seeing the new faces that had arrived in town.

As the quiet solitude was broken, the small town woke from its slumber, and more people appeared on the streets. The sounds of children playing in the city square could be heard ahead of them. When they arrived at the heart of the town near a small ornate fountain, a ball made of leather shot past them, with a group of children racing to catch it, ignoring their presence altogether.

When they found the inn that the *captain* spoke of, it seemed to Abella like a pleasant enough place, and knowing such dwellings from her past, she knew that there would be a brothel not far away. Many male travelers that stayed at these places would only have a short walk to the house of pleasure after an evening of eating and drinking their fill. *It seemed the case with our good Capitán Francisco, who appeared to be a little drunk or on his way soon. His slurred words when speaking to her father were an absolute giveaway,* Abella thought.

After getting themselves a room on the second floor, everybody retired to bed, exhausted from their ordeal. Even though it was just past midday, no one cared. Inside the room were two beds and a water basin near the window where one could watch. Other than that, the place had little in the way of conveniences. Being exhausted from sailing all night, Miguel instantly lay down on the bed and was soon asleep.

Abella and Mariana sat on the other bed, talking while they ate cheese, bread, and some salted meat brought to their room. Not wanting to venture out into the small town at night, they remained quiet, staring out their window at the streets below.

Feeling worried for the other girls' safety that they left back in Trinidad, all they could do was pray that they would all be safe. Many of these poor girls had no family waiting for them and were gladly accepted into their newly adopted family of harlots that all worked for Abella.

Abella herself had become the madam in charge when the original madam named Marie was murdered by an unsatisfied customer who complained that the girl he ordered wasn't a virgin. She knew that the man would go free for his crime and would have a story to tell his friends, then, as a result, expecting that he could treat any other harlot like human trash. Abella saw her friend dead on the floor with a dagger through her heart, wearing a blank stare as if pleading to be avenged. Without hesitation she reached inside her petticoat to withdraw her small musket and shot the man in the head, not feeling remorse for her actions. Then she disposed of his body in a pen of hungry pigs. Instantly, she was hailed the new madam by all the girls who witnessed the event. She was tough when she needed to be. She did her best to protect the working girls, who were mostly naïve about the world's ways; now their fate was unknown, a fact that haunted her waking thoughts.

As the blackness of night shadowed the small town, both women soon fell asleep in the small bed. They both dreamed of arriving in Jamaica, where they were sure they would be out of reach to the governor despite the loud noise from beneath them while the inn's customers drank on into the night.

THE FOLLOWING DAY THE STREETS below came alive with commerce when the sun rose. Everyone stayed in their room, not wanting to venture outside in case the governor had sent military soldiers searching for them.

Sometime that evening Miguel left the room to meet with Francisco to discuss payment for their voyage and returned a while later smelling of alcohol. He was told everything was in order, and they would board the ship the following day, bound for Jamaica and freedom. Payment for their voyage was Miguel's fishing vessel, including a few silver coins he managed to have with him, which the *captain* eagerly accepted.

It was sometime in the early morning hours when a knock was heard upon their door. Awaking with fright, Abella looked about the room, staring at the door. She waited and listened carefully. Then another knock, louder than the first, was heard. She reached for her blanket to cover herself. She grabbed the small candle near her bed to light her way and slowly crept toward the door.

Unexpectedly, there was another knock from the persistent stranger. Quickly, Miguel shot out of bed, confused and disoriented; he looked about the room in the dim light and saw Abella holding the candle.

"Who's pounding on the damn door?"

"Father, I do not know."

Walking up to the door, Miguel asked, "What do you want?" and waited for a reply.

On the other side of the door he could hear female voices whispering something that he couldn't quite make out.

"You are in grave danger and must leave immediately," someone said.

At that point Miguel reached for the knife on his belt to assure himself that it was there in case he needed it. Slowly, he unlatched the creaking door and looked outside into the hallway. There, he saw a young girl he recognized from the night before as the daughter of the tavern owner, who went by the name of Sofia.

Looking at her puzzled, he asked, "What did you say about us being in danger?"

"Quickly let me inside now, please," the girl cried out.

Without waiting for permission this girl named Sofia pushed her way inside and quickly reached around to close the door behind her. Standing there, she looked about the room and saw Abella with the small candle, staring at her oddly.

Ignoring her, she looked at Miguel and said, "Listen to me, please. I overheard my father making arrangements to throw you all in irons! Your friend, this Capitán Francisco, has betrayed you and has received news that there is a bounty on your daughter's head. My father and the *captain* are planning to surprise you in the morning, arrest all of you, and take you back to Trinidad."

"Are you sure?" Miguel asked, not believing the news about his old friend.

"Yes," Sofia responded, "I'm telling you the truth. My father would kill me if he knew I told you this, but I do not care because he mistreats me and often beats me. I cannot stand to be his slave any longer; that's what I am to him and nothing more."

Not sure what to do next, Miguel turned back to stare at his daughter, looking lost. Abella knew there was little in the way of choices so raced over and awoke Mariana from her sleep, saying, "We must leave immediately."

Mariana, still half asleep, yelled out, "What now?"

"Quickly, we must leave. Get dressed," Abella responded.

After walking over to Sofia, Abella gave her a stern look and asked, "Are you sure what you've heard is true?"

Now fully awake Mariana said, "Yes, we cannot just merely disappear into the night with no place to go."

"Listen to me, please. Francisco has returned to his ship to gather his men. When he returns he will place all of you in chains."

"That is not right. Francisco would never betray me," Miguel shouted.

"Listen, sometime in the morning hours while you're sleeping, Francisco plans on returning to the inn and, with the help from my father, they intend to enter your room to arrest you all."

"What now? Oh, where shall we go?" Mariana questioned.

"My father was offered a piece of the reward for your capture; if he agreed to help the *captain* and if you value your lives, you must leave here quickly or else you will be discovered."

"Where shall we go?" Miguel inquired.

"I know a way back to the pier where your boat is anchored. You can escape that way while it's still dark. Few people know about a small inlet on the other side of the island. You must get to your boat and sail it to the other side of the island. I will meet you there with supplies that will aid you on your journey, but you all must hurry and leave before it's too late."

Miguel looked intently at Sophia for any sign of treachery but saw only the fearful expression of a troubled youth.

Sofia cried, "Now do as I say and follow me."

Abella came forward and said, "Tell me first, what

is it you hope to gain by helping us? I do not trust anyone; it's how I managed to stay alive all this time. So tell me, what is your reward for helping us?"

"I want you to take me with you," Sophia said plainly.

"What? There was no room in the boat with everyone including Pablo," Mariana announced. Then after realizing what happened to the man, she suddenly remained quiet.

Miguel addressed Sophia directly and said, "You can come, but you must do as I say."

"I will do anything, but we must leave at once," Sophia responded.

Without objection everyone crept out of the room and down the stairs, following the girl through the village and out to the pier. When they arrived they gratefully found the small boat unguarded, exactly where they had left it.

Miguel then looked at Sophia and said, "I shall see you at the inlet on the other side of the island. You must hurry; it will be daylight soon."

She added, "Listen to me; I want you to look for a signal from my lantern. I will be moving it side to side; please hurry." Then she ran off.

Looking about the pier, they saw no one around and ran over to jump inside the boat. As Abella began untying it from the dock, Miguel grabbed ahold of one of the oars and pushed hard against one of the timbers of the pier in the direction of the open water. After taking the second oar and shoving them both into the rowlocks, he faced the stern and slowly rowed away from the small dock out to sea.

Treachery is everywhere; even an old friend could turn pirate any time and sell you out for a price. Now he thought, *Can we trust this young girl or did she set a trap for them all to follow?* These questions were first and foremost on Miguel's mind.

The fluorescent waves splashed on the rocky shoreline on a moonless night, providing little to no light to navigate. Experience taught Miguel to steer away from the splashing waves upon the rocky shore rather than toward it. An offshore breeze regarded them regrettably, hampering their progress and pushing them closer to the shoreline. Seeing her father struggle, Abella quickly sat next to him and grabbed ahold of the other oars to paddle.

It took a little time but they finally reached the open water. Then Miguel looked back toward the small harbor and gazed at the ship called the *Morning Star*. He could see a buzz of activity aboard the ship from his vantage point. Suddenly, he glimpsed a small group of torches being carried upon the water, as the group of men must have boarded a small boat and paddled toward town.

Miguel's anger burned as he thought, *If ever I run into Francisco again, he won't live to see another day.*

However, they still could be caught at any moment so with that in mind, they continued in their struggle to get away, dipping their oars into the dark water and rowing with all their might. After some time the small boat seemed far enough away that they could engage the sail.

In the fading darkness they saw the outlining palm trees near the beach and the crashing waves racing toward the sandy shoreline. Gratefully, it was a moonlit night; Miguel was most grateful for that. Being a sailor he had mastered the art of sailing and was soon tacking the boat in different angles to make the most out of the offshore breeze.

From their position on the water, they continued searching in the darkness for any sign of Sophia. Could this young girl be trusted, or was there an alternative motive? Truthfully, after hearing the news of his old friend turning into a traitor, it was not something that Miguel wanted to consider. After all, being played the fool was everyone's regret. The realization of being found by the governor and tortured to death when they thought they had made their escape was very disheartening.

Looking over at his daughter who struggled continually with the oars while trying her best to paddle the boat forward, Miguel felt that their attempts to get away were futile. The truth was that his decision to toss Pablo over the side of the fishing boat made him feel as though he was still haunting them.

Miguel thought that it was wrong, and yet he did it anyway. All of this was a result of him wanting to save his daughter. Regrettably, it weighed heavy on him. Desperately, he searched the shoreline for any sign of light.

Steering the boat far enough away so as not to hit the coral beneath was treacherous by day, but it was still dark, and at any moment he felt that they would run aground and all would be lost for sure. He couldn't tell precisely where the coral was except for the splashing of the waves that crashed upon it. It would already be too late if he misjudged their location and got stranded on the rocky reef while the onslaught of waves continued to slam against the boat until it became nothing but useless splinters.

As he maneuvered around the outcropping of rocky shoreline, the landscape suddenly changed; he could see a small inlet appear before them in the dark shadows.

Mariana was the first to spot the lantern glowing on the beach and yelled out, "There's Sofia!"

Unfortunately, as they looked for a way inside the inlet, they unexpectedly saw another group of lanterns moving toward the small channel, to everyone's dismay. The expression on everyone's face was not visible, but the disappointment couldn't be missed as they all sighed collectively.

The young girl named Sofia either played a part in catching them or was trapped in her effort to help them escape. Suddenly seeing the lanterns racing toward the inlet, Miguel instinctively knew what to do: He quickly steered his small boat away, back out into the open water.

After sitting back down on the wooden bench, Abella felt disappointed. It had become evident that their plan to escape to safety was now dashed to bits. She looked over at the figure of her father at the helm and wondered if he, too, was distressed.

Miguel, without a word, steered the small boat away, hoping they had not been seen, and never looked back.

Now the question arose: Where to go and who to

trust when your only friend turns on you? At that moment they all felt alone and vulnerable as they had nowhere to run. Their plan to escape from Trinidad seemed so simple at its creation. They were going to catch the *Morning Star* and sail to Jamaica. Once they arrived there, they would start a new life—but now it was not to be.

The only thing to do was to sail away as fast as they could and not get captured. But the question came again, where to go? Although he was once a sailor, Miguel was not a ship's *captain*; he didn't have the use of charts and a large boat to sail to safety. Instead, they had a small fishing boat that they put all their trust in. For now, it would have to do; it was their only way to stay alive.

As Miguel looked out into the open sea for which direction to chart their course, nothing mattered except to become invisible into the blackness that remained. Admittedly, it could have been a trap laid for them. But they would never know the truth as they sailed away from land. Was the bait Sofia, who played her part perfectly by placing them in the hands of these treacherous men, or was she just a pawn?

But why did Sofia lead them to this outlet? They already had them in their clutches back at the inn; why not just take them then? Unless Sofia's father had his agenda to get the bounty on their heads and sell them to the governor, cutting out Francisco, the *captain* of the *Morning Star*, altogether. These were treacherous waters they traveled. At any time they could find themselves unable to escape the clutches of the governor.

As Miguel was grabbing the rudder and piloting the boat out to sea, the island slowly disappeared from view. He felt relieved and grateful that they had managed to escape unharmed. Seeing the morning dawn appear, Miguel wondered what future they had left them. This uncertainty left him feeling sick.

Now everyone aboard the small vessel realized that they had barely escaped death. It was as if the grim reaper was giving chase. Try as he will, Miguel steered the little boat away from danger to escape calamity. However, he felt that soon his life would end, regardless of how fast he ran to avoid it.

CHAPTER 8

EDWARDO SANTOS FÉLIX ESCOBAR, THE governor, sat at his desk writing upon a parchment. Halfway through he dipped his pen into his inkwell and continued writing out the warrant for the arrest of Abella Sanchez. After hearing the news of her escape, Escobar wondered how a mere prostitute overpowered Pablo, his lieutenant commander. The more he thought about it, the more he gritted his teeth in response. For her treason, she would suffer the most. However, for her actions against the crown, she would hang.

Suddenly, he heard a knock on his door; without looking up he yelled, "Come in."

After opening the door, in walked Diego Carlos Espinosa, the captain of the ship named the *Reina Isabella*. After coming to a stop, he removed his hat and bowed, a customary salute to his superiors.

After looking up briefly, the governor pointed to a chair and ordered him to have a seat.

After sitting carefully, Diego positioned his sword to rest on his side and stared at his commander, waiting for a response.

After sprinkling some pumice on the wet ink for it to dry, Escobar blew off the remainder upon the floor and said, "I've just finished writing out a warrant for the arrest of Abella Sanchez, the prostitute from Marie's, that I'm ordering you to put in chains and return to Trinidad."

"As you wish, Your Excellency! I will bring this woman to justice," Diego answered.

"I want you to understand that she has had help from unknown accomplices, who have assisted in her escape. If it is your judgment, Capitán, to bring them back alive or dead, it does not matter to me," the governor said.

"I understand completely. Will there be anything else?" was Diego's immediate response.

"No, not at this time, Capitán."

After standing to his feet, Diego bowed, then placed his hat back upon his head and said, "Very well, Governor. I must leave at once if I hope to overtake them."

"Thank you, Capitán. I have your arrest warrant; it's almost complete. I only need to place my official stamp upon it."

Escobar, after pouring some wax upon the parchment, took a bronzed tip-carved mallet and dug it deep into the hot wax. Afterward, he handed it to Diego. Within his grasp Diego had all the orders he needed with the official seal on the document.

Holding the warrant in his hands, he asked, "Governor, do you have an idea where I should start my search for these desperados?"

"It is my understanding, Capitán, that Abella's accomplice was no other than her dear father, Miguel Sanchez, the fisherman. I believe it was he who aided her escape and sailed her away using his fishing vessel."

"A fisherman, you say?" Diego asked.

"I have ascertained that in the evening she was arrested by Pablo, my trusted servant; her father not only took Pablo but a young prostitute as well. Sometime before dawn they were assisted by a local fisherman named Escondido, who helped them launch their small fishing vessel."

"I don't believe I know him," Diego stated.

"No matter, Escondido's tongue became loosened using my torture techniques, and he fully divulged his part in their escape. I'm sad that the young man did not survive my truth device. I believe you will find them at Puerto Cabello in New Granada."

"How could they have sailed that great distance in such a small fishing boat?"

"I have no idea. But as I explained, Capitán, do as you wish with these scoundrels; they're no concern of mine. This betrayal is something that I do not take lightly.

It begins to crumble the foundation of the law, and I will not stand for it."

"I understand, Governor."

"You have your orders, Capitán. Bring back my commander named Pablo alive or the head of this prostitute."

"I will carry out your orders without delay, Governor." Having said this, Espinosa saluted, followed by the clicking of his black boots, and disappeared out of the room.

Leaving the governor's mansion, Diego had to go home to gather his things before he departed. Knowing the small fishing port, it wasn't that far and would take no more than four days to sail there. Arriving at his home, he packed some personal belongings for his journey in a travel bag and set it by the door. After walking over to his armoire, he took out some clothes, packed them away in a large duffle bag, and tied it closed.

Camila, his wife, stood by as he packed for his journey and said nothing until he had finished.

After setting down his duffle bag, he was ready to part with a kiss. However, before he could leave Camila grabbed him.

"Diego, I see you have your orders from the governor; listen to me, my love, the town is all in an uproar because of what that pig, Escobar, has done to Escondido and his family."

"I have nothing to do with that, my love," he replied.

After looking away briefly to remember the poor man and his family, she returned her gaze to her husband and said, "That young man did not deserve to be tortured and killed, nor his family abused and thrown out into the streets. Now you are obeying him to do what?"

"Please listen to me, wife; I have my orders. It seems that you have forgotten that I almost lost my command already. To disappoint the governor now would surely mean that I would be thrown out of the naval service and be forced to become a farmer or some other lowly occupation just to survive."

"I understand you're under a lot of pressure, but I

fear what the townspeople must think of us. I see it already in their faces when I go to the markets or when I go to the well for water. They smirk at me and give me dirty looks, knowing that you work for that murdering dog," Camila announced.

"I do not have the time to discuss this matter; I must get to my ship. We can continue this conversation when I return. Listen, I'm not sure how much longer I will be Capitán of the *Reina Isabella*. Perhaps it's time to consider the offer from Mateo, my cousin, to work as a merchant *captain*; at least I wouldn't have to do the bidding of this Escobar."

Camila kissed her husband lovingly and said, "Please return to me safely, my love; it's all I ask."

"I have to go. Please don't listen to the townspeople; they are old women who are bitter that their husbands don't love them any longer and want to ruin our happy lives with gossip and backbiting."

"I love you and will return soon. I promise you!"

After walking over to his wife, he again kissed her, as was his custom not knowing if perhaps today would be the last time he saw her. After leaving his home, he followed a small grassy path to where the docks were located. There, he saw a boat with two sailors waiting for his arrival. Diego handed his gear to one of the young men and stepped inside. Sitting near the transom, he looked on as the two sailors began rowing the small boat toward the *Reina Isabella* anchored just offshore.

The *Reina Isabella* was a Spanish galleon that served the dual purpose of being both a man-of-war and a treasure merchant ship. Within the Spanish flotilla, the fortified galleons had a striking design with its hull shape that tapered to a narrow top deck. The plan aimed to concentrate the weight on the ship's centerline and improve its stability.

The *Reina Isabella* was heavily armed with its forty heavy guns, with twenty on either side of the ship, including deck guns mounted on the railing used to repel anyone trying to board. Despite her heavy armament, the ship was easily rocked by the sea; her upper decks were extremely high, with an even higher stern. The boat's design caused it to pitch and roll more than other ships of foreign design. Diego's men under his command were too often prone to seasickness.

Diego was not the governor's favorite *captain* among the many others serving under him. Over several incidences in the past, he proved not to be as reliable as other ship *captain*s and seemed to be a disappointment overall. He realized that someone of lesser rank could handle this matter with just a few men in a small boat, but perhaps it was the governor's way of giving him a second chance to prove himself worthy.

Sitting ahead, the two sailors under his command paddled the small dinghy toward the waiting ship. There was a warm offshore breeze with no clouds in the sky. It seemed thus far to be a beautiful day. As they approached their boat, ropes from above were tossed over the side. A small gangway was lowered near the water. Immediately, all the sailors aboard the Spanish vessel came running in two distinct rows and stood to attention as Diego stepped up on the wooden planks.

Suddenly, his premier official, Carlos Salinas, ran up, saluted him, and stood to attention, waiting for his *captain* to address him adequately.

"Is everything in order, Señor Salinas?"

"Yes, Capitán, the ship is ready to sail, awaiting your command."

"Very well."

Salinas inquired about their orders, "What's our course, Capitán?"

Diego turned to him and showed the sealed arrest warrant from the governor and said, "We are to capture escaping criminals in the small fishing port of Puerto Cabello in New Granada. Set course immediately."

Given the coordinates of the location of the fishing village, Salinas quickly yelled orders to the crew to raise the anchor and set the sails to get underway. At that point Diego shared a customary salute with Salinas and walked away, allowing the workings of the ship to engage in bringing the *Reina* to full sail.

Every sailor on the *Reina Isabella* performed their duties without question; quickly, the ship began to move forward out to sea. After taking his place on the forecastle, Captain Espinosa was soon brought his spyglass. He looked into the open water to see signs of *piratas* or any other vessel that would take them by surprise.

Many of the men aboard the Spanish ship, mainly the officers, all knew of an inevitable fact that to rise in rank as a *captain* or admiral was either reached by being a member of a wealthy family or by serving many years aboard a ship and devoting oneself to the service of Spanish crown. Only then could one hope to gain rank by performance, exceptionally above and beyond the call of duty, which was already expected of oneself.

A seasoned officer spent many years serving in the Navy to reach the rank of *captain*. It was the case with Diego, who always performed his duties flawlessly. In addition to losing his ship to *piratas*, Diego survived a battle at sea in which many of his friends had perished and it had severely wounded him.

Being cast adrift in a small boat, he and the remainder of his crew had floated helplessly for several days until they finally reached the safety of a small fishing port, where he stayed for several weeks until he was well enough to return to Trinidad.

He felt a worrying sense of dread at repeating the loss of a ship under his command. In response he relentlessly had his crew practice firing drills of the heavy cannons every time they were at sea. Still, on their last voyage his crew reported to their stations slower than he liked; however, Diego felt that his men would perform brilliantly in battle when their real mettle would be tested as a fighting force.

He looked one final time at his lovely home, which was slowly became smaller from view as they had already traveled ten miles out to sea, only to change direction as they caught the southerly trade winds that flowed along the continent.

THE SUN ABOVE FELT HOT, and soon Diego began perspiring beneath his colorful jacket, along with the heavy saber with its bronze handle strapped to his side and his tight clothing, which felt burdensome. As Diego stood on the upper deck, he gazed out at the horizon for any sign of sails approaching. Eight hours into their voyage the waves were choppy as the ship was tossed from side to side. Its three-masted sails filled with an offshore breeze that propelled them forward. Standing at such a height above water, he had an advantage point and could see far out into the horizon, spying out any signs of *piratas.*

Salinas, his premier official, paced back and forth on the main deck below him, watching the men at work. It was understood that he was second in charge; he performed most of the evaluations of every sailor, reporting only the most severe violations to the captain himself, which resulted in punishments that were delivered swiftly and with a stern hand.

Today the men seemed distracted by the news that they were to capture Abella, the madam at Marie's. Although the men did their duties as requested, they acted sluggish and unhappy. Placing such an admired individual in the hands of the ruthless governor would only mean one thing in the end: death to the beautiful lady for whom most men had a particular affection.

As Diego looked out his spyglass, the sea looked a deep blue as the subtle white caps created from the wind occasionally appeared. As if a sense of calm came over Capitán Diego, not seeing any dangers in the open waters, he thought, *Perhaps it's time to relax.*

He stood upon the forecastle and allowed the gentle swaying of the ship to give him a sense of peaceful tranquility that was never to be trusted. Yes, although it wasn't the fleet's largest ship, she still commanded respect among other vessels of the day. Diego knew that these miles traveled from shore; there was no safe harbor or sheltered shoreline to search for safety. However, there was a sense of security, knowing that below deck four, cannons ready to bring destruction upon any cowardice *piratas* or enemy of the Spanish crown.

HOURS LATER AFTER RETIRING TO HIS cabin, Diego

changed out of his uniform and sat in his chair for some time. Gathering his thoughts about his mission, he again doubted that it was a worthy assignment of his talent. He remembered when Escobar, the governor, took office and had a meeting with all his staff. Escobar planned to rid the Caribbean waters of all *piratas*. This task was a daring adventure for anyone new to the office, but the governor had to impress the Spanish crown. It was Diego's misfortune to speak his mind about Escobar's bold plan, and he was immediately chastised.

That evening after arriving at the officer's dining table, many junior officers were laughing about a joke involving the governor and his wife. First Lieutenant Mendez pranced about with his arms tucked behind his back, resembling a peacock, which looked like Escobar in his elegant attire. Diego walked into the room and laughed, seeing the humor in the joke. Soon the mood changed to more pressing matters, such as the morale aboard the ship.

A junior officer named Humberto de Hevia spoke up. "Excuse me, Capitán, but what profit is it to bring females back to Trinidad in chains? Wouldn't it serve the crown by fighting *piratas*?"

Everyone around the table suddenly grew quiet, including the cook serving the food. With attention drawn to Diego, he looked at his junior officers and said, "Listen to me, all of you. Orders are orders; despite my feelings about this situation, I must carry them out to the letter."

No one argued or said anything else; the officers silently ate their meal. Now it was getting late, and Diego felt tired. He soon retired to his cabin. After getting undressed Diego poured himself some aged port to help him sleep. When he was finished with his glass, he retired to bed. Maintaining their course toward an unknown destination, the ship's motion gently rocked him to sleep. Just as he was about to doze off, he heard a crew member announce, "Twelve bells, and all is well." He soon was asleep, oblivious to this world and its disappointments, dreaming instead of his home and his loving wife, Camila.

Diego assembled his men the following day and ran through a firing drill, still slower than he liked. That evening he asked his first mate, Salinas, to join him for dinner in his cabin. Once their meal was over and the cabin boy removed the dishes, both men got comfortable. After pouring each of them another glass of wine, Diego asked Salinas for any suggestions on what they could do to quicken the men's pace during the firing drills.

"As I explained to you before, Capitán, the men are disappointed by the orders to capture a gentlewoman. They feel that their talents would be better served in combat against the *piratas* or even the British or other enemies of the crown."

Diego looked upset by the response and said, "I understand the crew's concern, but this should not affect their efficiency at firing the cannons." After taking another sip of wine, he continued, "Now tell me, did you have time to go over the supply manifest as I requested before we left port?"

"Yes, I'm sad to report that they were still running low on supplies of gunpowder. I wanted to bring this up during our last firing exercise, Capitán, but you seemed more concerned about how quickly the men could fire the cannons than our gunpowder stores used during practice firing drills themselves."

"Tell me, Salinas, do you not realize that without gunpowder we are helpless to defend ourselves in any engagement we face? It is our only protection against *piratas*," Diego shouted, being frustrated by the news.

"You must believe me, Capitán, I tried to get us more gunpowder, but the supply officer had direct orders from the governor that only so many barrels would be given to each ship. It seems that there is a shortage of gunpowder."

"Tell me, how many barrels do we have left, Señor Salinas?"

"I'm sad to report only sixty barrels of gunpowder left, Capitán. This tally is a more exact amount after our last firing exercise."

The news was disheartening; however, not wanting to show his anger toward his premier official, the captain stood to his feet, pacing back and forth while looking at the floor, with his hands locked behind his back. He realized that this job was Salinas's alone. Why he couldn't tell him before they wasted more gunpowder on another firing exercise was a dereliction of duty. He looked at his first mate and said, "That will be all, Señor Salinas."

"As you wish, Capitán." After quickly finishing his glass of wine, Salinas stood to his feet, saluted, and then walked out, knowing that he was negligent in his duties.

The following day the morning sun's rays barely showed through the dense covering above. The salt spray from the waves burst upon the ship's bow and filled the surrounding decks with the salted aroma. Above, the squawking seagulls flying above the wooden masts called out as they searched for a free meal beneath the churning waves.

As captain on this ship, Diego felt an uneasiness that haunted him throughout the night. *How could I be so stupid as not to realize we were running low on gunpowder?* Thinking back upon it now, Salinas kept asking him for an audience but being busy sulking over his latest orders, he refused to listen. No, the blame, indeed, was his own, and he would have a word with Señor Salinas about the matter.

Ahead of them by tomorrow, they would reach Puerto Cabello sometime in the evening hours. Diego felt within his heart that capturing these escapees would be no trouble. The truth was he had no reason to dispute his orders. This Abella, whom the governor seemed most anxious to capture, would be brought to justice for whatever reason.

As the ship maintained its course toward the small fishing port, the captain seemed more accessible to his crew. He appeared on the deck wearing a smile, which was quite unusual. Sometime before midday, standing alone on the forecastle, Diego eyed a group of seagulls and watched them fly above the admiral's pennant. Unexpectedly, Carlos, the premier official, approached and stood near; he said nothing but looked up, admiring the flying spectacle.

"I have known you for many years now, Carlos. I

can always tell when something is on your mind. So please tell me, what's troubling you?"

"I understand, Capitán, orders are orders, it is as you say. But still, I must inform you that we could have a hard time persuading the men when it comes to imprisoning the madam of the local brothel."

"I see."

"Capitán, this Abella, I have known for many years; she has always provided the necessity for men's entertainment at a fair price, I must say. I would be lying if I did not say that I have a soft spot in my heart for this woman," Carlos admitted.

"I understand your concerns, but for now, we have our orders; we must obey them, regardless of our feelings."

"As you wish, Capitán." Having said this, Carlos disappeared and was soon overseeing the cleaning of the deck.

Feeling frustrated over the situation to arrest this woman, Diego took out his spyglass to survey the horizon for any sign of danger. To his disbelief he saw a white sail some distance away. Straining at the spyglass to look a second time, he not only saw one sail but a smaller one appeared next to the first ship.

It was well known in these Caribbean waters that seeing two separate sails together only meant one thing— *piratas de Iron Born*—and none other. Immediately, Diego yelled out for Carlos, his premier official, to come to him at once.

Hearing their captain scream out orders caused the crew to cease what they were doing to stare up at the forecastle deck, where they saw a frightening sight: the commander prancing back and forth with fear written upon his face.

After running up to the forecastle deck, Carlos suddenly said, "What is it, Capitán?"

The man in the crow's nest above yelled, "Ships approaching off the starboard bow."

Diego, staring through his spyglass, turned away briefly, looked upon his premier official with distress, and said, "Señor, prepare the men for battle, for we will soon be having company."

"What do you mean, Capitán?"

"These ships that approach, who they are, I have no idea; they're still too far to judge, but if they are *piratas de Iron Born* as I suspect, then I want the men to be ready to give an account of ourselves to these dogs."

"What, Capitán? What is it that you're saying? *Piratas de Iron Born?*" Now looking off into the distance, Carlos could make out a small set of white sails approaching. Instantly, he jumped into action and shouted orders to the men to go below, commanding everyone to their combat stations.

The whole ship erupted into chaos. Screaming voices yelled back and forth as every man scrambled down below decks, leaving the soapy buckets behind. Suddenly, each cannon was loaded with the twelve-pound musket balls and was poised to fire, awaiting the word from Hugo, the master gunner.

Above the main deck other sailors ran to the swivel guns and quickly loaded them with a shot of iron pellets. Now every crew member stood at their battle station and waited. An eerier hush fell over the ship as it maintained its course, unable to escape.

Standing on the quarterdeck, Diego turned back toward the navigator whose hands were grasping the giant ship's wheel. He ordered him to maintain course, not to divert or change the ship's direction.

A sudden rush of exhilaration overcame Diego, suspecting those approaching sails belonged to the most notable *piratas*. These particular *piratas* had undoubtedly hoped to capture a fatted Spanish galleon ship filled to her upper decks with golden treasure. Recent sightings of these cutthroats sailing these waters were reported to the admiralty. However, it was mainly sightings from nearby fishermen and nothing more.

Today if they could outmaneuver and destroy these *piratas de Iron Born*, it would bring Capitán Diego recognition and perhaps a commission. He looked down at his junior officers, Humberto de Hevia and Matias Hernandez, who had never tasted battle. They both stood there looking up at Capitán Diego as if searching for strength, frightened to move from their posts. Wanting to diminish their fears, Diego yelled down at them, "Have courage, for the battle is already won."

Then a nervous smile appeared on both their faces as they turned to look at one another, desperate for their young lives.

With eyes fixated on the approaching danger, Capitán Diego did not move from his station and was poised to give out commands to his men. He ordered his sword to be brought to him, along with his belt containing musket pistols. The main deck below looked empty of life as every sailor was poised for action, standing alert at their battle stations. Below decks, each station housed three sailors to load and reload the heavy cannons as they waited nervously for the battle to commence.

Capitán Diego felt confident that Hugo, his master gunner, would have the heavy guns ready to fire once given the word. His primary concern was the lack of black powder. Why hadn't he paid closer attention to the words of Salinas? Running out of black powder at such a critical time would be disastrous. Every shot fired from their cannons would have to find its mark. There was no room for near misses; every shot fired would have to hit their target precisely.

With nervous anticipation, he gazed through his spyglass. The sails continued to approach, and the infamous pirate flag was now visible, displaying the iron maiden and crossed swords flying off the ship's transom as if proud to be a murderous pack of dogs set loose on the innocent.

Today if they were victorious in this battle and sank these murderous cutthroats, he would be the hero to the crown. Regardless of this, before him was the real test that he and his men were soon to experience.

Looking again through his spyglass behind, he saw that the two *pirata* ships had shortened the distance between them. Their white sails grew more prominent as he saw their infamous Captain Redbone standing alone on the forecastle, directing his men. As he glanced through his spyglass, he saw the man staring back at them, no doubt studying their strength as a fighting force, looking for any weakness in their defenses.

At this time Capitán Diego's visionary plan was to take the offensive stance and part the two approaching ships in two, thereby giving a full blast of his roaring cannons broadside as they met the enemy head-on. Proud as he was to provide a fight, he stared back at his enemy with determination, ready to destroy the coward.

In reality, Diego uncharacteristically laughed at seeing the approaching danger. It was a complete surprise to his men that it was within earshot, and those close to him looked up with bewilderment. Glancing away from the spyglass, Diego turned to the helmsman, yelling a command to steer the vessel starboard directly between the two ships. Suddenly, Carlos reappeared on the main deck and looked up at Diego, awaiting the order to fire the barrage of cannons.

Then unexpectedly came the sound of several cannons going off in the distance, and Diego turned to see a white plume of smoke erupt from both the enemy ships. An eerie sound cutting through the air came whistling past, which soon gave way to several large splashes that landed helplessly in the sea, narrowly missing their ship.

It seemed that the *piratas de Iron Born* wanted to be first to fire their guns, hopeful of delivering the first set of cannonballs down their throat. But for now, this insult must be ignored because of the gunpowder shortage.

Diego ordered his navigator, "Maintain your course. Do not deviate left or right!"

Traveling close to twelve knots, this course and speed would eventually bring them head-on into a collision with the bigger *pirata* ship. The outcome of this battle, only God knew. Saying a silent prayer at the time seemed logical as Diego whispered a small one; suddenly, he was interrupted by another blast of cannons going off, which unfortunately hit their mark upon the mainsails. The cannonballs cut a perfectly round hole through the fabric and narrowly missed the mainmast.

After turning again to see his helmsman gripping the ship's wheel, Diego yelled, "Maintain course between the two ships!"

The man watched the approaching ships set on a

collision course, getting closer than before. Without showing fear the navigator didn't flinch or turn away. Now the approaching vessels were less than fifty yards away; they soon would careen into one another. However, was there enough time to avoid a collision? There was no time to change or divert their course, and Diego watched as the two ships suddenly began to part.

Diego had gambled everything. *One way or another, today, you Iron Born shall be destroyed*, he thought.

Looking down upon the deck, Diego shouted to Carlos, "Steady, do not fire; wait for my signal!"

"Yes, Capitán, we are awaiting your orders."

Now that the ships were within sight, it became evident that the second *pirata* vessel was a smaller two-masted schooner. Although she had a complement of eight cannons on either side of the haul, she was no threat to their ship. Diego watched as the schooner began to steer clear of their large vessel.

After running to the quarterdeck, Diego positioned himself near the navigator, relentlessly determined to maintain their course. A barrage of cannon fire sounded from the enemy ship, sending cannonballs crashing into their railing around their forecastle, bursting into their hull, and sending wooden fragments careening all over the deck.

How many of his men had just died because of his actions? He hadn't a clue, but they would all be lost in this war if he stopped considering the young lives lost. Now without any recourse left to them, Diego's decision to steer between the two ships was set in stone; he ordered the navigator to stay his resolve.

The enemy was left with little recourse but to divert their course to avoid colliding with their ship. The small space between the two vessels grew broader as if they were threading a needle, and the *Reina Isabella* steered forward at an imaginary target.

Drawing out his saber, Diego pointed it directly between the two vessels. Standing proudly in the noonday sun, his steel blade glistened as he held his weapon high. He yelled to his navigator, "See there your target.

Maintain your heading between the two ships."

Dressed in the finery of a captain in the Spanish Navy, Diego nervously screamed the command to ready the guns; his voice echoed within the timbers below decks. To the navigator's astonishment, the two *pirata* ships widely separated as if Moses was parting the waves.

As they entered the small space, Diego screamed the command to fire the cannons. Fuses were lit, and a moment later massive explosions erupted, sending iron balls of death into the enemy's ships, which tore into each ship's superstructure.

Cannons rumbled with loud booms and smoke filled the air, making everything hard to see as each naval force shot cannonballs careening into one another. Unfortunately, the men below decks were the ones who suffered most because the massive shots burst upon them, sending pieces of metal shrapnel and large chunks of wood that impacted the tight spaces. Afterward, ear-piercing screams of death erupted from the first barrage of exploding cannon fire from both ships.

Quickly came more cannon fire from the *pirata* vessels. Aboard the *Reina Isabella*, the mainmast and mizzen mast suddenly tore loose from their stays, collapsing forward with their large white sails blanketing the main deck, some dragging in the sea.

The *Hell's Fury*, whose bowsprit and top yard of her mainmast were blown away and parts of her poop deck destroyed, still managed to sail under her power and quickly came about for another onslaught of cannon destruction. The smaller *pirata* vessel, whose main deck was below the galleon's waterline, had suffered from cannon fire that took out most of her quarterdeck and the mainmast, losing over half their sailing power from that single barrage.

As the *Reina Isabella* sailed through the narrow impasse between the ships, she exited out the other side, barely able to maneuver. With several of her guns on her starboard side destroyed by the larger pirate ship cannons, Capitán Diego ordered his ship to turn back around for a second barrage. Not hearing a reply, he looked over at his navigator, only to see that part of the ship's wheel that controlled the rudder was torn away from the man that steered the boat; all that was left was a bare hand gripping the wheel.

He looked desperately for Carlos, the premier official, who had gone below decks to care for the men; not seeing him anywhere, Diego ran to the ship's wheel and grabbed ahold just as the *Reina Isabella* suddenly lifted and tilted starboard, free from its steering mechanism beneath.

Black smoke suddenly appeared as a fire raged below decks. The remainder of the black powder magazines erupted, sending a giant fireball out the cargo decks to the main level.

Wanting to fire a second barrage on the enemy's ship, Diego did his best to turn the ship back around. But now, unfortunately, the steering mechanism seemed dislodged and nonfunctional. The *Reina Isabella* lunged forward into the open sea, drifting upon the waves, helpless to steer a course.

Diego stood alone on the quarterdeck. There seemed to be fire erupting everywhere about the ship's main structure, which was torn away in many places. He heard screams from his men trapped below decks, dying; fear gripped him, and he could not move. He looked upon the two enemy ships that were still a formidable fighting force and watched as they turned about for a second chance to strike at them.

Now floating helplessly upon the crystal blue water after having survived the first barrage from their enemy, they lumbered along with one remaining sail—yet no rudder to control the ship's direction.

Looking toward the stern, Diego saw the *pirata* ships turning. They had sustained notable damage but still managed to come again to strike another blow. This outcome wasn't what he expected; although he was outgunned from the start, he felt within his heart that his superior Spanish ship would have destroyed these *piratas'* dogs.

Now waiting for the inevitable outcome, Hugo, his master gunner, unexpectedly appeared on the main deck dressed in black soot from the burning embers below. He looked up at Diego and announced, "Capitán, we're ready to strike once more at our enemy."

Looking down at the man, Diego felt astonished at hearing the news. Although he recognized that their enemy was turning to have a second go at them, he still managed to hold his sword aloft and yelled out, "Let us give a reason for our proud heritage. We are superior to these accursed bastards; let us deliver death at the edge of our swords. Listen for my command; I will give the word to fire."

"As you wish, Capitán," Hugo replied, then returned down below decks.

As the superior *pirata* ship completed her turn, Diego looked behind and saw the captain screaming his commands to his men. Their cannons drew outward from their portholes when they appeared alongside, displaying the large hollow black openings pointed directly at them. Given the same response in return to the *piratas*, every surviving sailor aboard the *Reina Isabella* pushed what loaded cannons would return fire out their portholes.

When the ships were in close proximity, both captains yelled out the command to fire. The second series of cannon fires erupted, causing irreparable damage that killed even more men who survived the first confrontation.

Having lived through the onslaught of cannon fire, Capitán Diego once again found his ship floating helplessly upon the waters, unable to gain any speed. Unfortunately, the *Reina Isabella* was severely listed to one side as she took on water.

Diego knew that his ship was sinking. Somehow she sustained more damage than the *pirata* boat. Looking beneath the decks, he saw flames blazing wildly out of control. Few men could have survived this latest attack. It would've been honorable for any man to give his life fighting for Spanish royalty, especially during battle. He felt pride swell up within his heart, knowing that they would be remembered for their bravery and devotion to their king and queen in the end.

The *Reina* floated lifelessly atop the waves as it began leaning on her port side. Diego knew that his hopes of bringing death to the *piratas* were now a distant dream. He would undoubtedly face death if these cowards boarded their ship, and he alone would lead the fight with the few remaining sailors to kill what they could of these *piratas.*

He could hear the screams below the decks that seemed to echo louder than roaring flames. Diego no longer saw his first mate, knowing that he served in a most distinguished role and died honorably. Although few would know of his sacrifice this day, Diego himself would go to his grave knowing how every man under his command had fought.

No longer able to give a response from their silent cannons, Diego looked downward at all the devastation and said a prayer for those men whose death had quickly taken them. Now reduced to nothing but burning timbers of a forgotten vessel, the *Reina Isabella* would soon go under the waves, a forgotten memory.

With little or no fight left in him, Diego took his saber, burying it deeply into the planks of oak timbers that were once a proud deck. Whatever the outcome of this day was to be, his death was now inevitable, and he only wished for it to be over quickly.

Then he heard some commotion behind him; as he turned to look, he saw the two *pirata* ships maneuver into position, steering toward his vessel to overtake it. With most of their sailing power still intact, their movability to change course was now evident.

Just as the bigger *pirata* ship's bow moved past them, Diego expected to hear the blast of cannon fire to assure their destruction. But to his surprise, their boat suddenly slowed, and boarding lines were thrown over to his main decks.

However, as this was happening, to his surprise, the smaller gunship moved forward on their port side, and an array of cannon fire erupted, blasting away the ship's bow.

Helpless to move, Diego's saber still vibrated in the hard planks of solid oaks. He realized that he would soon feel death at the sword's edge and waited for it earnestly. *Let it come now*, he thought. *I'm ready!* Looking down at the fiery depths of his bow, he saw the flames flickering upward as the fire began to eat away his ship.

At that moment the most surprising thing happened: He heard some commotion below decks. Suddenly, a hatch flew open and out crawled no less than forty of his men, screaming a war cry as they piled onto the deck. Instantaneously, his crew met the approaching *piratas* that jumped onto their ship and fought them mercilessly.

Musket fire began erupting everywhere as opposing forces met for the first time. Screams of men in pain or being murdered echoed throughout the ship as musket balls slammed into men's bodies, some dying instantly.

Suddenly, Carlos, the premier official, appeared. After seeing his friend whom he thought had perished earlier, Diego cried, "I'm so glad you're alive. It seems that we're in dire straits."

"Capitán, down below there are many men still trapped, unable to help defend our ship. But were—"

Just as the words left his mouth, a musket was suddenly fired from the pirate ship that struck Carlos in the head, sending splattered blood and brain matter across Diego's face.

In horror Diego looked down at his friend, who was now bleeding out of his head wound. Grabbing his cutlass, he ran toward the first *piratas* he saw, digging his long blade deep into his body. After withdrawing his sword, he raised it above the man's head and came crashing downward in a single stroke, removing his head from his body.

Now with the taste of blood upon his lips he searched out another invader and pounced, killing him quickly. Unfortunately, there seemed to be more *piratas* surviving the battle than his men; the combat fought upon the *Reina*'s decks was suddenly altered. The few remaining members of the Spanish Navy that fought on only died much too quickly.

There never seemed to be any time to fire the deck guns upon the approaching *piratas* as they swarmed onto the ship. Now the last few remaining sailors under his command realized that the battle was lost. Suddenly, his crew threw down their weapons, knowing that the outcome was already decided.

However, Diego fought on and swung his blade at another *piratas de Iron Born*, who was able to block his attack in time. The remaining opponents in the battle for life and death had tried to outmaneuver the other. Diego, however, was the best trained in swordplay; against a lowly *pirata*, he was superior in every way. With a shrewd move much like the game of chess, he dodged an approaching blow and swung around, burying his long cutlass into the chest of the *pirata*'s dog.

After withdrawing his sword, he heard the man scream as he removed his blade. Just as Diego was about to lift his head, two large *piratas* unexpectedly grabbed him from behind and knocked him to the ground, then wrapped a noose around his neck.

Now a captured prize, the *Reina Isabella* and its captain, Diego Carlos Espinosa, were nothing more than a defeated enemy. He knew that being captain meant he would face certain death. The *piratas* were not known for their leniency toward the one man aboard a ship that would bring destruction.

Surprisingly, a wooden plank was brought forward between the two ships as Redbone, the *pirata* captain, proudly walked across and approached. Diego wrestled to get free but to no avail. Then Diego looked about to see the dead and dying on the deck of the once-proud *Reina Isabella*. A group of twelve men had surrendered and were tied together as they waited for their fate. Among them was the youngest officer named Matias Hernandez, who was not sure what had happened to his counterpart, the other young cadet, Humberto de Hevia, on whom he was ordered to keep a wary eye to make sure he came to no harm.

Now there was nothing except burning timbers beneath the decks. Looking up at the *piratas*' Captain Redbone, whom he despised for his cruelty, Diego spat at him and was suddenly punched in the ribs by one of the *piratas* holding him.

Redbone laughed, enjoying the mistreatment.

After walking over, Redbone said, "Capitán, there is no benefit for you to struggle. Surrender your ship to me at once or else I run you through myself. Any leniency toward ye men will be forgotten, and they will be snuffed out as if they be a candle."

"You scoundrel dog, I shall fight you with every last bit of strength I have within my body," the proud Diego shouted.

Redbone turned to his first mate, Mr. Schmidt, and asked, "Arrrr—is it true that a captain should go down with ye ship?"

Mr. Schmidt quickly agreed with the captain's estimation and said, "It is certain that all seafaring capitáns should go down with their ship!"

"Arrrr, Mr. Schmidt, then let it be so," Redbone ordered.

What happened next surprised Diego as he was quickly bound to the mizzen mast and tied all around, with ropes about his body. Spikes were driven through Diego's hands and feet and pounded hard into the oak deck of the ship.

After looking about the sinking ship, Redbone ordered his men to salvage any remaining wealth that could be found including what was inside the captain's cabin, taking any charts and compasses or sextons that would be valuable prizes to retain. Afterward, the search resulted in little bounty or treasure. Diego's saber, a prized possession with its gold inlaid handle, was taken by Redbone and slipped inside his belt, regardless of the wet blood dripping off its cutting edge from its last victim.

As Diego watched, several crew members of *Hell's Fury* appeared to transfer their dead *piratas de Iron Born* back aboard their ship. Suddenly, two men lifted Diego to his feet and dragged him to the mizzen mast of his boat. Then they made him hug the wooden mast, as it were. As he resisted another pirate appeared with a long rope and formed a knot, then wrapped the cord around his waist several times and tied him securely so he couldn't escape.

Suddenly, another man appeared on his ship, whom Diego guessed was the ship's carpenter, wearing a leather belt with a hammer strapped to his side. This carpenter stood next to him. Unexpectedly, he took Diego's left hand and stretched it around what remained of the mast. After reaching inside his leather pouch, he withdrew a solid metal spike.

This new insult to one's only character didn't seem to affect the captain as much as losing his ship; he looked at this so-called carpenter with cold-blooded eyes and gave no response as the man set the sharp spike atop his left hand and slammed the large nail with his hammer, driving it the wooden beam.

Diego, drenched in pain, remained steadfast as the carpenter continued to hit the nail head repeatedly, driving the nail more profoundly into the wood until only the large head remained visible. Grabbing another nail inside his bag, the carpenter held his right hand against the mast and repeated his assault.

Knowing what would happen next, Redbone yelled, "Avast thee timbers, man, why waste a perfect pair of boots? Take them off his feet and secure him fast to the deck. Perhaps they will fit you or some other worthy *pirata*."

After looking at Redbone wearing a smile, Mr. Schmidt without hesitation reached down to pull Diego's boots free and yelled back at his captain, "Sir, they're much too small for a man of my size. Perhaps a young lad would have use for them, maybe our cabin boy?" Then he took the boots and draped them over his shoulder, ordering the carpenter to continue his work.

Placing Diego's bare feet on the main deck, the carpenter set a steel nail atop his right foot and slammed hard against its head, driving the longer nail entirely through, causing Diego great pain, then repeating the process for his other foot. Diego was soon secured into place.

Now any movement he made sent searing pain coursing throughout his body. With the nails securing him, Diego was guaranteed to go down with his ship. Turning to yell insults at the enemy pirate Redbone, Diego cursed his mother and his entire life.

In response Redbone walked away, laughing and smirking at the helpless insults.

Then Mr. Schmidt asked, "What of the captives, Captain?"

Redbone stopped in his tracks and turned about to address the issue personally. "Arrrr, Mr. Schmidt, sir, ye know too well ye do man—that we do not take prisoners, sir. Kill them all and be done with it."

"As you wish, Captain," was the large man's quick answer.

He then looked over at the two men holding the small group and said, "You heard the captain, men; why the delay? We have a job; let's get on with it then."

Mr. Schmidt knew that if they were prisoners aboard a Spanish military ship, they would all face a firing squad, which was customary, or death by hanging. With no time to waste, he ordered the prisoners to stand at the railing. Shouting orders for an equal assemblage of pirates to be armed with muskets, a line of armed men soon appeared with rifles loaded.

It was as swift as death could be; each Spanish sailor met their end with a shot into their heart, and soon everyone lay dead or dying atop the main deck, although when it came to the youth the cruelest of all *piratas de Iron Born* would hesitate in his duties and wasn't sure what to do. After seeing their reluctance about murdering the teen, Mr. Schmidt stepped forward and heartlessly lifted Matias Hernandez by his neck, looking into the boy's eyes as he struggled to breathe.

Schmidt considered how easy it would be to snuff out his life with a simple snap of his neck. But apart from this, the Iron Born weren't monsters in any sense. Considering the boy couldn't speak English, Schmidt spoke in Spanish, "*Hoy te convertirás en mi sirviente personal,*" meaning today you will become my personal servant. After sitting the boy on the ground, he quickly moved his head up and down as his way to agree to Mr. Schmidt's terms. It was all that was needed.

After Redbone reached his ship, he stood by the gangway. He ordered the lingering men aboard the *Hell's Fury* to cut the mooring lines to send the Spanish galleon adrift, then watched the remains of the burning Spanish vessel drift helplessly atop the waves.

Soon the two vessels separated, and those aboard the *Hell's Fury* safely steered away from the once elegant ship, the *Reina Isabella*. They never looked back, believing she would soon disappear beneath the waves. Soon they began celebrating their victory, opening barrels of rum taken from the Spanish ship.

The Dutch attaché, who had a front-row seat, watched the whole affair without as much as a word spoken. Not playing a part in the victory, he decided it best to return to his cabin to drink the night away.

Diego had no recourse left to him; he prayed for his soul. Mounted to the mizzen mast, he did tug at the rope and steel shafts that held him tightly for any sign of weakness. Unexpectedly, the ship pitched to one side as the forward compartments continued to fill with water. Fully realizing his predicament, he knew his life would be over soon.

The brutality of these *piratas de Iron Born* was no tall tale. He was now an example of such an encounter. After a short time Diego ceased his resistance to being free, accepting his fate. Looking at the starboard side of his ship, he could see *Hell's Fury* sailing away.

He wished to curse the pirate Redbone with his last breath, besides his wretchedness and fortitude. However, he closed his eyes and listened to the creaking timbers beneath him, slowly becoming silent as the saltwater rose. Now he thought of his men and the sad outcome of this battle. For whatever reason these *piratas* dogs had for being in these waters, so close to his homeland, he would never know.

Suddenly, the entire vessel moved forward as it seemed ready to plunge deeper into the abyss. Diego suddenly held his breath, filling his lungs with precious air. But strangely, after a few moments had elapsed, he had to exhale as he was sure his ship was going to plunge deep into the cold water, and his life would soon be over.

He waited patiently, but nothing happened; the ship rocked, tossed about by the passing waves. Unexpectedly, he felt something bump into his leg; he saw, to his horror, José de Viera, a young father of three, whose head was partly blown away.

His cold, dead eye was looking up at him as if to say, "Why have you allowed me to die, Capitán?"

More than ever, he wished for death. "It must happen quickly," he prayed. *How is it possible that I'm alive while so many of my men are dead?* he thought.

Back aboard the *Hell's Fury*, the first mate, Schmidt, addressed the captain, "Where to now, sir?"

Looking about the damaged ship, Redbone knew they were no longer a formidable fighting force. The damage his ships received from the Spanish had to be repaired. He intended to sail into Trinidad to retrieve the one Iron Born Pirate that escaped.

However, they had to retreat into a port of safety for repairs. Redbone turned to Mr. Schmidt and said, "We sail for Port Royal."

"Is that all, sir?"

"Aye—have the men begin what repairs they can; I fear that Spaniard was able to extract more damage upon us than I expected. Send word to the captain aboard the other ship of our intentions. This evening an extra helping of rum for our men; they all have fought bravely."

Mr. Schmidt then stood erect, his giant statue now visible, and replied, "That be true, Captain, except for the men dealing with the Spanish youth. I fear some haven't the stomach to follow your orders to the letter."

"Arrrr—that is a problem I shall deal with soon enough. For now, we have men to ferry off to the spirit world so make merry with the song as we are about to send our Iron Born brothers to the other side."

"Aye, Aye, captain. There is no finer a reward on this earth than to die an Iron Born. Let us drink and be merry for today; they have died worthy and true, as any Iron Born Pirate should."

Sometime later the small image of the ship's silhouette was still seen against the colored horizon. What was most disturbing was the faint laughter and song coming from the *Hell's Fury* crew. There was no remorse or regret for what they'd done; they seemed joyful somehow for killing his men.

In the darkness that soon blanketed him completely, Diego thought of his men and how no one would sing them any song nor give a prominent funeral. Instead, the sharks had arrived. In the still silence he could hear the splashing waves as these predators fought over the remains of his men. No song or dance for them, just a forgotten memory of a life once lived in the service of the Spanish Navy.

CHAPTER 9

WHEN THE CAPTAIN OF THE pirate ship *Abraxas* appeared on deck, Thomas was surprised to discover that he was French and spoke with a heavy accent. As the captain approached both men were brought to their knees, forced to look down at the deck. A pair of black boots stopped before them, and they heard a man's voice say, "What fish have you caught in your net today, Monsieur Stark?"

"It seems that one of these fishes claims to be an Iron Born Pirate, Captain. Sir, he bears the mark upon his wrist!" Elijah Stark answered.

"What is this you say, Monsieur Stark? He bears the mark?"

"Yes, sir, it is true," he said, ordering the men that held Mauricio down to unroll his sleeve to show his captain. Then Stark stood by, seeing the expression on his captain's face.

Now eyeing the branded cross swords on Mauricio's wrist, the captain ordered him to be released. Mauricio stood to his feet, thanking the captain. It was then that the black boots appeared next to Thomas. Regrettably, he heard the notorious Captain Lafayette Beaumont shout.

"What of this English codfish, Monsieur Stark?"

"He was sailing with the young Iron Born, Captain."

Unfortunately, Thomas heard the man pull his cutlass from its sheath as Beaumont shouted, "Off with his head!" Then grabbing hold of Thomas's hair, he pulled his head upward and looked him in the eye to say, "If you allow one of these English to live a moment longer, you have to believe me when I say they will invade and conquer your homeland from you. It is a sad truth, but this man should die."

"Wait, Captain, I beg you to give leniency in this matter," Mauricio shouted. "This man saved my life; I owe him a debt. Do you see the small chest of gold before you? It's his reward for saving my life; it is an honorable thing to keep him alive. Please, I beg you."

Beaumont eyed Mauricio devilishly and said, "Although it goes against my will, still I understand your Iron Born promise is your bond; if this man lives, then he is your responsibility. Do you understand?"

"Yes, Captain, I thank you for your graciousness in this matter. Although I believe you should keep what little gold Thomas was rewarded as a ransom for his life, I'm sure his life means more to him than a few trinkets of gold."

"What do you say, Englishman? Is your life worth more to you than the small chest of gold?" Beaumont questioned.

Pushing away his captors, Thomas stood upright and said, "First of all, let me introduce myself. My name is Thomas Banish; it is true what the Iron Born Pirate said. You can keep the gold. Betrayal of a pirate, sir, does not surprise me."

"Take them both down below and put Thomas here in chains. Why will I decide whether he lives or not?"

"Thank you again, sir, for sparing my life," Thomas answered.

"Perhaps you shall live, but what I cannot say is the quality of life you shall experience, Mr. Thomas Banish. You must understand that many of my men have suffered under the dominance of the British Empire that you are a significant part of. Upon this vessel, sir, is a dangerous place to find oneself."

After stepping forward, Mauricio announced, "Captain Beaumont, believe me when I say that your reward shall be great for rescuing a fellow pirate. Redbone is most gracious on such matters."

"You tell me, young Iron Born, how is it that you

find yourself so far from your ship and in the hands of this Englishman?"

"It is a simple thing. You see, my sister, Mariana, is a harlot. I sought to rescue her, but in my failed attempt I was stabbed. In Trinidad they brought me into their prison. There, I was mistreated. Thomas saved my life; even though I am a pirate, he rescued me."

"Interesting ," Beaumont said. "But I must ask, how was it that Redbone, a man known for his supremacy over his men, allowed you to take this quest to save your sister and abandon your post aboard ship?"

"I'm afraid to say, señor, that my captain was not privy to me deserting," Mauricio replied.

"Deserter, I see; yes, take our young pirate in irons as well. Perhaps there shall also be a reward for this little fish."

"No, Captain, you cannot return me to Redbone, please. Can't you see he would hang me or worse?" Mauricio begged.

"It is not my concern on what your captain decides your fate shall be nor that of your Englishman; I am only concerned with the gold I shall be rewarded."

Both men struggled against their captors. But tried as they might, they were dragged below the ship and locked away in their cells.

Appearing near his captain, Mr. Stark asked, "What course shall we set?"

"The last reports I've heard of Redbone was that he sailed off the waters of Trinidad. It is the area we should find our Iron Born Pirates. Set sail for Trinidad," the captain bellowed as he returned his cutlass to its sheath.

"As you wish, Captain."

Then after returning to his cabin Beaumont poured himself a cognac. After walking over to a small table, he removed his wig and set it on a wooden replica of a human head. After scratching his itching scalp, he removed his heavy colorful jacket. His feet felt sore within the stiff leather boots, and he sat upon his bunk, struggling to get them off. Afterward, standing in his hosiery, his feet hurt badly.

After walking about his cabin, he poured himself

some cognac. After opening a small silver box, he removed some snuff and inhaled it into his nasal cavity. A sneeze erupted; then he took a silk handkerchief to clean his nose. After setting down upon a small chair, he glanced out the back of the ship.

As he considered his options a realization occurred to him. For years he had known that several countries wanted the notorious Captain Redbone. Every pirate captain had a price upon their heads including himself; it was the nature of the business in which they made a living. Alone in his cabin, he gave off an unexpected chuckle as he thought, *You take your friends where you can find them.*

Looking out the small windows at the distant horizon, Beaumont contemplated his new predicament, which Stark brought on board his ship. It was clear to him that the young Iron Born Pirate was a wanted man. This Redbone was a man you would not want to cross. No doubt, he would cut off both his legs, this young pirate, for deserting his post.

Taking a slow sip of cognac, Beaumont thought, *It just doesn't seem right, someone that young scurrying around the deck upon a pegboard. His punishment for a crewman deserting his post would be fairer by only cutting one of the lad's legs off; there be differences between Redbone and himself,* Beaumont thought.

For that fool, hearty souls that perform the ritual of the Bloody Hag and live to tell the tale of their survival should be proud to bear the marks of honor of the iron maiden, that ruthless bitch!

After emptying his glass of cognac, he poured himself another and considered the Englishman down below in irons for the moment. *What shall be done with him?* he thought. *Perhaps ransom, although the British are not known for their generosity in saving their kind. No, we pirates are genuinely honorable among our kind, unlike us swashbucklers who consider their fellow buccaneers something of value above all else.*

At that moment he heard a knock on his door. "Who be there?" Beaumont yelled.

"It is I, Captain, Mr. Stark!"

"Come in, you scurvy dog!"

The door creaked open upon its hinges. Cautiously walking into the room, Mr. Stark said, "Captain, if you have a moment?"

"Yes, but you see I'm busy."

"Yes, of course. To the point then, sir. The men don't see it reasonable that you take one of our own and set him in chains below. Why would you turn over this poor lad to Redbone to pay the price for his betrayal, captain?"

"Monsieur, I, and I alone, decide the young man's fate. You must understand the dangers we face sailing under the black flag. It is our doom if a military ship belonging to a country seeking our heads happen upon us. You understand we cannot take desertion of one's post so lightly, nor would I accept this insult upon my ship. And my men understand that lesson," Beaumont answered with a scowl.

"I understand, sir, we all have a job to do; I shall do my best to explain to the men your reasoning behind this decision to return the true Blood Pirate."

"Good, see it be done. Now I have things on my mind; you must leave me to it."

"As you wish."

Bowing down, he saluted his captain and left his quarters. After returning outside, Mr. Stark saw several of his shipmates waiting near the door for an answer. Grinning back at them, he said plainly, "The captain's made his decision; we sail for Trinidad to search for the Iron Born. If any want to question the captain's orders, please knock on his door and see the answer you get!"

No one dared question their orders any further, and every man returned to their duties, knowing the course was set right and shall not be changed or challenged, leaving it to their captain to decide what's best.

MEANWHILE, SPENDING THE FOLLOWING DAYS in a dark, musky cell sat Thomas and Mauricio. The only light in the dark space came from a small lantern that hung from a chain swaying back and forth with the ship's motion. What little food was offered only came once a day and was slid underneath the small cell's bars.

Thomas expected this treatment from his pirate captors, but Mauricio was surprised by it all and never expected to be locked away in a dark cell.

Their outcomes looked dismal as Thomas could only guess his future. Being an English sailor imprisoned aboard a pirate ship, he didn't expect to live long, no more than a burning candle in a typhoon would extinguish itself. The whole reason for being in these dangerous waters was to capture such pirates as these.

Looking over at Mauricio, Thomas said, "My friend, it looks like we traded one prison cell for another. This whole thing has me disheartened in so many ways I cannot say. Somehow we must escape our bonds if we expect to live!"

Mauricio, nodding his head in agreement, asked, "How is it possible that we can escape from this cell?"

"That is the question; perhaps we can bribe one of the guards? It is a practice that is not uncommon among pirates; some are often persuaded to change their loyalties for a promise of gold."

"Yes, you're right."

Suddenly, two men appeared near their cell and shouted, "Our captain has decided, Mr. Englishman, that you would be more comfortable topside."

Letting out a sinister laugh, one of the men unlocked the cell door, displayed a pistol, and pointed it at both of them as a show of force.

After grabbing ahold of Thomas by his arms, they dragged him out of the cell. When Mauricio objected he was smacked in his mouth for his troubles.

After shoving Thomas upstairs to the main deck, he saw the entire crew looking at him when he arrived topside. Each wore grins across their face. Then the crowd of men suddenly separated, and Thomas caught a horrid sight: an iron cage with a small door opened, waiting for an unfortunate soul that he realized could only be himself.

Standing by the small iron door wearing a devilish grin was Captain Beaumont. He turned to his men and proclaimed, "Mr. Englishman! The crew and I wanted you to have the same pleasures aboard our ship that your English captain would offer us. In consideration of this, I have decided that you shall spend the rest of your voyage on the mainsail's yardarm."

Turning to his first mate, the captain said, "Mr. Stark, I believe you wanted your pound of flesh. See to it now, sir."

Stark slowly approached; the men holding Thomas down let go of their grip and cautiously stepped backward. Suddenly, the first mate swung his fist and struck Thomas across his jaw, sending him reeling onto the hard deck. Without mercy Stark grabbed Thomas by his hair, lifted his head, and said, "Englishman, I want you to understand the reasoning behind my vile hatred toward you and your country. At nine, while living on Tortuga as a boy, my mother was abducted by a drunk British sailor and raped maliciously, then murdered afterward."

Another crushing blow to Thomas's face sent blood spatter streaming onto the wooden deck from his broken nose. Instantly, the swelling upon his face prevented him from seeing his attacker, only a blurry image. The pain was torturous; he could do nothing but listen to the man's hatred leveled upon his person.

After lifting Thomas to his feet, Stark suddenly slammed his fist into his body, and he felt his ribs break. Reeling back in pain, Thomas recoiled from the assaults. However, in mounting a defense, Thomas administered a punch across the man's jaw when Stark advanced for another strike. The effects were dismal at best. Stark laughed aloud and struck Thomas across his jaw again, sending him backward onto the hard deck, where he could not get up from the floor.

As a demeaning gesture Stark approached, undid his trousers, and began spraying Thomas with his urine. The humiliation didn't end there, as each pirate aboard the *Abraxas* whose hatred matched Mr. Starks joined in. Soon Thomas was soaked from head to toe in the urine. His stinging eyes and cuts became unbearable.

Afterward, Beaumont yelled out, "Take him now. Throw him inside the cage. We shall see how our little bird sings on his perch, high above the deck."

Thomas fought and struggled against those men trying to throw him inside the small cage, but they overpowered him with a rush, and the door was locked into place with a click.

Thomas was immediately taken aloft, high above the deck where he was tied off around the mainsail and slowly began to swing back and forth. Looking down below at his captors, he searched for pity but found none. Truthfully, if the situation was reversed, they knew there would be no pity for them.

The smell of urine upon his person was horrid. Still, the humiliation at seeing the old, crusty, toothless men laughing among themselves as they relieved their bladders was the most troublesome.

Later that day while baking under a scorching Caribbean sun, Thomas felt himself being cooked raw as he struggled to get comfortable inside the cramped space. His sore ribs ached him badly, and the smell that continued to fill his nostrils made him uncomfortable. His thirst was everlasting; he longed for a drink. His mouth became parched and dry as each passing hour gave him no relief from his misery.

Down below in his cell, Mauricio pondered the question of what happened to Thomas, his friend. He could not be sure, but if Thomas were aboard his ship, the *Hell's Fury*, no doubt he wouldn't suffer the same fate or worse. Pirate captains sailing the Caribbean waters had a hateful loathing toward the British. Their laws set in stone always carried the same judgment of death for any pirate captured.

A cabin boy appeared that evening, carrying a small bowl of stew or some other creation with dead bugs floating in the mix. Mauricio did his best to befriend the young lad as he desperately questioned him about Thomas.

The young boy, looking for anyone listening, gently whispered, "I'm sorry about your friend; it seems that he is nothing more than a caged bird hanging about the sails."

Mauricio didn't understand what he meant at first

and asked again for an explanation.

The young lad whispered, "He's sitting inside a cage, hanging off the yardarm." Then, being frightened to say any more, he hurried away.

Regrettably, Mauricio understood his meaning. Could it be true? Thomas exposed to the elements above the deck would be cooked raw. From the pirates' view, it would make perfect sense that he only needed to be alive for the pirate captain to get his reward. The thought of his friend hanging above decks troubled him significantly. He promised he would find a way to bribe one of these buccaneers and save his friend from death.

The lad who brought him his food seemed friendly enough, but would he be willing to betray his comrades and help set Thomas free? How then to escape a ship filled with pirates? It was to be their real dilemma.

These waterways were a favorite hunting ground for Caribbean pirates. With a broad array of ships traveling these waters, a pirate captain was almost always successful in plundering when a merchant ship contained tobacco or spices from the Orient but, most of all, a Spanish galleon full of gold. He and Thomas had not sailed that far, and no doubt they would soon run into the *Hell's Fury.*

It was now that Mauricio became committed to saving his friend Thomas. Over these past days he befriended the ship's doctor, Tjerk Hiddes, a Danish man captured and brought aboard to serve the pirates who sank his boat.

Mauricio had also discovered that neither the lad nor the ship's doctor was joyful with their arrangements aboard the pirate ship. It seemed that they were refugees left alive to serve the needs of these pirate cutthroats. It was a Dutch schooner, the *Batavia*, that these brigands had captured; they killed everyone aboard except those who had practical skills to serve their interest.

Their fate of certain death was only diverted because of vacancies that had arisen when the pirate ship's doctor had died of infection earlier; the young cabin boy was killed in a fight with a Dutch ship's crew.

The French captain, Lafayette Beaumont, who was

newly appointed, hadn't accepted his responsibility for the young cabin boy murdered in their last battle. The cabin boy was liked by many; they all mourned his death.

Mauricio, counting the cost of such a treasonous plan, approached the doctor with great caution. After hearing of Mauricio's plan, the good doctor only agreed to help if he promised to bring the cabin boy named Bram with them.

Tjerk offered his ideas on how to get away clean. He knew they would go past an island that would provide sanctuary for two days. He would have to bribe members of the crew. A few men owed him their lives aboard ship, being saved from the fever. Besides this, a few pirates were Dutch; they felt responsible for the death of the *Albatross*'s crew when they did nothing to help their compatriots.

Now it had been several days since Mauricio had seen Thomas alive; he wondered how his friend had fared since he last saw him. On his last visit with the doctor, he pleaded for Tjerk to look upon Thomas to ensure he was still alive and breathing.

The doctor explained, "It was not that these pirates desired to kill him outright but to give him ill treatment. However, he promised to check on his friend that evening. If Thomas wasn't strong enough to survive his ordeal, Tjerk was sorry for his loss."

Mauricio answered, "Tell me, how alive can a man be placed in a cage exposed to the elements?"

THAT EVENING APPEARED AS A moonless night. Sadly, the only way to see if Thomas was still alive was to climb the central mast. Tjerk stood upon the deck eyeing the height of the yardarm that Thomas was hanging, and he realized that it was a task more suitable for Bram than himself.

The doctor who appeared on deck was looked upon with little concern by the night watchman, a Mr. Bakker, another man the doctor had saved. When Tjerk appeared carrying a small gunnysack and began to climb the shroud up to the mainmast, the watchman merely turned his head to look away.

The middle-aged doctor wasn't as spry as he once was and struggled to get up to the mainmast. Now reaching the yardarm, he darted across the sizable wooden shaft, with his feet dangling off and balancing himself from falling off. Finally arriving at the single rope wrapped around the yardarm, he looked down into the cage and saw Thomas, who appeared unconscious and unresponsive.

Tjerk called out his name several times before Thomas finally responded. Looking half dead, Thomas suddenly looked up at the man calling his name and saw a stranger he had not known straddled upon the yardarm.

"Here, take this quick or else I'll be discovered," Tjerk whispered.

Thomas thought it was a dream and barely moved or acknowledged the small bag lowered into his cage. He was sure that he had died since he felt completely numb. Still regaining his senses, he quickly realized that this wasn't a dream after all for something unexpected was sitting in his lap that was hard to believe.

The man's voice said, "Your friend, Mauricio, is very concerned for your safety. Be of good cheer; we are devising a plan of escape."

Thomas drowsily looked up, then asked, "What are you saying about an escape?"

The stranger's voice said in the dark shadows of night, "I haven't the time to explain."

"Thank you, stranger, for your gracious gift," Thomas muttered.

After opening the small sack, which contained cheese, bread, some meat, and a small flask of wine, he could barely believe his eyes. After lifting the wine flask he drank several sips but decided not to finish it all at once; he then slipped it inside his shirt, hiding it from view. Thomas hungrily began eating.

Looking up, Thomas watched the man struggle across the yardarm, stopping several times to rest. The man carefully crawled down the shroud to the main deck below and disappeared.

Thomas thought of a true friend among these

cutthroats, his friend Mauricio who now had as much to lose aboard this ship of mysteries.

The following day was much like any other, staring down at the French captain Beaumont whom Thomas instantly hated. He watched the man plot a course upon a map, using his sextant to navigate. There seemed to be an argument between his first mate, Mr. Stark, and the captain, and Thomas wondered why.

From his perch high above, Thomas could barely hear their conversation down below. It seemed that Mr. Stark wanted to stop getting provisions from a nearby island. He tried his best to persuade his captain of their need for supplies. However, Beaumont was more adamant about continuing their journey toward Trinidad in search of the Iron Born Pirates.

Amid all this upheaval Thomas realized that a quarrelsome, unhappy crew toward their captain could be a weakness he could use to his advantage.

The following day while maintaining a course toward Trinidad, Mauricio was visited by the good doctor. While the two men spoke about what lay ahead, Tjerk announced they would be passing by an uninhabited island sometime in the morning. It would have to be tonight that they would make their escape or not at all.

After hearing this, Mauricio felt overjoyed at the news. Although it was dangerous and everyone involved could lose their lives in the attempted escape, it was still worth it; they would take this one opportunity to be free, no matter the cost.

Much later Mauricio heard a man's voice yelling from the above deck: "Twelve bells, and all is well." Afterward, everything grew quiet on the ship, except for the usual creaking noise from the timbers that formed the ship's hull.

Suddenly, the doctor appeared with a set of keys and began searching for a particular key that would unlock Mauricio's cell door. With him was young Bram, who held the lantern within his grasp, frightened that they would be discovered at any moment.

Unlocking the iron door, it squeaked open.

Tjerk said, "Hurry, come with us; we must leave."

Following the doctor out on the deck, Mauricio hid behind a tarp, having been sure he was seen by the ship's night watchman, a Mr. Pelletier, who stood by the railing looking outward. Glancing upward, Mauricio could see the ship's navigator standing at the wheel. However, the good doctor seemed not to be bothered and waved at the man, acting as if they weren't there.

Then something unexpected happened. Tjerk approached the night watchman from behind, the man Mauricio learned to despise because of his mistreatment toward him. Then as he watched, he saw the doctor quietly remove a belaying pin from the railing, crept up behind Mr. Pelletier, and come down with a crushing blow to the man's skull, causing him to fall to the deck, unconscious.

Then approaching the navigator, the doctor slipped him a small leather pouch with what must have been gold inside. Mauricio overheard him say, "Mr. Stromal, per our agreement." And the man took hold of the small leather pouch and tucked it inside his belt. Then, surprisingly, the man looked directly ahead as if he saw an unknown object that held his attention.

Knowing what was to happen, the navigator cried out, "Doctor, make your aim true, man."

Without saying a word the doctor took the same belaying pin and struck him hard, knowing where to strike without causing permanent damage. The navigator collapsed to the ground, unconscious. It seemed to Mauricio that the doctor had his plan in place after all. He turned the ship on a new course, away from the island, then took a single rope and tied the steering wheel.

Looking upward at the mainmast, Mauricio saw the iron cage that held Thomas aloft; he ran over to where the rope was bound tightly around the mast and grabbed ahold of it, calling out to Tjerk and Bram to give him a hand so he could lower his friend to the deck.

Without hesitation everyone grabbed ahold of the rope as Tjerk unexpectedly displayed a knife and began cutting the cord from the mainmast. A moment later Thomas was lowered to the deck of the ship.

After looking inside the small cage, Mauricio

yelled, "Thomas, are you alive?!" At the time he looked dead and unresponsive.

Quickly, Tjerk displayed a key to unlock the iron lock to the small cage and swung the door open. "Hurry, come with us at once!" he yelled at Thomas, but he didn't move.

Not having a moment to waste, both Mauricio and Tjerk grabbed ahold of Thomas by his arms and began to pull him free. Once outside the cage, Thomas remained comatose; he collapsed forward, not moving.

Tjerk checked Thomas for a pulse and responded, "He's still alive; we need to get him away. Stay here and brace him as best as you can." He ran toward the stern to grab ahold of a rope tied to a small wooden boat that floated upon the water below. Gripping the line tightly, he brought the boat to the port side of the ship and tied it securely.

"Quickly, let's get into the boat," he cried out to Mauricio.

After grabbing ahold of Thomas, they lifted him upward. Bram quickly joined in, carrying him to the ship's port side together. Thomas was kept inside that small cage these past days and couldn't move or walk as his limbs and legs were cramped beyond use.

After running over to the iron cage, Tjerk cut off the remaining piece of rope, returned to Thomas, and then wrapped it around his chest, asking Mauricio for help. His grunts and groans were quickly ignored by dragging Thomas across the deck, then moving him up and over the ship's gunwales. After being lowered into the small boat, Thomas sat there in pain and was soon joined by the others. Suddenly, it became apparent that there wasn't much room left inside the tiny boat. But regardless, it was their one ticket to freedom, and they were grateful to have it.

While hurrying to the transom of the small boat and grabbing ahold of an oar, Tjerk cried out, "Push off quickly; we haven't much time left before sunbreak." Then pointing toward a distant island, he said, "We must paddle over there if we ever hope to have a fighting chance at getting away."

Mauricio took the remaining oar without hesitation and heaved it hard against the ship's side.

Now adrift, they watched the ship slowly move past them on an unknown course.

Quickly, the men paddled their small boat away. After close to two hours, Tjerk and Mauricio both became tired. Without hesitation Bram showed maturity by taking their oars, shoving them into the metal cleats, and rowing hard as he could. The pirate ship, whose image was soon lost in the morning darkness, faded from view.

From what anyone knew, the island was uninhabited. Hopefully, it would provide a haven in which to hide. They hoped that by steering toward the island's backside, they could find a hidden cave or another undiscovered place to vanish.

These pirates were no fools. Assuredly, they would turn back around once their disappearance was realized. The only question on everyone's mind was: Would they pay for their escape with their lives?

As the small boat made its way toward the shadowy island, Thomas suddenly whispered, "Thank you. Thank you all for saving my life."

Then nothing else was said as he fell asleep, exhausted from his endurance.

Tjerk patted him on the shoulder and said, "You're safe now."

"I hope we are safe away from that hellhole," young Bram whispered out, relentlessly rowing and refusing to stop to rest.

"Yes, let us be free or die trying," Mauricio said.

Chapter 10

THE COLOR OF THE WATER beneath his small fishing boat was the darkest blue Miguel had ever seen. He'd never sailed this far from home; the menacing dark clouds ahead looked worrisome. He knew that a storm was coming in their direction; although the girls seemed unbothered by what lay ahead, they couldn't understand the danger they faced and laughed about it like schoolgirls.

Miguel didn't mind the songs they sang; it was a relief from the anxiety he still felt from killing Pablo. However, over the next hour the wind increased, causing the waves to become choppier and more substantial in size. After looking about the small boat at what little provisions they had aboard, Miguel began securing the satchel by tying the bag to a small cleat. Unfortunately, having lost the use of an anchor, there was nothing to stabilize the boat when things got rough.

Miguel looked at his daughter and said, "Listen, I have something to say. Do you see the approaching darkness? It means there's a storm ahead of us. It is not my choice in the matter; it is God's wrath upon us all for the innocent life I've taken. I cannot say whether we shall survive, but I want you ladies to understand we are in for a rough ride."

Abella reached back to grab her father's hand and said, "Miguel, you only wanted to save us. This Pablo was a monster that you should not feel bad for destroying. You have no way of knowing, but there are stories of him stealing young girls away from their families, and when the father objected, he would stab him through with his sword and laugh while the man was bleeding to death. So, no, Father, you did the world a favor."

However, the look on her father's face spoke volumes; he was still struggling with what he did, and no matter what Abella said, he would not forgive himself.

Mariana looked at the approaching doom, turned back, and said, "Tell us, Miguel, what we can do to survive this?"

"Take anything of value and store it in the small compartment toward the bow. Search the same compartment for some rope; I believe that I still have some leftovers from my last fishing trip. Take the rope you find and tie yourselves to your seat. That way when the waves knock about the boat, you won't be thrown overboard and drown."

Immediately, the women went to work searching the small compartment; they soon found the remains of a short rope and set about securing themselves to their seats, as Miguel had suggested. Sometime later the wind changed direction from the warmness of the Caribbean trade winds to a colder north wind that blew violently. Ahead of them they could see the changes affecting the shape of the waves as large swells climbed upward and passed underneath their small boat.

Now all they could do was wait until the storm's fury came crashing upon their heads. It was unknown if they could survive, but soon they would discover the outcome. In times past Miguel would avoid such a threatening display and steer to the safety of a small port of call. As it was, he had little choice in the matter but to remain and tough it out as they trudged ahead.

Now more than ever Miguel had to protect the mainsail, for if it were lost, their ability to maneuver would be lost, too. Soon the wind would be howling hard, trying to bend or break the mainmast. Gratefully, he had chosen the hardest of woods that would withstand such harsh conditions and would resist snapping in two. However, nothing could be done to confront their fury if the winds were strong enough.

It was a larger boat than most—this seagoing

fishing vessel he had built to catch fish out in the outer banks. At that place the giant waves could be monstrous, but the reward was well worth the risk, especially when he returned with a much larger catch than all the fishermen of his village.

He knew the planks were fastened more securely than typical for boats this size, and they would hold fast; for that, he was confident. However, the battle against nature was one in which man often lost; this was a truth in life that Miguel accepted, and having lost friends that encountered such natural disasters as these, he never returned home again.

Abella felt confident in her father's abilities, knowing he had many years of seamanship behind him. Nonetheless, she had never been part of that life, having chosen a much easier way to make a living while lying upon her back. However, she was about to experience a lesson in humility, which her father had already been tested.

After looking about the boat, the food and wineskin were secured in the small hatchway. Abella was hopeful that the saltwater wouldn't penetrate. She felt helpless and did not know what else to do.

"Father, I have stored the food in the little cabinet, but I don't know of anything else to do to secure our safety."

"Listen, you and Mariana need to keep your ropes tightened securely; your lives depend on it! What you must understand is the waves will be monstrous. If at any moment while we're in the middle of the storm and you fall out of the boat, I will not be able to save any of you."

The look of fear gripped both women.

After seeing this, Miguel said, "All I can say is to check your bindings, tie yourselves several times around your waist, and secure yourselves to the hull. As I suspected, this storm is shaping up to be large."

A short time later Abella announced, "We have taken what rope we could find and left some for you, Father. Here is what's left. You need to tie yourself securely."

Without argument and taking the small amount of

rope, Miguel wrapped it around his body several times, then tied himself to an iron ring hanging from the transom. Looking up into the sky, he announced, "Already, I can see the lightning erupting within the clouds a distance away and the waves continuing to change shape."

Unknown forces seemed to battle for supremacy. Mariana listened to the father and daughter discuss their possible doom and was terrified. Silently, she began to pray within her heart, wanting restitution for her sinful life, and begged for mercy from the good Lord above if he would let her survive this approaching storm, which again had changed the wind direction.

Abella knew how to tie specific sailors' knots; her father had taught her. She secured herself to the seat, but before making the final knot, she helped Mariana, who knew little of this, and helped her tie herself to a hard plank.

Afterward, while both women grasped their seats, things became rocky as the boat was tossed from side to side; all they could do was sit, unable to affect the outcome.

Miguel steered within the wave's trough and drove the boat up and over to the top. Soon the wind blasted hard against their sail as they gathered speed, advancing into the storm's fury.

The waves began crashing over the bow as the boat crested the waves and arrived at the top, where they would experience the full effect of the wind gust that battered against them, causing the fabric sail to flap about, trying to undo the lines that held it into place.

Then, as if climbing up a mountain of water, the boat struggled to reach the top. Afterward, it plunged into the churning sea that foamed at the bottom. Now darkness surrounded them, with only brief illuminations of lightning strikes erupting above.

Miguel realized that they had entered the eye of the storm. The wind howled as the waves slammed hard against the small boat. Soon they were taking on water at an alarming rate; if they didn't bail it out, they would surely sink.

Miguel shouted over the howling wind that the boat was filling up with water. He instructed Abella to take the only bucket in the boat and bail out as much water as possible. Unfortunately, as she bailed out water, more was replaced; soon afterward it became a losing battle. The boat traveled deeply into another trough, between two enormous waves that became separated by the blowing wind. Miguel gripped the small rudder and positioned the ship on a new course that moved down into the bottomless abyss with less resistance—maneuvering into the next approaching wave that seemed more massive than the first.

The whole situation felt hopeless, and Abella was soon tired of bailing out the water. She asked Mariana to replace her; without hesitation Mariana instinctively began to fill the bucket and emptied it over the side. Abella continued bailing as she now cupped her hands together and shoved a minuscule amount of water out.

Miguel struggled to steer the boat with the small rudder until suddenly, the wind snapped the rope holding the mainsail; as a result it began flapping violently in the wind. Abella reached out for the line and held it tightly as the boat again drove down into another monstrous wave.

Mariana continued bailing out the water from the boat, then a bolt of lightning suddenly came crashing down in a thunderous crackling boom all about them. Abella and Mariana both jumped in fright, nearly out of their seats, thinking the worst had come. Then the rain suddenly began pouring down upon them in sheets of the watery deluge, which felt cold and harmful.

Abella struggled to hold the rope of the sail as the wind continued blasting against the fabric. The coarse line burned into her hands as the saltwater sprayed everywhere. Then again, another wave crashed over the bow, sending unwanted water inside the small craft.

Now to survive each had their job to perform; all they could do was find the strength within themselves to continue, for if any of them faltered in their duties, they would all perish.

Secretly, Miguel had accepted their fate and knew in his heart that a wave would appear at any moment that would destroy them all. Regardless, he maneuvered the boat on an actual course. He knew all too well what would happen if the boat capsized, leaving them all to bobble atop the waves until exhaustion overtook them and they took their last breath underwater.

Mariana continued bailing the water until the bucket became so heavy that she could barely reach the gunnel's edge; helplessly, she spilled some water back inside the boat. There was no time to rest; with each attempt to bail the water out of the boat, she prayed to God above for the strength to lift the bucket high enough to pour it out. However, she knew all would be lost if she stopped her efforts.

It was then that one felt closest to God, knowing how close He was to them. Each examined their sins and felt the regret of wasted lives. They struggled to continue as the storm's relentless power seemed unstoppable.

Then after some time a nervous calm overcame the elements; the wind slowed, and the rocking waves abated. Miguel knew they were coming into the middle of the storm; the worst part was soon upon them.

"Continue your efforts and do not stop; you must continue finding the strength within yourselves to continue," he yelled.

Their bodies, soaked to the bone, left them feeling weak. Then Miguel yelled to Abella to take his knife and cut the rope on the other side of the sail to let it fly free. Now it was more important to keep the boat afloat because there was too much water inside.

Quickly, Abella cut the small rope that held the sail in place, and soon it was slapping wildly in the wind. Her hands were now bloody and hurting; she knew there was nothing to do except help bail as much water out of the boat as she could. After handing the knife back to her father, she readied herself for the remainder of the storm.

Miguel knew that something had to be done to get the water out of the boat and yelled to Mariana to give him the bucket. After untying himself from the iron ring, he asked Abella to replace him and grab ahold of the rudder while bailing the water from the hull.

With renewed vigor and purpose, Miguel dug into

the pool of water that filled the inside of the boat as he bailed as much water as possible until he could see a change in the boat's lift. However, bailing soon became tiresome; even for Miguel who grew tired and weary as the small vessel struggled over another massive wave.

After taking his place at the rudder, Miguel handed the bucket off to Abella and grabbed ahold of the small rudder, preparing for the second half of the storm soon upon them. Again, the wind picked up and began another relentless attack upon them without mercy.

It was several more hours of hard labor until they finally saw a break in the storm.

The wind suddenly changed direction, and the merciless forces that fought against them gave up the battle for omnipotence, allowing them to win the day. Once the rain had decreased and the waves diminished, there wasn't any way to determine where they were, but no one cared for now.

Now utterly exhausted and with no strength left, they could finally relax. However, Abella took over the last duties of bailing the remains of water that had filled the boat. She suggested that Miguel take some time to rest. He obliged her and tied off the small rudder; then he lay down inside the small space between the bench and transom.

When Abella had finished removing most of the water from the boat, she, too, laid down. Looking over at Mariana, she noticed that she had fallen asleep and slumped over while still secured to her seat. For now, everyone was utterly exhausted, with no energy left. The boat drifted on an unknown course; it floated above the water as its occupants drifted into sleep. The storm that had lasted for several hours gave way to a crystal night sky with twinkling stars above and calm waters.

MIGUEL OPENED HIS EYES THE following day as the sun's glare shone about them. There was no land in sight or way to know where they were. Miguel tried to stand erect, but his sore, aching body resisted movement. Stepping forward, he opened up the small hatch that held the supplies and began rummaging through one of the sacks. Inside, he pulled out a compass, opened it, and saw the needle pointing south.

Without a map he knew that the ocean current would carry them back into the hands of the dangerous governor, who sought their heads upon a spike. At least having the compass allowed them some directional tool in which to sail. He knew of several small fishing villages south of their location.

Looking about, he observed the women still asleep. Abella lay where she was previously bailing out the water and hadn't moved. The small bucket still lay there near her head. Still tied and secured with the rope, Mariana laid her head on the wooden bench and remained asleep.

Miguel felt exhausted; he knew that their journey was far from over. While he stood there stretching, he felt the waves rocking his vessel beneath him. Gazing out into the vast openness of water, he fixated upon a course that would take them to safety.

As he tied the sail, something off in the distance caught his eye. It was large and dark and floated just above the waterline. This unknown object was too far to see with the naked eye so he reached back inside his satchel to remove his spyglass. The body looked large enough to still be visible at such a long distance away. It seemed utterly black. *I should investigate this strange thing; perhaps there's something there that could aid our escape,* Miguel thought. Changing direction, he tied the sail to the mast and steered toward the object. The sail soon filled with a slight passing northern wind, and the boat lumbered onward.

It took some time to reach the object, but as he got closer, to his amazement, he recognized it as being the remains of the Spanish galleon, entirely burnt and blown apart in many places. It was just a hulk of burning timbers, but somehow remained afloat, no doubt air trapped beneath its decks, acting as ballasts.

Why was it remaining afloat after the storm that they survived? Miguel thought. Perhaps it just caught the tail end of the storm and wasn't affected. The closer he got, the more he could make out the ship's superstructure that hung just above the waterline. Still, there was something else that sent a shudder coursing through him.

Upon the mizzen mast, he saw a man looking dead.

As they got closer, he could see the actual size of the ship and the man fastened with ropes. However, dead bodies hung over the railings and the deck while some floated headfirst in the water, their corpses bloated from the sun. Miguel looked at the gruesome sight and felt sick. He wanted to turn away but felt a need to investigate the carnage. It was apparent what he saw was from a battle at sea, the relics of the loser in the fight that lost it all.

He wondered if it wasn't too late to save what must have been the ship's captain strapped to the mizzen mast. He maneuvered his boat near the sinking bow and gently banged into the wooden structure. He quickly grabbed the rope he used to tie himself and tied it to the large vessel.

After crawling upward upon the sinking ship, Miguel hurried to the man; when he arrived there, he saw no sign of life. He checked the man's pulse, only to discover that he was still alive. Although he had a faint heartbeat, the man seemed unaware of his presence.

It was the work of pirates; their brutality and cruelty were well known. Examining the man's condition, he quickly saw the protruding nails sticking out of the man's hands, pounded hard into the wooden mast of the ship.

Without a moment's notice Miguel grabbed his knife and quickly cut the rope fastening the man to the wooden mast, then felt his body go limp. After taking his knife he buried the blade inside the man's hand, cutting deeply into his flesh until he could pull him free. Regrettably, the only way to pull him free was to pry his hands through steel nails.

A small whimper was the only sound made as blood poured out of the wound and dripped down his elbow, forming red droplets in the water. Then Miguel repeated the process until the captain's upper body was free. Now the man collapsed in his arms. But sadly, as Miguel pulled hard to free him, he didn't budge but moaned in pain.

This unlikely event couldn't be realized until

Miguel reached into the water and felt the head of another nail protruding above the man's foot. "Those cursed *piratas*," he snarled under his breath.

Looking among the dead bodies floating helplessly side to side on the rocking ship, Miguel searched for something he could use to pull the nails out of the man's foot. Near one of the bodies he saw a marlinspike in the hand of one of the dead Spanish men. This man must have tried to use it as a weapon and lost.

He placed the marlinspike under the head of the nail, then tied the small line attached to the handle around the nail head and strained hard against the steel rod; he soon felt it move upward, eventually coming out of the man's foot. Now free the blood dripped from the top of his foot, turning the water red. He ran over and took it from the body, returning quickly.

Checking the other foot, he found another nail precisely as the first and repeated the process until the man was now free to move. Miguel dragged him to the ship's side and yelled to Abella to wake up. After hearing her father's cries, both women suddenly awoke and looked upward at him, astonished, still half asleep. They soon realized they were fastened to a Spanish galleon, which left them stunned.

Miguel again screamed aloud for them to give him a hand. Suddenly, they saw Miguel lifting a man over the railing. After Grabbing his feet, both ladies guided the stranger downward into their boat.

Recognizing the man's uniform, Abella knew he was the captain of the ship. She didn't know what cruel providence he played in that battle. However, this stranger was closer to death than life; seeing the scars on his hands and feet made her feel that death would be a welcomed relief.

Looking at the captain he saved, Miguel felt within himself that perhaps this was God's way of allowing him to make restitution for killing the soldier, Pablo. Maybe this was the one saving grace allowed him; he would do what he must to save this man.

Just as Miguel was about to return to his boat, he heard a faint voice calling for help from inside the captain's quarters, a call Miguel could not ignore. He stood there silently and listened, hearing nothing except the splashing waves upon the ship's hull. He then called out, "Hello, is anyone there?"

Again, a voice called out for help, sounding faint and far away. Looking about the cabin, Miguel saw no one there, as if the spirits of the dead were beckoning him to come closer. He was sure that everyone was dead and became frightened by the sound. Deciding it was best to get to their boat and get away, he turned to leave. Miguel suddenly heard someone calling out; there seemed something different about the call as if a young boy was screaming out for help. Refusing to play a part in this game of the dead, he again turned to leave but could not leave without investigating the source of the call, even if it cost him his own life.

CHAPTER 11

THE HMS *DEFIANCE* WAS ANCHORED at Port Royal, gathering supplies. They loaded various fruits and grain crates into the ship's cargo hold. Their captain discussed the supply list with his newly appointed boatswain, Mr. Blackwood. After hearing a commotion, he looked to see a British man-of-war approaching the harbor. He recognized it as the HMS *Dolphin*.

Already trimming her sails, she approached slowly, coming into view on their starboard side.

Captain Edmonton announced to his boatswain, "Well, it looks like we shall have guests for dinner, Mr. Blackwood."

"I shall inform the men to be ready with a boarding party, sir."

"Very well, then. That will be all, sir," Edmonton replied, handing the supply list back to Mr. Blackwood.

After concluding their business, the junior officer saluted and walked away.

Edmonton somberly watched a clear view from the poop deck as the HMS *Dolphin* continued its approach near the port. Then, just as the ship began to enter the mouth of the channel, she turned easterly, changing her course somewhat, slowing her travel, until the boat had slowed enough to set its anchor.

Then there was a loud, rustling noise as the heavy anchor chain was released, spinning downward through the hawser hole, being run out until the bitter end as the powerful ship ground to a halt.

From his position Edmonton could see the captain aboard the *Dolphin* addressing his first mate and crew, no doubt explaining the proper procedures for docking a ship. Turning his attention to his men loading supplies, he watched two of them struggling with a large rum barrel. Each man would get a quarter-pint a day, the reason for so many barrels. It was an essential commodity aboard a ship. Besides the cartons of fruits and baskets of chickens still waiting to be loaded, the goats were bleating.

As Edmonton stood watching, he noticed the port master tallying up all the goods he supplied on the pier in front of his ship, including coffee beans and other spices. When he was finished he began conversing with Mr. Cornwall, the ship's commander. With him was a large negro he had in his employment. The shoremen loading the ship were entirely his responsibility. The port master wore a white suit and white stockings with his black-buckle shoes, including a large white hat to shield him from the intense tropical sun.

When the final supplies were on board, Edmonton yelled to Mr. Cornwall to bring the dockmaster to his cabin, where they could conduct their business privately. A customary salute later, the small group left the pier toward the captain's cabin.

Glancing behind his shoulder, Edmonton saw the crew of the HMS *Dolphin* securing their ship. A short time later a small boarding party began to form near the gangway. He expected their captain to arrive within the hour. After walking down the wooden steps to the main deck, the captain retired into his stateroom and waited. Sitting at his table, he glanced at the nautical charts, thinking of their next port of call.

They had left Bristol several months ago to rid these waters of the pirate scum that were miraculously able to vanish before their eyes. About two weeks ago they encountered a violent storm in pursuit of these pirates. Sadly, though they would've engaged these Iron Born Pirates in battle, it wasn't to be.

Thinking back to that dreadful day, a passing thought of Mr. Thomas Banish falling overboard was the only logical explanation for his disappearance. He was boatswain by title alone. This Thomas appeared to have his ideas of what a sailor in the British Navy should be. He was disorganized in his duties; *truthfully, I am glad to be rid of him*, he thought. However, being captain, Edmonton needed a reason for his vanishing and recorded in his journal that Thomas had died at sea during a tropical storm, perhaps a personal delight to an annoyance he disliked.

Suddenly, a knock on his cabin door was heard. Edmonton yelled out, "Come in."

The door opened, and Mr. Cornwall, the ship's commander, walked inside and quickly saluted.

"Captain, Mr. Dominguez, the dockmaster, is here for his payment. All the supplies listed upon our manifest have been fulfilled."

"Very well, sir, please show him in."

Mr. Cornwall left the room briefly and returned with a tall Spanish-looking man he escorted inside. Followed by a large negro, they greeted the captain.

"Good afternoon; I hope you're having a pleasant day."

"Thank you, Mr. Dominguez; I am, indeed."

Turning to his commander, he asked, "Mr. Cornwall, are all the supplies loaded on board?"

"Yes, sir. Captain, everything upon our list has been loaded; we are now ready to set sail."

"Very well, Mr. Cornwall. Thank you. That will be all."

Turning to his guest, Edmonton said, "Would you care to join me in a glass of cognac, Mr. Dominguez?"

"Yes, thank you, Capitán, that is very generous of you. I, too, appreciate the finer things in life and would enjoy a glass."

Edmonton then walked over to a wooden cabinet and opened its ornately carved glass door. After removing a crystal glass canister and three small glasses, he poured each guest a glass of his finest cognac. After giving each of them a drink, he proposed a toast: "Sirs, to your health."

"Thank you, Capitán, to yours as well."

And everyone took a sip.

"Remarkable vintage, Capitán; the cognac tastes very smooth."

Edmonton smiled, nodded his head thoughtfully, and called to Mr. Stanley to come to his cabin. Quickly, a young cabin boy appeared and was given orders to fetch the ship's Paymaster. In a rush the lad ran off, only to return a few moments later with Mr. Bixby in tow.

"Yes, Captain, you called me, sir," the man said.

"Do you see this man seated here before me? I need you to pay him this amount for supplying our ship. See to it at once, sir."

After handing the manifest over to Mr. Bixby, he looked down at the paper and said, "As you wish, Captain."

Mr. Dominguez looked down at the paper and said, "The total should amount to three hundred and fifty pieces of eight."

"Very well, sir, I shall return momentarily with your payment."

Mr. Bixby left the room to return quickly, displaying a large bag full of silver. After he paid the dockmaster, Mr. Dominguez, and with their business completed, the dockmaster tipped his hat to the captain, drank down what remained of his expensive cognac, and left the cabin, with his associate following closely behind.

Walking over to the rear windows and glancing out, Edmonton could see the HMS *Dolphin*'s boarding party entering a small boat. He knew the captain of the HMS *Dolphin* personally, having served on the same ship for a short time—not as friends but with mutual respect for one another.

Something was troubling about the fact that Mr. Thomas Banish was the brother-in-law of the HMS *Dolphin*'s captain. This relationship alone was a meaningless nuisance as the outcome of the boatswain was the same no matter what port they sailed. If Captain Harrington asked of Thomas's whereabouts, it would be explained that he fell overboard during a storm. Sadly, both these men were close, and the news might shock Captain Harrington.

This arrival of the other ship was an unexpected turn of events. The HMS *Dolphin* anchored off the starboard bow. It didn't matter that both boats were on the same mission to destroy the Iron Born Pirates. Now having two formidable men-of-war anchored near one another, it would defy any approaching buccaneer's foolish attempt to attack. However, on his command, he had men scouring the horizon for any sign of approaching sails.

With one final glance back out the window, Edmonton could see Captain Harrington seated in the middle, looking proud as a peacock, as his junior officers sat behind. After drinking his last cognac, he sat down the glass and left his cabin. After walking back into the open sunlight, he stood at the railing eyeing his men, then called Mr. Cornwall, the ship's commander, to have them appear at their stations. A commotion soon erupted on deck as every seaman scrambled to their places, standing shoulder to shoulder, looking straight ahead with shoulders back.

The distance between the ships was shortened as the small boat suddenly came alongside. A whistle sounded at the gangway, alerting everyone of their presence. A detachment of sailors from the HMS *Dolphin* soon reached the top of the stairs and piled onto the deck. The *Dolphin*'s Captain Harrington appeared, saluting the officer on watch, who then stepped back into the row of sailors.

He was met by Cornwall, who ceremoniously saluted, then stood to attention at the head of the column. Captain Edmonton then appeared on deck and gave a military salute; afterward, he and Harrington shook hands with one another as if they were old friends.

"Come, let us get out of this blistering sun and retire to my cabin," Edmonton said. "I have a bottle of delicious port and a cigar that I've been waiting to try."

"That's a splendid idea," Harrington replied. Then addressing his men, he said, "Dismissed, relax yourselves; you're among friends."

While the two walked across the deck toward the captain's cabin, Edmonton let out a hearty laugh and said, "Harrington, how have you been, you old sea dog? It's been too many years since I last saw you; it looks like life is treating you well, sir. I notice the few pounds of gluttony on your soul and body, man."

"Oh, yes, I cannot deny that truth," Harrington responded with a joyful laugh.

As the two men walked together, they began reminiscing about old times back at the naval academy, in which they both admitted their disappointment at not having reached the rank of admiral.

After arriving at the captain's cabin, Harrington took a seat in the available chair near the window and sat quietly watching the movements of his host.

Edmonton walked over to his desk and reached for a small cedar box filled with cigars. He took one in hand. After taking a box of matches made of pinewood and impregnated with sulfur, he struck it against a small stone, causing a flame. Taking one cigar in hand, he began rolling it between his two fingers until the end was red. He then gave it to Harrington, who thanked him. Then he took one for himself and repeated the process until he was able to inhale a long draw into his lungs.

Smoke began filling the room with the sweet smell of tobacco leaves. Edmonton, putting out the match, sat the burning stick inside a spittoon and turned back.

"I have a matter that I must discuss with you."

"Yes, go on."

"How can I say this lightly? It's distressing news, but I'm sad to report that your brother-in-law, Thomas Banish, was lost in a storm some weeks back."

Harrington took another long draw from the rich tobacco and exhaled the smoke into the room; his puzzled countenance showed concern as he gazed at the floor.

Edmonton continued. "We encountered a hurricane; sadly, a rogue wave washed Thomas overboard."

A nervous tension filled the small cabin more than the tobacco smoke. Suddenly, Harrington stood to his feet and walked over to the window to stare across the bay at his ship. After taking another draw into his lungs, he exhaled the smoke out the window and turned to face his host.

"I retrieved my brother-in-law's uniform from a madam back in Trinidad. When I saw Thomas's name on the collar, I wanted to know what happened to him. But sadly, the governor refused to tell me anything about his whereabouts. Thomas is alive; don't ask me how but the man is resilient at best. No, he survived somehow, to end up in Trinidad."

"Why, Trinidad?" Edmonton asked.

"Why, indeed. No matter where I found Thomas's garment. But sadly, things between the governor and myself got heated; I felt that it was best to depart, not wanting to declare war over a uniform."

"It seems we have a mystery on our hands, does it not? This Mr. Banish has beaten the odds and survived being washed overboard, lost at sea to only end up in a Spanish port of call. Now, however, what trouble the man has found himself in is the question."

"I had an opportunity to dine with the governor of Trinidad, both he and his wife. I thought that honesty was foremost in our communications. But sadly, I was mistaken. However, being the clever man I am, I discovered Thomas's uniform in a brothel."

"His uniform in a brothel? That's quite strange, sir, I must say."

Edmonton replied, "Yes, strange, indeed, captain. I agree."

"Tell me, man, of your plans. We are fully supplied with new provisions to continue our search for Iron Born Pirates. As far as I'm concerned, your brother-in-law is a deserter! When I return to England, I plan on having him court-martialed before the admiralty."

"Good God, man, isn't that a little harsh? The man should be dead. Tell me, truthfully, why your hatred toward the man?"

"Dereliction of duty. The night Thomas fell overboard, it was reported that he had too much rum to drink. The man deserted his post through his actions. Aboard my ship, I require more from my men than he portrayed," Edmonton answered.

"This matter of desertion does not sit well with me; it's unfitting conduct for any Royal Navy men," Harrington pointed out. Then added, "I hope to discuss this matter further over dinner this evening if you would like to be my guest. For now, put aside any differences that we feel toward Thomas."

"Thank you, Harrington, but sadly, circumstances have arisen where we must depart quickly. Recently, I received reports that the pirate ship *Abraxas* has been spotted near the Antilles. If this is true, I must investigate."

"I understand, sir; I wish you success in your pursuits. Let us enjoy a glass of port before we part with one another."

Edmonton nodded in agreement as he poured each of them a glass. Afterward, they lifted their glasses to the King of England, George II, and drank the glasses empty. After their visit, Harrington announced that he intended to return to Trinidad to discover the whereabouts of Thomas.

Captain Edmonton said, "Mr. Banish, I wish for the man's safe return."

Somehow, however, his comments seemed mendacious. Harrington shrugged his shoulders afterward.

Their business concluded, and both men walked back to the gangway where sailors were standing about conversing with one another. Suddenly, seeing their captains appear, everyone stood to attention, forming two separate rows. Harrington turned to his host to shake his hand, thanking him for a pleasant visit.

After returning to his ship, Harrington watched as the HMS *Defiance* pulled anchor and left Port Royal, sailing toward the Antilles, a familiar hunting ground for pirate dogs.

Harrington sought to control his anger at hearing that Edmonton wanted to have Thomas court-martialed before the admiralty. Besides this, he thought, *the man survived being thrown overboard; I'm not sure what my next course of action should be.*

Though the relations between the two nations of England and Spain were often problematic, it was the very reason that Harrington felt uncomfortable, suspecting perilous danger if they remained in the port of Trinidad from this Governor Edwardo.

When they return to Trinidad, he decided he won't accept any excuses on where Thomas was being held in secret. Now recognizing the dangers acquainted with returning to the Spanish port, he realized that approaching the situation in a calm demeanor would be the proper approach.

The next day after the ship was adequately supplied, Harrington ordered the *Dolphin* to raise the anchor. The boat slowly traveled out of Port Royal, traveling southwest. The navigator plotted a new course for Trinidad. *There, the truth shall be known by saber or cannon, whichever the governor decides,* Harrington thought.

Chapter 12

MIGUEL PAUSED TO LISTEN WHEN he heard a distant cry from the ship's bowels. Immediately, he ran toward the sound. He was arriving at the door leading to the captain's cabin. There, the exterior door was partly torn from its hinges, barely hanging loose to one side. Looking inside the dark space, he saw several bodies piled one upon the other.

Miguel called out, "Is anyone there?"

Listening, he waited for a reply; surprisingly, he again heard a call for help coming from deep within the interior of the ship. He quickly stepped into the dark space to begin his search within the commissioned officers' quarters where numerous bodies lay dead—their faces looking distorted as the instruments of their death remained buried deep within their bodies. Still, others were murdered by heavy muskets fired at close range. The floor beneath was coated with blood as the smell of death lingered in the tight space.

Finally, Miguel reached the captain's quarters where the door was missing entirely. Glancing inside the dimly lit space, he saw broken furniture thrown about, with a pile of bodies in the center of the room. To his amazement, he suddenly saw a hand begin to wave at him from beneath the pile of remains.

Miguel raced over, grabbed ahold of a body, and pulled it off the pile. Beneath the collection, each corpse looked bloated due to the beginning stages of decay. Hurriedly removing several more bodies, he finally came upon a corpse of a large man with a saber sticking out his back. Miguel struggled to pull him free, discarding the body near the doorway. When he returned he looked down and saw a young lad, no older than fifteen in age, trapped beneath. A saber had pierced him through his side, pinning him fast into the deck. His voice was hoarse as he begged for help to be set free.

Miguel realized that to save the young boy, he would have to remove the saber pinning him to the floor. After scrutinizing the blade, Miguel could tell that it didn't puncture any vital organs, only that it was lodged below his rib cage.

The ship's creaking sounds signaled that the boat was sinking. What caused it to remain afloat was anyone's guess. But for now, Miguel did not concern himself with that matter, only the situation that lay before him.

Looking about the room, Miguel found the captain's uniform in a cabinet and quickly cut off a small section. He then wound it tightly into a ball. After handing it to the youth, he ordered him to insert it into his mouth and bite hard against the pain. Shaking his head, knowing what was about to happen, the young man closed his eyes and waited.

Miguel grabbed hold of the saber's handle and placed his foot on the boy's chest. The youth, gritting his teeth, looked up nervously as Miguel began to pull. A few anxious moments later the saber dislodged from the young man's body and pulled free. After casting the blade aside, Miguel quickly examined the wound; gratefully, there was little blood. But what couldn't be helped was the cry of searing pain afterward.

"We must leave immediately," Miguel informed the boy.

He nodded in response, saying no words as Miguel lifted him off the floor and hurried out of the cabin and over to the ship's port side. Looking down inside their small boat, he again yelled out for Abella to give him a hand as he lowered the boy into the arms of the waiting women.

Now safe from certain death, both the boy and captain were quickly attended to by both Mariana and Abella. They began to dress each of the wounds by ripping parts of their clothing away to make bandages.

While Miguel stood on the main deck, he again yelled out, hoping to hear a cry for help from the many corpses that littered the half-sunken ship. This time, however, there were no cries for help, nothing but the slow rocking of the vessel with its creaking timbers and nothing else. Afterward, an eerie silence was all that was heard.

Doing all he could for the lost and helpless, Miguel stepped inside his fishing boat, untied the line that held them secure, and pushed off. They sailed away from the remains of the sinking Spanish galleon, never to return to the horrid sight where death and carnage were all that remained.

The captain's expressionless stare didn't seem to change, even with the discovery of the young boy Miguel found alive. The man remained speechless, yet realizing he was alive should have made a difference. However, all his crew didn't fare as well. In such times it was well known that whoever wasn't murdered would be sold by the pirates as slaves. Nevertheless, he was grateful for seeing his junior officer, Humberto de Hevia, alive. There was something special about this lad that he never entirely understood. He was undoubtedly the son of a noble or perhaps some sea captain who wanted his boy to experience the life of a naval officer. The admiralty had given him orders to keep a wary eye upon him.

Miguel again stared at the burned-out hull, asking himself, *Why hasn't the storm sunk the ship?* An act of God's tender mercies, he concluded. *A miracle is the only answer.* Staring at the waterline of the half-submerged ship, he knew that it wouldn't be long before it would take all the corpses down into the cold depths, never to be seen again. Their laughter and songs of life would forever be silenced, with only the tears of wives and mothers back at home to keep their memory alive.

The Spaniards fought this sea battle hard, but in the end one could easily see that the *piratas* took what they desired of the once beautiful ship and burned what was left. The dead that littered the deck were horrible to see. After watching the two men he was able to save, Miguel thought, *Two lives for the price of one.* Keeping these two from certain death was a resounding accomplishment; he felt grateful for having the opportunity.

Now what course to set was the real question. He understood that both men needed medical attention, which no occupant in the boat could administer. Then he looked over at the captain, whose face looked deep with wrinkles; the man sat quietly, not speaking. The complete loss of his crew must've weighed heavily upon his shoulders. After looking over at his daughter, Miguel suggested she give the man something to drink.

"Yes, father, you're right," she remarked.

After reaching for the wineskin, Abella turned to look at the man with compassion, then softly said, "Señor, excuse me, would you care for something to drink?"

He stared back at her as if she was a phantom with no life existing within her. His parched lips looked cracked as his face was burnt red from the sun beating down upon him.

Without saying a word he reached for the wineskin to take a small drink. Then he continued staring at the floor.

Mariana was already dressing the young boy's wound on his side as he moaned slightly. She knew how to attend to the knife wounds that her clients would often receive, bidding for her attention from other suiters.

The captain's wounds had bled. His hands still bore the marks of the holes that Miguel had to cut open to release the steel spikes. Abella had cleaned his wounds by pouring some wine upon them and wrapping them tightly to stop the bleeding. The proud captain didn't seem to notice her attending to his injuries. The alcohol, which must have burned painfully, had little effect; he gave only a slight moan in response.

Miguel turned his small boat south. He considered any safe harbor nearby would be an excellent place to take the two needing medical care. However, having a cousin in Caracas, New Granada, who was a doctor, seemed the logical solution to their problems. The one reason he hadn't considered him before was due to a quarrel they had when they were both young men and hadn't spoken for many years because of it.

Along the way over the next few hours, Miguel concentrated on his new course near the Puerto de La Guaira, which lay approximately two days away from their current location. His new crew before him consisted of a despondent captain, the young lad that mostly slept, his daughter, and her young friend. Now all together sailing to an unfamiliar destination, the passing hours soon gave way to a brilliantly lit sky full of twinkling stars that looked much like diamonds against a black velvet sky.

He received help from the women. Each managed to take a turn at the helm, maintaining a course Miguel had assigned them. After pointing to a particular star on the horizon, he merely gave instructions to line up the mast, steering the boat in that direction.

Once their course was set, the small boat floated along, pushed by a gentle breeze from the north. Miguel managed to get some sleep or what little he could as his bones felt tired and sore from being in the cramped space for so long. But now with newfound determination, he was steadfast in reaching Caracas to save the lives of those aboard.

THE FOLLOWING DAY, AFTER ABELLA had relieved her at the rudder, Mariana, being the consoling angel, spoke with the captain about his troubles. At first he was reserved, only responding with grunts and moans at her inquiries. But after some time everyone heard him describing the last moments of his ship, the *Reina Isabella*, including how the Iron Born Pirates attacked them.

He described how they honorably fought in a sea battle but were outgunned by two ships more forceful than themselves. In the hand-to-hand skirmish aboard his ship, he described seeing his men cut down by musket fire while most fought on until the bitter end until only he remained. A ruined man before the world, he now bore the scars of his losses.

Mariana then described their plight to the captain about how she and Abella had run away from Trinidad because the governor had an arrest warrant out for their capture to put them all in prison.

Suddenly, Diego looked up at Mariana and announced, "I know this because I was the one sent by Edwardo, the governor, to imprison you all, including your father, Miguel Sanchez!"

Mariana looked about the boat with dismay, especially at Abella who, upon hearing the news, looked on with shock, not believing her ears.

Abella moved closer to Diego, looked the man directly in the eye, and asked, "So you are the one who was sent to arrest both my father and me? See now how events have changed; we were the ones who have saved you from certain death, señor, but it was your duty to bring death upon our heads instead!"

Miguel, hearing the entire conversation, remained quiet. His thoughts on the matter were dismal as he suddenly realized they had saved the individual who was to bring destruction upon them—this game of fate. No one spoke for some time as the small boat headed toward Caracas.

The following morning they passed an island some distance away. Miguel knew it once housed a small leper colony but was now deserted; he felt it was not worth investigating so he continued toward New Grenada.

That evening the last of the wine was drank from the solitary wineskin; what remained of the food was rationed in small bites, knowing that it would have to do until the next day. They couldn't afford to eat their fill but had to make it last.

The following morning the young boy moaned in pain as he awoke from his sleep. Not sure where he was, he looked up at Mariana to inquire about who it was that he owed his life.

A smile appeared upon Mariana's face as she pointed to the elderly fishermen and said, "It was Miguel who saved your life; he was the one that rescued you from your sinking ship, señor."

Looking at Miguel, the young lad said aloud, "I must thank you, señor, for your courageous act."

Then the boy stopped, remembering the bloody

battle.

Suddenly, noticing his commander for the first time, he said, "Capitán Espinosa, you're alive! But what of the others, our ship?"

Then came a startling revelation as he understood for the first time that everyone aboard the *Reina Isabella* was dead or captured; they had lost the battle. This new realization was too much for the once-proud junior officer, Humberto de Hevia, as he kneeled and sat quietly.

At that moment Miguel, seeing all the mouths they were to feed, informed Abella to open the small hatch up near the bow of the boat. "Inside, you will see a small wooden barrel; could you retrieve it for me?"

With nothing said, Abella crawled over to the bow of the small boat and opened the hatch; there, as her father had said, was a little wooden barrel with a lid. Grabbing ahold of it, she brought it back to Miguel.

He looked up at her and said, "This is a fishing boat; after all, let us see if we can catch something to eat."

Inside the hull's lid was a long fishing line with fishing hooks baited with salted mackerel. After unwinding the fishing line, Miguel allowed it to fall over the transom trailing behind. With barely a breeze to fill their sails, their process was slow. However, perfect for fishing, it allowed them to troll for fish. When the fishing line was out, Miguel tied a small bell to the end of the line.

As they drifted along a soothing calmness shrouded everyone as the boat gently floated above the waves and backed down again through the small troughs. Gazing at Espinosa, who was now asleep, Miguel wondered what it would've been like if he had imprisoned them. Would Espinosa have mistreated them or beat them while they were in irons aboard his ship? To have one's adversary in your hands and the freedom to treat them as they would treat you was a choice he struggled with making. He could easily apply the same treatment to the captain and the young lad he gave to Pablo; he knew he would receive little argument—well, perhaps not when it came to murdering the lad.

Unexpectedly, the tiny bell began ringing. Just as Miguel took ahold of the line, he heard Abella excitedly ask, "Do we have a big fish, Father?"

"I believe so. Let us see what we have caught."

After pulling hard on the line, the big fish resisted, struggling. After looking inside the small bucket, Miguel took out a single piece of wood, wrapped the cord around it several times, pulled hard, then wrapped a loop around the stick and pulled hard once more. After seeing her father struggle, Abella hurried over and began rewinding the line inside the bucket.

The whole commotion suddenly awakened everyone aboard the boat, eagerly looking at what must have been a large fish on the line. A bluefin tuna weighing close to forty pounds appeared on the surface. Miguel heard cheers from each of the hungry passengers. However, he needed help bringing it aboard. Gratefully, Abella reached over the rail to grab ahold of the fish's tail, but it fought hard, not wanting to surrender. Regardless, she was determined, and as Miguel pulled the fish upward into the boat, she again grabbed its tail and heaved the fish inside.

As the fish fought for its life, Miguel was quick to ease its pain with a single knife thrust into its brain. When the fish was dead, he quickly went about cleaning it. When he was finished he again asked Abella to return to the small hatch at the bow; inside, she would find a little metal box to bring. She hurried over to open the hatch, and there, as her father had said, was the metal object that she soon discovered was quite heavy. Struggling to bring it to him, she appeared with the article in hand.

Miguel had finished cleaning the fish and took hold of the metal box. He put two small rods from the bottom of the box inside metal rings under his seat, balancing the metal box. After opening the box's lid, he saw white sand inside that filled the bottom with a bed of small wooden splinters; on top of those were pieces of charcoal. After taking a bit of raw cotton, he laid it over the charcoal. Then after removing a portion of flint and a steel rod, he struck it hard, sending sparks onto the cloth. Soon a small fire began that ignited the wood and coals beneath.

Miguel, taking his knife, cut off a piece of the bluefin. He placed it over the small fire to slowly cook it.

The smell was divine; suddenly, the mood aboard the boat changed as everyone knew they were about to be fed. The ladies were the first to eat; then everyone had their fill of the fresh fish. The remains were salted and stored inside the small hatch along with the wooden barrel and stove.

Sometime that evening, off in the distance, the lights from Puerto de La Guaira could be seen brightly against the surrounding dark peaks. They would have to pass through the mountainous terrain just nineteen miles ahead to reach Caracas.

It was late when Miguel finally docked the small boat at the pier. He quickly exited the boat and ran to the nearest doctor, looking for help.

Returning a short time later, Miguel appeared with a man wearing his sleepwear, holding a lantern. The man, a local doctor, stepped inside the boat to examine both wounded men. A horse-driven carriage appeared, driven by a woman. Stopping suddenly, the woman jumped off the cart to assist the doctor. With everyone's help, Captain Espinosa and young Humberto soon were off to be treated, following the small cart through the sleeping town. It soon stopped near a small house. The doctor jumped off and hurried the two wounded inside. Nothing could be done now but to wait to see if they survived their injuries.

The following day Miguel sent word to his cousin, Ramón Cardenas, the doctor in Caracas. He begged him for help, unsure who else he could turn to in the strange town.

It took a day before he got a response. A man appeared on a horse, knocking on their door at the inn. When the messenger gave Miguel the letter from his cousin, he read its words: *Miguel, I have patients that I must attend to; I cannot come at this time. You are welcome to come to Caracas and stay with my family. I hope you understand.* It was signed by Ramón.

The news was disheartening to everyone in the small group, especially Miguel. The wounded were well cared for, but still, Miguel had hoped that his cousin would come to see him. The disappointment left him saddened and reserved.

Staying at the small port guarded by a Spanish military presence left them all to realize that they were in dangerous waters. However, it wasn't until a company of soldiers appeared at the doctor's house to inquire about Captain Espinosa and who had saved him that their fates were sealed. Sadly, they didn't have to wait long before another detachment of soldiers appeared at the inn to place everyone in irons.

This betrayal was never more heartfelt than with Miguel, who was the one that saved both Captain Espinosa and the young officer's lives. Now it seemed that the local official had heard of the arrest warrant to bring them all back to Trinidad, regardless of their heroic acts, to lock them away.

While both Abella and Mariana shared a jail cell, Miguel sat alone across the way in the darkness and hardly spoke to anyone. Their escape attempt to freedom had led to nothing but disappointment. Sadly, as the hours drifted by, he remained silent as they all awaited their fate.

Miguel knew that soon Pablo's demise would become common knowledge, no doubt by the torturous methods that Escobar, the governor, was known to enjoy. The whole dilemma was frightening. A man his age wouldn't last too long on the rack or any other torturous device that the notorious governor had in his game room.

Miguel looked at his beautiful daughter and wondered where everything went wrong. He thought of her growing up without a motherly influence; it was no wonder she turned out the way she did.

It was all his fault. Miguel accepted this responsibility; he felt more misery in his already worsening condition. Watching his daughter being tortured would be the final nail to his coffin. No matter why he chose to keep them alive, none of what he did before mattered any longer; each day that ended with the setting sun only brought him more regret, knowing that he had to wait for his life to be over.

Abella and Mariana would sing songs during their

lengthy stay. The other prisoners inside the small jail seemed to enjoy the diversion from the tedious waiting, cheering at the end of every song they sang.

After a week had gone by, Miguel had a visitor. He was surprised to see his cousin, Ramón Cardenas, being led into the prison by two guards one morning. Now stopping in front of Miguel's cell door, Ramón looked at him sorrowfully.

"Are the charges against you true?"

Miguel didn't speak; he just nodded his head in response. After seeing Ramón, whom she had heard so much of, Abella stood to her feet and called out to him to help her father get out of prison.

"My father is innocent of any crimes."

Ramón turned to her and said, "I cannot help him because the charges are severe. He is being charged with the disappearance of a military officer, but so are you. You see, not all of you have been arrested but also the Spanish captain Diego Espinosa, who shall be court-martialed for losing his ship."

Miguel appeared at the iron bars and asked, "Please, tell me of the young Humberto. Is he still alive?"

"Yes, thanks to your efforts, Cousin, but there is something else that I must tell you. This governor, Escobar, is traveling from Trinidad and will arrive here next week. He has given explicit orders that all of you are to remain here. I understand that you will be tortured until you confess the whereabouts of Pablo Garcia, the captain of the royal guards. Subsequently, you three shall be hanged on the gallows as murderers."

Suddenly, Mariana yelled, "Murderers, we're no murderers but saviors of the helpless! Why does that pig Escobar believe us to be murderers?"

"I am only telling you what I have heard."

Abella walked up to the iron bars, looked directly at Ramón, and said, "Thank you for coming." Then she sat back down on a small stool, feeling disgusted and afraid.

A guard appeared to tell Ramón it was time to leave. He thanked the man and turned to his cousin.

"Miguel, I have paid money to have you fed, both you and the ladies. The guards are to bring you fresh water and food each day. I'm sorry to see you in this condition; please believe me when I tell you I'm doing everything I can, but it all looks hopeless."

Miguel looked up at Ramón, thanking him, "It's all in the hands of God to decide our fate. Only He will judge us with the truth. I'm glad that the young lad is alive and doing well. However, I realize the captain will take some time to heal; in my heart I know that man has suffered enough already."

Unexpectedly, the guard watching the whole affair stepped in front of Ramón, ordering him to leave. He had no choice and walked away, promising to return when he could, leaving them to contemplate their destiny.

Abella called out to her father and asked, "Tell me, what do you think our chances are of getting out of this alive?"

Miguel, the realist, turned to his daughter and said, "I fear that there is no escape for any of us. We have acted the fools and will receive a fool's reward."

"I should have never asked for your help; it was my problem alone and no one else's."

"Daughter, I do not want you to blame yourself for this. You came to me for help; I could never refuse you in your time of need. I want you to have faith that we will not see the gallows, but as I say this I know that there is no escape for us."

Miguel returned to the corner of his cell and sat in the darkness, being hidden from view.

A few minutes later Abella could hear her father's faint cries. She wondered about her life and the time wasted on selfish pleasures of the flesh, never considering her father's love that she so freely received. His fatherly love, however, meant nothing to her because of the blame she placed upon her father; he was never there when she needed him most—during her pregnancy.

She looked at her young friend, Mariana Barros, who stared out the small window at freedom just beyond her reach, Abella thought of her young life ending tragically. Even though she played no fundamental part in the escape, no doubt Escobar would give no leniency to any of them since the murder of Pablo Garcia, the captain of the royal guards, would eventually be discovered.

Then a commotion was heard outside their cell. Unexpectedly, a detachment of military soldiers appeared in the jail, forming two separate lines as they came to attention. This military action was the usual display of stringent soldierly practice. Seeing this, every prisoner inside the small space stood to their feet. Then a plump man wearing a red silk jacket with matching pants, a white-colored wig, and shiny boots appeared, twisting his thick dark mustache. He passed through the middle of the line. After taking his time to eye his prisoners carefully, he suddenly stopped in front of Miguel's cell and said, "Are you comfortable, señor?"

Miguel looked back at him and said, "Let me ask you, is any of this humorous somehow?"

"I do not understand your answer," the man replied.

"Why have we been thrown in prison? No one has explained the charges brought before us."

"Please let me introduce myself. My name is Felipe San Sebastian. I am the local magistrate here in Puerto de La Guaira. I received reports of your escape from Trinidad. I wanted to capture you before you left our beautiful city."

"You have no right. We're not citizens from your city and have broken no laws," Abella shouted.

"The district governor had issued an arrest warrant for you all. I plan on keeping you in custody until he arrives."

"Why should Escobar come here?" Abella shouted, being concerned.

"Oh, yes, he should arrive by the end of the month," the magistrate announced.

After hearing the news of their appending doom, no one else spoke, and each sat down, absorbing what it all meant.

"Let me leave you to consider your destiny and make peace with God. If any of you wish to confess, I can send the local priest to see you. Each prisoner shall have the opportunity to confess their sins."

"Thank you, señor; I need to see a priest; I have

many iniquities for which I'm willing to seek forgiveness," Miguel announced.

"Very well, I'll send Father Basilio Alvarez to see you."

Then, turning to the women, he said, "I'm sure all of you need forgiveness for one reason or another." After his remark, a smile appeared on his face. After walking away, he left them to their misery.

"Father, do you believe that we can survive this?" Abella asked, being more worried than before.

"I'm not sure any of us will survive, but let me say that now would be the time to make peace with God. I want you to take this opportunity to speak with the priest when he arrives," Miguel suggested.

Looking out her small window through the iron bars at the harbor below, Abella thought of her lost child. For the first time in many years she wondered how her life would have been so different if only the man she loved had married her as he had promised. Her bitterness toward men, in general, seemed to ooze from her pores; she wasn't sure if giving confession would soothe the antipathy she felt.

All was lost; Abella's time to be judged was near. She gripped the cold iron bars and felt a bitter hatred for being trapped in her cage. Outside the walls meant they could escape their fate, but with no one to help, their future was inevitable: torture, then death.

CHAPTER 13

THE CLOUDY SUN APPEARING JUST above the horizon brightened the early morning hours. The pirate ship slumbered along on an unknown course. It would arise atop the waves until its total weight was discovered, then come crashing down upon the ocean wave beneath that helplessly gave way. The large steering wheel of the ship strained at the rope holding it in place, with no one to control it.

Waking to relieve himself, Elijah Stark, the first mate of the pirate ship *Abraxas*, stood urinating over the poop deck. For some unknown reason he felt something was out of place as he looked over at the navigator's station; he in horror didn't see anyone steering the ship. After running over to the ship's wheel, he immediately noticed it was secured with a long leader line. At that time he saw Mr. Stromal's body lying on the ground, looking dead. He raced over to check the man, kneeling beside his body; he discovered that the man was still breathing. Relieved to find him still alive, he thought, *Whoever assaulted this man would pay for their treachery.*

Then, unexpectedly, something else caught Mr. Stark's attention; there, a few feet away, was the body of Mr. Pelletier, the man whom he assigned to be the night watchman. After examining that man, he discovered he had similar injuries.

There was nothing else to do for the wounded men; he knew he had to alert the captain. Waking the captain wasn't a task he enjoyed, especially at such an hour as this. The man always awoke in a sour mood when he was interrupted in his sleep. This attack on the two crew members wouldn't help his disposition.

Mr. Stark then observed the discarded iron cage that the Englishman was kept in; he thought this would undoubtedly anger the captain even more, seeing that his prized pigeon had flown the coop.

Leaving the evidence where it lay, he ran to the captain's cabin and began pounding on the door, a light beating at first, but then hearing no response, he hit harder, knowing the man was a sound sleeper. Suddenly hearing a commotion inside, with a blast of cursing at the intruder, Mr. Stark stood there silently, knowing any moment the door would open to a bear of a man not wanting to be woken.

Then, as expected, the door flew open, and an angry Lafayette Beaumont stood holding a pistol at Mr. Stark's head, cursing the day he was born.

"Captain Beaumont, sir, I'm afraid I have some bad news to give you. It seems that someone aboard has assaulted the ship's navigator and night watchmen. Besides this, our Englishman, no doubt the young Iron Born Pirate, has escaped. I have not confirmed the latter as of late, sir, but it stands to reason that he would be gone."

Lowering his musket, the captain said, "Monsieur Stark, they had accomplices helping them perform this cowardice act. Check the good doctor's quarters; tell me if you see him there sleeping. I suspect he will also be missing."

"As you wish, Captain. I will alert the men to search the entire ship; what if I find the men hiding? What shall happen to them, sir?"

"Death, of course, Monsieur Stark."

"Very well, Captain."

Understanding his orders, Mr. Stark yelled and kicked the sleeping crew out of their bunks. However, Mr. Pelletier and Mr. Stromal remained on the deck, unaware of the commotion throughout the ship.

Sometime later that morning the doctor and cabin boy was discovered to have been gone missing, plus the Iron Blood Pirate kept below. Captain Beaumont realized these escapees must have brought together a conspiracy, not acting alone; they had to have had accomplices.

The entire crew was alerted to the main deck and stood quietly around the unconscious men. Mr. Stark gave the orders to wake the men. Appearing over each of them with a bucket filled with seawater, a pair of pirates soon stood over them and carelessly dumped the entire icy mixture across both men's faces.

Quickly spitting out the seawater, each man awoke, lying there, regaining their senses. When they opened their eyes to focus on their surroundings, they saw all their shipmates standing around them, wearing frowns of hatred.

Mr. Pelletier was utterly unaware of how he arrived there the following morning. At last he looked around and said, "What the hell is going on?"

The navigator, Mr. Stromal, barely able to stand, stood up to address the captain. "I'm sorry, Captain Beaumont, I seemed to have fallen asleep at my post. I suppose that's what happened, sir. But then again, why this pounding head of mine, sir? I do not know."

"Take hold of them both!" Beaumont ordered his men.

"What is this all about?" Mr. Stromal yelled out as he struggled to get loose.

However, at that very instant, unfortunately for him, a bag of gold paid by the doctor to look the other way had unexpectedly fallen out of his belt and landed with a thud upon the wooden deck. Looking down with disbelief that he could be so careless, the man realized he was a dead man standing.

After seeing the small bag of gold that could have only been the payment for allowing the doctor and the others to go free, Captain Beaumont instantly understood who betrayed him. His anger was kindled as he yelled, "Take hold of the traitors and tie them securely to the anchor chain."

After picking up the small leather pouch of gold within his hand, Beaumont ordered the boatswain to appear on deck.

Struggling to be free, both men fought for their lives, but to no avail. They were soon taken to the ship's bow and bound to the heavy anchor chain by their arms and feet.

Everyone aboard the ship suddenly ran forward and shouted: "Kill the traitors!"

Captain Beaumont followed the procession to the ship's bow and stood watching. When the boatswain appeared the captain ordered him to retrieve his ship sail's repair kit, including the sewing needles, and to do it quickly.

Each prisoner looked on with trembling nerves, knowing that whatever the captain devised for them would not be pleasant.

When the boatswain reappeared the captain ordered him to stand ready. After taking his dagger from his belt, Beaumont knelt over Mr. Stromal, holding the small leather pouch of gold. He yelled out for all to hear.

"Monsieur Stromal, I would not want you to leave behind your payment for your betrayal, sir. Instead, you can give it to Charon, the ferryman of Hades, as you leave this life for the other."

The captain's laugh sounded chilling for all to hear. After ripping Stromal's shirt off his body, the captain stuck his blade into the man's abdomen, making an incision large enough to fit an orange. Then he shoved the leather pouch into his body and ordered the boatswain to sew the man together.

Without showing concern for the amount of pain he was causing Mr. Stromal, the boatswain dug the big needle into his skin and slowly pulled the thick line through the opening. The blood dripped outward but was ignored as the boatswain again jammed the needle into his skin and jerked the string ever tighter. Stromal groaned in pain as each new hole was created in his abdomen. Finally, the boatswain finished sewing the wound back together; the man stood and nodded to the captain, signaling he had finished his work.

"Very well," the captain said. Looking over at his first mate, he said, "Monsieur Stark, do your duty."

"You heard the captain," Mr. Stark yelled out. "Trim the sails and be ready to set the anchor."

Looking down at the two men secured to the

anchor chain, Mr. Stark knew their horrible fate.

When the ship eventually slowed and became motionless, Mr. Stark grabbed his knife and walked over to Mr. Pelletier, whom he had known for many years as a friend. However, when he was about to slice his wrist, Mr. Pelletier screamed.

"I'm innocent of this treachery, man!" Looking up, begging for pity, he cried, "Captain, you know me, please, show me mercy!"

"Mercy, you say? Do you want me to extend mercy? Yet, while we felt safe in our bunks, you betrayed us all. No, sir, no mercy but a lesson for all to see. All be warned, this happens to any buccaneer who is a night watchman and allows himself to be knocked unconscious. Mr. Stark, do your duty."

Despite his feeling, Mr. Stark, detached from any opinions, reached down to cut both men's wrists. Now bleeding all over the deck, the red color oozed outward, causing several men that stood near to back away from the life-giving liquid that appeared near their boots.

"Outstanding, Monsieur Stark!" the captain yelled. Then, looking over at the men standing by the bow, he ordered them to release the anchor. As everyone watched, the heavy anchor was released into the murky deep. The men bound by their feet and hands had no recourse but to slide along the deck toward the bow. When the rusty chain unraveled, they soon came to the bowsprit and weren't sure if they would fit beneath the railing. But that problem was overcome by a piece of railing removed earlier; over the bow both men were soon ejected into the watery depths.

Beneath the waterline each man struggled to be free, knowing that the hungry sharks would be feeding on their helpless bodies at any moment. The heavy anchor took them down and lower into the cold darkness. Holding one's breath underwater, no man could do it for long. What little breath they had in their lungs, it, too, would soon be spent.

The unwise decision to grant a favor owed to the doctor was now the most dreaded of choices Mr. Stromal had ever made. Looking upward into the blue sky that turned a darker blue as they traveled downward into the abyss, he cursed Captain Beaumont, whom he never liked nor trusted.

Suddenly, they felt themselves crashing onto the sea bottom as the heavy anchor reached its limits, no more than twelve fathoms deep. Still able to hold a breath of oxygen into his lungs, Mr. Stromal looked over at the sudden commotion next to him as he realized Mr. Pelletier had just released his last breath of oxygen. Sadly, the man then filled his lungs with the salty water. In response he kicked and struggled at his bindings, wanting to rise to the surface but was pinned down instead as he took his final dance of death, kicking his feet wildly, trying to free himself. A few moments later the lifeless body floated, just above the chain that held him captive, no longer making any movements to be free. Soon to be dead, Mr. Stromal had accepted his fate, recognizing that at any moment he would breathe the salty coolness into his lungs and become food for the sharks.

Then he saw a flash of gray swimming past him in a blur. He knew that his dinner guest had arrived; although the water had turned a dark red from their cuts, he could still see the blue sky above. Then, in a flash, he suddenly saw the gray shape appear, and in an instant the shark struck his dead partner, digging its teeth into his lifeless body. The murky water turned a dark red color. The image not far from him was hard to see; a flipping tail or two and the jerking of the bodies—both Mr. Pelletier's and the shark's—were all observed.

Feeling light-headed from the blood loss, Mr. Stromal knew his time was up, and he waited for the grim reaper to show his face. *Would it hurt badly?* he asked himself. With death now near, his vision blurred as he floated, releasing his final breath outward in the form of tiny bubbles. Then, suddenly, he heard a loud muffled booming from above. Looking back up to the surface, he saw wood fragments raining downward into the watery depths. Another booming noise followed in rapid procession. It was then he realized that his ship was being attacked.

While delivering the death sentence to him and his

mate, they allowed themselves to become unaware of their surroundings, no doubt, and were caught off guard; now they, too, shall share in his fate of death.

After releasing his final breath, he accepted his demise. No longer was he able to feel his own body, which seemed a welcomed relief as he realized his dinner guest had arrived and began jerking his body side to side as they dined on what remained of his flesh. He could suddenly feel light-headed; everything around him became blurry and unclear. He closed his eyes, never to see this world again.

CHAPTER 14

While seated in his royal palace, Governor Escobar received word about Capitán Diego Espinosa having survived a battle with the Iron Born Pirates. The news was disturbing at best. The entire ship named the *Reina Isabella* was lost with all her crew except a young officer named Humberto. However, the one piece of news that pleased the governor most was that Abella, the prostitute, had been captured along with her father and the other young prostitute. Although still no word of Pablo Garcia, the captain of the royal guards, that truth would be known soon enough, thanks to the torturous techniques he planned on implementing.

It took a few days before he could arrange passage upon a Spanish galleon to take him to Puerto de La Guaira to arrest Capitán Diego for his duty misconduct. When the news came that his ship had arrived, Escobar said his farewells to his lovely wife, Countess Maria Consuela Anita, to board the vessel named the *Nuestra Señora de Begoña.*

The Spanish captain, Sergio Ramos Arconada, performed his ritual of honoring his guest brilliantly. That evening he had planned a special dinner in his honor. The voyage to Puerto de La Guaira would take over two weeks; they sailed on the morning tide.

The voyage was pleasurable, as was expected, and the governor had no complaints. No complaints until he appeared on the quarterdeck one morning to breathe some fresh air. While refreshing himself he caught a glance of the first mate and a deckhand looking his way, making humorous gestures and laughing at his expense.

Perhaps it was how he looked in his powdered wig and affluent attire, but regardless, it was unacceptable so he stormed off to address the matter with the ship captain.

While pounding upon the captain's door, he yelled, "Capitán Arconada, there's a grave matter that I must discuss with you." After getting no response, he pounded harder and said, "Capitán, it is Escobar, the governor; open the door!"

Still no response.

Angry frustration set in, and he beat upon the door, demanding entry into the captain's quarters. Suddenly hearing some commotion behind him, Escobar turned around to see Capitán Arconada and a cabin boy coming down the narrow hallway.

"Capitán, there's an issue I'm having with Midshipman Adrián Salinas and his cousin, Emilio Fernández, that I must address with you, sir. It seems that they have not learned to respect the man that holds the governor's title; I want this matter brought to your attention immediately, señor."

Arconada, somewhat frustrated and troubled by other matters aboard his ship, gave little thought to the man's complaints.

After seeing his dismal response, Escobar quickly stood in front of the captain, blocking his attempt to enter his cabin, and said, "Señor, do not forget whom it is that's addressing you; you would be wise not to ignore my complaint!"

Capitán Arconada looked at the man with restraint and kept himself from laughing. However, he replied, "I understand who I'm addressing, señor. What I'm not understanding is your complaint against my junior officers. I do not understand what they had done to offend you, but I'm sure that the matter can be quickly resolved with a simple apology."

Then Arconada added, "If I recall, you seemed to get along with the two of them splendidly at dinner the other night."

"No, Capitán, you do not understand," Eduardo complained. "This insult is not the first incident on your ship. I have seen expressions of disrespect among your ranks. I want you to know that I am not pleased with these reprehensible insolent stares toward myself, nor will I tolerate this matter any further, so I demand that something is done."

Capitán Arconada looked at him with disgust and simply asked, "What is it that you wish me to do, señor?"

The governor looked with raised eyebrows and said, "Any time I have witnessed such disrespectful attentions from lesser persons among my rank, I intend that they should be taught respect from those of higher authority. I believe twelve lashes across their backs would make them understand who they have smirked at and made a joke of, señor."

"Let me understand your meaning, Governor. You wish me to have my man flogged for simply laughing at a joke they were sharing? Could it be, señor, that you misunderstand their intent in this matter?"

"No, señor, I do not misunderstand the laughter at my expense. You would be wise to remember who it is addressing you. Now I was hoping you could take action in this matter and have these men flogged immediately. Let's see if they still wear smiles after the sting of the cat o' nine tails has danced across their backs."

Arconada, feeling angered, was reasonably upset after hearing the punishment brought upon his officers. Still, sadly, Escobar was the governor and in charge of the entire region, which gave him no recourse but to obey his wishes. After looking back at Escobar, he gave a customary bow, then replied, "I shall take care of this matter immediately, señor; you have my word."

"Thank you, Capitán. I regretfully have to command this sort of respect upon your vessel, but I'm sure that as this matter is handled quickly and efficiently, all else shall fall into place, and it should be a delightful voyage, señor."

Arconada did not respond; instead, he turned back to address the cabin boy, giving him orders to have Javier Pérez, the master-at-arms, brought to him at once. Without hesitation the young boy ran off, returning a few moments later accompanied by a seasoned-looking seaman in his late forties. His appearance gave the impression that he had seen many things. His many tattoos, a deep scar above his eyebrow, and the golden ring he wore in his left ear made one believe that he was a man not to agitate or cross paths.

After walking up to Capitán Arconada, the man saluted and came to attention. "What is it that you need, Capitán?"

"Señor Pérez, there is a matter involving Midshipman Adrián Salinas and his cousin, Emilio Fernández; both of these men are to be put in irons and brought to the gangway ladder. There, I want the crew assembled to witness the punishment for conduct unbecoming an officer."

That was all that was said; quickly, the master-at-arms disappeared to carry out the captain's orders.

Within the hour the entire crew stood to attention on the main deck. The sound of a drum was heard, pounding a rhythmic beat that was slow and steady. The two men that were accused were ceremonially brought forward as they read the charges brought against them. There was moaning and complaints from the crew as they watched their comrades' shirts being removed from them, leaving them both naked to the waist.

After removing the gangway ladder from its position near the railing, Adrián Salinas's wrists were tied fast with a lashing to the brass man-rope eyebolts, with his ankles to a small grating on the deck. In the meantime the boatswain produced the whip, a wooden handle about fifteen inches long, and a thick pack-cord that was twenty inches long, with the ends having shards of glass sewn into the cords not knotted. While standing his arms were stretched considerably above his head.

Capitán Arconada ordered the boatswain's mate to do his duty and not favor the man. Looking over at Escobar, he said aloud to give each man seven latches.

"Only seven?!" Escobar objected.

"You heard me, boatswain, do your duty!" came the stern reply from Capitán Arconada.

The boatswain's mate swung round and brought the "cats" down across Salinas's shoulders; the master-at-arms called out aloud, "One . . . Two . . ." and so on until

"Seven."

Then the captain said, "Stop. Take him down."

This judgment was repeated a second time with Emilio Fernández. Afterward, both men were taken away to be aided by the ship's doctor.

While the men were carried off with blood spilling down their backs, a smirk appeared upon Escobar's face, seeing the results of his simple complaint to the captain. He had been vindicated; now he enjoyed the savory taste of revenge. For him, it did not matter if these two men were laughing at his expense; no, what mattered most was that the crew trembled in fear at seeing him walk past—after all, he was the governor.

This unwarranted punishment of these two men sent an uproar among the men that could not be discounted upon the ship; the entire crew hated the governor because of it. Capitán Arconada quickly noticed the change in his crew and worried that perhaps he went too far by allowing this pompous ass to dictate to him what should happen to his staff. Yes, all his men went about their work duties as expected. But all wore expressionist stares and frowns, not lifting their eyes from the deck on which he stood.

However, the governor would stand each morning upon the deck, happily taking in the breath of salt air into his lungs, looking proud as a peacock upon his post, without regard for the painful disgrace he brought upon the two innocent sailors. Nevertheless, aboard the ship every seaman had a newfound hatred for the ostentatious passenger they wished to murder.

AFTER ABOUT A WEEK THEY finally reached Puerto de La Guaira. They soon heard a loud commotion approaching the ship when they docked at the pier. Deemed as a customary tradition in some circles, troops appeared in a steady marching of pounding boots upon the ceramic tiles. A large wooden coach was soon seen driven by eight white horses.

Dismounting the carriage, a plump man appeared, twisting his thick dark mustache and wearing a long, black wig, a long, buttoned brown jacket, opaque hosiery, and black shoes with high heels. He approached the governor.

After coming to a stop, the official bowed, removing his hat. After placing his hat back upon his head, he said, "Please let me introduce myself. My name is Felipe San Sebastian. I am the local magistrate here in Puerto de La Guaira. I'm the one who informed you of the capture of the two harlots and the fishermen that I hold in my jail."

"That is good news, magistrate," Escobar replied. "Tell me, what of Capitán Diego Espinosa?"

"The man is resting in a house owned by a widow not far from here. He poses no real threat of escaping; after all, the man cannot walk."

"Very well, I am pleased with your results, Felipe San Sebastian. Soon I shall have all my little birdies back in their cages." After patting the magistrate on his back, Escobar let out a devilish laugh and abruptly left with his new companion.

As the carriage left, followed closely by the military troops, Capitán Arconada and his men were glad to see Escobar depart. However, losing respect from his crew was a small price he had to pay to keep his command; he knew of the governor's reputation and what it meant to cross the man. Arconada recognized there was little choice in the matter but to follow orders that were entirely unreasonable and unwarranted. Still, having survived his encounter with the devil, he came away with his command and his life intact—both he felt grateful to have.

CHAPTER 15

ALL ABOARD THE *ABRAXAS* TURNED back toward the cannon fire. To their horror, they saw the British man-of-war, HMS *Defiance*, blasting their cannon fire directly at their ship, which had already received noticeable damage.

Elijah Stark shouted orders for everyone to get to their battle stations. The pirate crew assigned to fire the cannons scattered below decks. Shouts of cursing from the master gunner erupted. Pirates were tripping over one another to get to their designated stations to load their guns, knowing that their lives depended on giving a response to the British man-of-war that were attacking their pirate ship.

After seeing the anchor holding them fast, Captain Beaumont shouted out the order to raise the anchor. After hearing the captain screaming out the command, no less than twelve men immediately grabbed ahold of the oak beams, shoving them inside the capstan. Hurriedly, they strained at the mechanism, turning it around. Then they heard loud booms from down below their ship as the pirate crew sought to return fire upon the British.

More cannon fire erupted from the British ship as they came alongside and fired another salvo into the *Abraxas*. The pirate ship's cannon fire was useless as they could not directly aim their cannons into their enemy while struggling to bring up the heavy anchor.

Another barrage of cannon fire blasted into the *Abraxas*'s superstructure, ripping away its two mainsails. The mizzen mast was cut into two, tumbling down upon the deck. The mainmast had its upper sail blasted in half and toppled, hanging lifeless. Specially designed cannonballs welded together with a chain were intended for such a purpose, causing most of the damage to the sailing mast. However, with the right master gunner directing their cannons, there was little chance of surviving the attack.

Finally, the anchor was secured into place, including the horrid remains of the two crew members brought aboard the ship with their bodies ripped apart and their eyes looking like dark orbs, wide open, staring back. All who saw it became instantly sick to their stomachs.

Ignoring the men's remains before them, Beaumont had to concentrate on what was happening to his ship. In a desperate race to gain control of the battle, he ordered his navigator to turn back toward the cannon fire, maneuvering the *Abraxas* toward the British man-of-war. The navigator gripped the giant wheel to turn it over and over in a circular motion, guiding the massive ship to give their enemy a shot broadside.

The ship turned back around as quickly as it would, gradually gaining speed and hopefully achieving an advantage. Time was not a luxury they could afford; if there were any hope of surviving this attack, they had to act quickly or else everything would be lost.

Another salvo of cannon fire erupted from down below decks. Beaumont knew his master gunner, Monsieur Esmée Bouvier, was the one responsible for orchestrating their defenses. If there were a chance of escaping this nightmare, it would be due to the man's expert marksmanship as a master gunner. The man was the most excellent marksman he'd ever seen in action.

Still, the damage to his ship was mounting. Regrettably, Captain Beaumont had to take desperate actions to save her. Then he ordered Mr. Stark to discard the damaged sails overboard; they were slowing his ship. After looking over at the navigator, the one man controlling the vessel during the sea battle, Beaumont ordered him to maintain his course. Hopefully, they would intersect the British ship to fire their cannons into its haul, destroying their ability to inflict more damage.

IN THE MEANTIME ABOARD THE HMS *Defiance*, Captain Edmonton gave the orders to his navigator to stay his course. Their cannon fire was utterly destroying the hated pirate ship *Abraxas*. Each sounding blast into the insufferable pirates gave Edmonton a sense of relief, knowing that at last his prized enemy ship was soon to be his. He continuously gave orders to fire, not relenting until he saw them strike their colors and a white flag appeared off their stern castle.

If they sought to surrender, they would have to remove their pirate flag, the very one they proudly displayed.

"The black flag with the skull and crossbones," Edmonton yelled.

The master gunner, Gottfried James, took his job seriously as he again yelled out the command to reload the cannons on the port side. Although none of the pirate cannons fired at them had found their mark upon the *Defiance*, he knew that if the pirates were to get underway, they, too, could be impaired.

Aboard the *Defiance*, down below decks, each battle station comprised three to four men at a time. After firing their cannons, a man standing by would take a ram at the end of a stick and dip it into the water to ease the burning embers. A black powder charge was quickly loaded into each cannon. Next, a twelve-pound musket ball was dropped inside the hollow tubes. With the guns loaded, a silent uneasiness shrouded the small spaces while they waited for the master gunner to give the command to fire. They would only ignite the fuse to set the cannons ablaze upon his signal.

The *Defiance* was still maneuvering into position, to close within fifty yards of their prey. Suddenly, the master gunner lifted his hand. A moment later he yelled out the command to fire. So began the loud booms and thunderous roars of the rolls of cannons that were systematically ignited, sending out fireballs encapsulated with iron projectiles erupting out the end of the barrels.

Looking intently to see what damage was caused by their latest firing, Gottfried James stared out the wooden hatch as their cannonballs flew through the air, crashing into their enemy's ship, hitting it broadside. The damage caused was immediate; numerous cannons were thrown backward in disarray as heavy musket balls careened through the ship's hull, killing several pirates instantly. More and more fires erupted inside the *Abraxas* as their chances to return fire slowly dwindled along with their ability to wage war.

After looking back again at his men operating the guns, Gottfried James ordered them to reload their cannons for another firing. Once this task was performed, the men pulled hard upon the ropes to extend the barrels out the hatchways. Everyone watched and waited for the following command to fire but already, the racked *Abraxas* was slowly dismantling before their eyes. Several flames tore at the wood timbers beneath the decks as giant plumes of black smoke filled the air, with the sounds of men dying, screaming out in pain to be free.

Mr. Blackwood had armed the militia aboard the *Defiance* as they drifted closer to their enemy, readying the armed boarding party for a final battle. Each deckhand was supplied a musket and bayonets as they stood at attention awaiting orders as the two forces were about to clash.

Although the enemy tried their best to gain the upper hand by maneuvering their ship to fire their cannons, it was too little, too late. Instead, they had to contend with raging fires down below decks, besides the wounded they had to ignore. Captain Edmonton continued to gaze out his spyglass at the *Abraxas*, whose crew seemed confused, madly running about the ship. How fortunate it was to find them unaware of their approach. The imprudent reality was that they had never taken down their pirate flag—a straightforward evaluation of to whom the ship belonged, seeing the skull and crossbones flying off the transom. There had to be some distraction that kept the crew's curiosity. Still, it was a military advantage that he took to his favor.

Now drifting upon a collision course to board the enemy ship, a merchant mariner would occasionally fire his musket at any enemy that dared expose himself. Small attachments of soldiers stood by ready, along with the main deck's railing, ever observant to avoid being shot at by the cutthroat pirates. It was foolish to believe that these pirates were utterly disabled, not able to fight. Mr. Blackwood knew these pirates were ruthless murdering dogs; they would not surrender easily, fighting to the last man. The eventual outcome of their surrender would be a trip to the gallows, where they would hang. Death was the only ending of a pirate's life.

Unexpectedly, the master gunner, Gottfried James, surmised the need to fire a barrage of cannonballs again into the heart of their enemy; all cannons erupted beneath the main deck. With each salvo fired, the destruction caused by the iron balls was mounting.

Captain Edmonton observed the battle proceedings around him. Glancing over near the railing, he saw Mr. Blackwood with his saber in hand in front of the merchant mariner, standing ready to pounce upon the enemy ship to end these Iron Born Pirates.

The last barrage of cannon fire from the *Defiance* ripped apart the *Abraxas*'s mainsails, including a large part of the superstructure, leaving behind wooden fragments that littered the sea. The helpless *Abraxas* had fired her guns, but the *Defiance* was much too agile to sail back out of range for their assault to be effective. Nonetheless, the *Abraxas* quietly lumbered along with little sail to give her speed or chance of escape.

The time had come to take his prize. Edmonton ordered Mr. Cornwall, the ship's commander, to ready the mooring lines and the boarding party. Immediately, twelve sailors appeared upon the deck with hooks tied with long riggings in hand. Sadly, they were met with erratic gunfire, killing several men instantly.

Regardless, the mooring lines were thrown over; the two ships were soon drawn together, meeting side by side. Shouting erupted throughout each ship's decks as men readied to meet one another to the death.

Mr. Cornwall ordered the gangways shoved across the gap; however, just as they were in position, the pirates were the first to jump across to battle them for supremacy, using musket fire in a smoke-filled event. Men began falling dead into the water below; others came across wielding cutlasses and shouting curses. Some never reached the British ship and died aboard the *Abraxas*'s decks.

Maintaining their ranks, the British again reloaded their muskets as pirates began pouring onto their ship, killing several merchant mariners who hadn't had time to recharge their weapons. Man-to-man combat erupted aboard the *Defiance* quickly as death screams rose above the waterline.

Edmonton watched as Mr. Blackwood was engaged in swordplay with a certain pirate. The pirate was quickly outmaneuvered and fell dead as Blackwood's sword ran him through, outsmarted by the ship fencing champion. Then Mr. Blackwood ordered the merchant mariners across the gangways onto the pirate ship. These sailors, who usually acted in a reserved fashion, suddenly let out their battle cries as they ran across the planks under a barrage of musket fire, engaging some with muskets and others with their swords as the battle raged on to the death.

From his perch above decks, Edmonton saw what must've been the French captain battling with several British sailors. Unexpectedly, the pirate captain withdrew a musket from within his coat and shot one of the men in the head, where he fell dead. The other sailor continued fighting but soon lost the battle as the experienced French captain, well known for his sword abilities, thrust him through.

Anger engulfed Edmonton sorely as he saw his men dying. In response he ran from his post toward the main deck; he soon encountered a solitary pirate coming up from the other side. The man had swung his saber and jabbed at Edmonton several times in an ill fate of swordplay. However, the experienced British captain blocked the pirate's thrust, burying his sword deep into the man's chest, where he fell dead onto the coated red and blood-stained deck.

After running across the gangway onto the pirate ship, Edmonton soon engaged in swordplay with another pirate, whose experience and abilities at swordplay matched his own. The sword fight began by blocking one another's blows, then dodging back and forth when possible. This pirate fought vigorously as he endeavored to kill him, with countermoves never seen by Edmonton, whose vast experience at swordplay was barely able to keep him alive.

Edmonton suddenly felt the blade slice into his arm as the man was able to penetrate his defenses. Ignoring the pain, Edmonton continued fighting as the two steel swords cut through the air in a blurry image, instantly smashing into one another. Edmonton could dodge one rushing advance and swung around to stab the man through his rib cage. The bizarre look upon the man's face showed amazement that Edmonton's sword had found its mark, and he gritted his teeth in anger as the long steel penetrated his body. The dying man tried to speak as a trickle of blood suddenly leaked out the side of his mouth. Then the pirate unexpectedly dropped his sword; after grabbing ahold of Edmonton's blade, he tried to pull it free. After drawing his dagger loose from beneath his coat, Edmonton shoved the small knife into the man's throat, where he heard a gurgling sound as air penetrated his lungs.

After pulling his sword free from the man's body, Edmonton looked to where he last saw the pirate captain. There, he saw Mr. Blackwood engaged in swordplay with the noted pirate captain. Just as Edmonton hurried to get there, he was suddenly blocked from his approach by another pirate swinging his sword madly at him. In response Edmonton calmly took his pistol from his belt and fired it at the man's chest, penetrating his heart, then he, too, fell dead upon the deck.

With the battle raging and men dying all around, Edmonton advanced toward the ship's railing and saw one of his junior officers dead, lying in a pool of blood. Poor Jason Jones, a young freckle-faced recruit from South Hampton. A young man of considerable stature, he fought bravely and was able to kill his attacker, as evidenced by the headless corpse lying next to him.

Another set of muskets firing close by interrupted his thoughts. Edmonton searched the ship for the pirate captain and saw him standing over the dead body of Mr.

Blackwood, whom he had just cut through. Disturbed by the image, Edmonton felt himself lose all reluctance and ran toward the French captain with hatred in his heart. When they met one another in battle, it was determined to be a fight unto death.

After seeing Beaumont grab his wounded right arm, this advantage gave Edmonton instant gratification as he realized that Mr. Blackwood did his best at swordplay and injured his assailant in the process.

Looking up to see Edmonton coming at him with fire in his eyes, the pirate seemed dislodged, taken back somewhat. He quickly lifted his sword in defense just as Edmonton came crashing down upon him. Swiftly, engaging swords met and rang out a reverberated distinct sound.

Momentarily pushing off, the two men stood, staring at one another with vile hatred, knowing that there could only be one left alive.

Rapidly, Beaumont swung his sword in full swiping motion to cut Edmonton's head off his shoulders, but he was blocked as Edmonton could fight off the attack. The two swords began rattling back and forth as they dug deep into their sharp cutting edges.

Edmonton struck hard in an attempt to strike at the French pirate but was countered and blocked. Unexpectedly, Beaumont withdrew his pistol from his coat and quickly fired his gun; the musket ball struck Edmonton in his bicep, ripping out a piece of the right arm. Ignoring the pain, Edmonton fought on using his left arm and battled with a newfound resolve that even surprised the pirate.

After several minutes of battling back and forth, Beaumont's abilities began to wane, and his strength diminished because of the blood loss from his previous wound. Each captain fought as hard as they could, moving in various positions to gain an advantage over the weakness of the other but to no avail. It seemed that neither man was willing to submit or forfeit their position.

Around them the pirate ship was shrouded with an eerie silence as the screaming sounds of men fighting among each other quieted; the battle was coming to an end. Both captains could not turn away or be allowed to see who was victorious in this battle to the death as they continued fighting.

Beaumont again advanced in another strike against Edmonton, who defended himself from the attack and shot past the pirate to slice into the man's leg; he stumbled only briefly and recovered, standing up, as blood poured out his wound. Seeing the change in his opponent's ability to fight, Edmonton stood there staring at the man.

As they paused to look about, something caught the attention of both men. Regrettably, there was a sudden change in personnel aboard the *Abraxas*, as all the men now staring back at them were wearing the British uniform with muskets pointing at the French captain.

Edmonton stood back, lowering his sword, and yelled out, "Captain Beaumont, you pirate dog, now is the time of your surrender. Throw down your sword; I promise any of your men alive shall be treated fairly."

Beaumont smiled crookedly and replied, "What makes you so sure, señor, that you're victorious?"

Edmonton stood back, laughed aloud, and said, "Look about you, man. Can you not see my men holding their rifles, ready to fire upon you, sir? I demand you throw down your sword; perhaps I shall allow you to live."

"I shall never surrender," came Beaumont's short reply.

"So be it," Edmonton replied. "This day you shall die; afterward, I shall have your head upon a pike proudly displayed over the mainsail."

Having said this, Edmonton advanced with a strength unknown, even to him. He lifted his sword and made it come crashing down in a single blow upon Beaumont with such fierceness that he knocked the sword from the pirate's hand. With his prey at the end of his sword, Edmonton again ordered the man to surrender and give up his fight.

Beaumont's answer was suddenly clear to everyone. He withdrew a pistol from his belt and lifted it toward Edmonton's head, cocking the trigger. After seeing the gun displayed, Edmonton moved at lightning speed to stab his sword deep into the pirate captain and quickly withdrew it back again in a single slice. At las, the end had come for one of the most famous and feared captains of all the Caribbean. After dropping his musket, Beaumont grabbed his chest as blood began to trickle out of his mouth. With his dying breath, he cursed Edmonton and all his men.

No honor is to be found at the end of a pirate's life. The killing and raping of the innocent were now forgotten memories of a dead man. The things he did in life amounting to a fearsome reputation as a bloodthirsty pirate were God's alone to judge.

After seeing the death of his enemy, Edmonton felt relief as the pirate's facial expression suddenly glazed over; his body collapsed upon the deck with a thud. Now standing there among his crew all around him, his senses returned; he studied the carnage of death that littered the deck.

The sickening smell of blood that leaked from the corpses of men filled the air with a prudent aroma. Edmonton surveyed the battle zone all around him; there, he saw the remaining British forces standing about, looking exhausted, knowing they had won the day alone.

Suddenly, a small attachment of soldiers appeared, leading some prisoners from down below—eleven pirates who were still alive that had not surrendered. One of his junior officers leading the party brought the men nearby, came to attention, and saluted Captain Edmonton, announcing that these were the last survivors of the pirate ship *Abraxas*.

"Very well, Mr. Jones, take them away."

Jones saluted and then escorted them down into the ship's interior to be set in irons. Among them was Mr. Stark, who looked upon his dead captain, knowing his fate would match his captain's.

Edmonton, feeling relief that they won the battle but also sadness about losing Mr. Blackwood, a loss that was hard to take. After returning his sword to his sheath, he slowly returned to his ship and ordered all the British sailors' bodies to be carried back to the HMS *Defiance* for proper burial.

However, the notable pirate ship *Abraxas* was to be set ablaze, including her dead crew who littered her decks. All of them would burn to Hell, thus a fitting end to their wretched lives.

The mooring lines were soon cut, allowing the ship to drift helplessly upon the open water. A powder charge was set down in the hull, and its fuse soon lit. A short time later a loud explosion was heard, sending massive timbers several hundred feet in the air as the remaining superstructure was blown apart.

Fire quickly engulfed the remaining parts of the ship that sent out a black plume of smoke into the Caribbean blue sky, which could be seen for many miles and served as a message to anyone who took a life of piracy that this would be their eventual end.

The carnage of the battle that was fought here was soon a distant memory. As the crew aboard the *Defiance* watched the pirate ship sinking, the pirates' bodies that were either blown apart or thrown into the murky water changed the ocean's vibrant blue color to a dark red. The pirates' proud black flag, the skull and crossbones that hung off the transom of their ship, dipped beneath the waves, not to be seen again.

CHAPTER 16

Standing high atop a mountainous peak, Bram was gazing outwardly toward the last known location of the dreaded ship *Abraxas*. The view of the surrounding coastline was visible for many miles out to sea. All morning long he stood on his perch, hoping that he didn't see the *Abraxas* appear.

Bram soon became bored with being on the lookout for pirate ships as the hours slowly passed with nothing to see except the driving the waves that crashed on the rocky shore. The sun felt hot and unrelenting. Half a day had passed, and there was still no sign of the *Abraxas*. He had told the others that he was staying at his post until he was relieved, keeping a wary eye out for trouble. Mauricio had promised to replace him sometime before the evening meal. Bram waited patiently as the hours trickled past with nothing else to do except sit upon a rock.

Sometime before the noon hour, from his lookout, off in the distance, Bram suddenly saw what appeared to be black smoke rising off the ocean surface. At first it was barely visible to the naked eye, but in time it became more pronounced, growing larger in form and intensity. He could hardly believe his eyes, not sure what it meant precisely, but he knew that he had to tell the others; perhaps they could make sense of it.

After running down the path he had discovered as a means to reach the highest mountain peak, he sprinted through the overgrowth of the jungle foliage and rocky outcroppings. Running too fast, he slipped, bruising his knee. Ignoring the pain, he soon hobbled into camp and excitedly yelled, "I saw black smoke. Black smoke is off in the distance from the ocean's surface."

Tjerk, fiddling with a trap to catch animals, shouted, "What did you say about black smoke?"

"I saw black smoke, which must mean that something large was set ablaze," Bram shouted excitedly.

Thomas heard the news and asked, "How far away was it?"

Bram answered, "I'm not sure; you'll have to come up to the rocky point to see yourselves."

Mauricio, who at the time was lying down under a shade tree, sat up, excited to hear the news. Then he became somewhat concerned and said aloud, "I hope it is not those pirates aboard the *Abraxas* destroying another ship! What chance would we have if they found us? I can promise you it will not be pleasant."

Thomas spoke to Bram, "Show us without delay. Hopefully, it's not a trick of the eyes!"

Everyone in the small party then followed Bram back up the rugged peak. It took time to make the journey, mainly due to Bram's sore knee and Thomas's lack of mobility. When they reached the area that Bram used as a lookout, the black plume was more visible than ever. Each man, staring at the dark object, came away with an interpretation of what it could mean. Tjerk pointed out that it was obviously a ship burning due to a piracy attack, or perhaps it was a sea battle fought to the death in which the loser was now burning in flames.

Thomas agreed and said, "Yes, for that much smoke to be seen at such a great distance away could only mean that something large was ablaze."

At this point no one knew whether it was friend or foe.

Mauricio stepped forward, gazing at the sight, and said, "I can tell you if it's the *Abraxas* burning. I only know of a few ships in this world that could destroy such a powerful adversary."

"Blessed be the British man-of-war!" Thomas quickly shouted, then added, "Yes, perhaps, a British man-of-war, but as late I've only known of two such powerful ships in these waters, the HMS *Defiance* and the

HMS *Dolphin*; both are a model fighting force to be reckoned with."

Tjerk surmised the situation and said, "We must decide on what to do next; assuredly, we cannot stay on this island forever! Yes, eating coconuts and bananas and the occasional fish patties is a delicacy I enjoy. However, I would not want to do it for the rest of my days."

"Nor I," Thomas yelled.

"We must find out who is victorious in that battle, but we have no way of knowing. I'm afraid, gentlemen, that we have to be on our guard from this moment on," Tjerk explained.

Mauricio spoke up. "Yes, be on our guard, that is correct, for we have no weapons to speak of, only that small pistol Tjerk is carrying with him, which is sadly, all we have to defend ourselves. Our choice to leave the *Abraxas* in such a hurry could cost our lives."

Thomas laughed and said, "Cost us our lives? Honestly, I've barely escaped death at the hands of the French captain aboard the *Abraxas*! I'm grateful to be alive. What does it matter now? We've been on borrowed time ever since we left that appalling ship."

Bram unexpectedly said, "Alive to fight another day."

Tjerk looked upon the companions and said, "If there was a way that we could make it to Porto la Cabello, I know that we could find refuge there. It's commonplace for Dutch smugglers. If we could reach their shores, it would be a place where we could feel safe. Sadly, it's so far away from here; I don't even know how far it could be."

Thomas turned back and stared at everyone, asking the obvious question, "Well, what shall we do then? It seems that our choices are limited, either die on this island or at the hands of those damned pirates. I don't see any other option! Although if it is the British man-of-war destroying the *Abraxas*, there would be no need to worry about our lives; we all would be safe."

Tjerk countered, "Yes, the decision is before us. We have to consider all our options."

Unexpectedly, Bram said, "What if I take the boat back into the water to act as a decoy? If an unknown ship approaches, I could say I alone survived from a sinking passenger ship."

Mauricio replied, "That wouldn't work! What if the pirates aboard the *Abraxas* capture you? Are you that confident, my young friend, to believe that you could convince the ruthless Captain Beaumont that none of us survived, that you alone made it to safety?"

Bram looked at Mauricio confidently and responded, "I know a secret that none of you know about. Back aboard the *Abraxas*, Captain Beaumont was once a father of a young boy named Peter. This Peter died of smallpox at the young age of twelve."

"That's interesting; I would have never guessed," Tjerk announced.

"The captain had shared this with me when he was drunk and crying over the memory of the young lad. Ever since that day, the man has treated me with nothing but kindness! I'm not fearful of any harm coming from the man."

Everyone suggested ideas in the small council that had formed, but none seemed feasible. Bram's plan was the most noteworthy and brave. Bram was well-liked and highly respected among the elders of the little party. He had already shown the courage that spoke of his integrity as a young man.

With little choices left to them, everyone agreed to allow Bram to take the boat out into the open water, ever conscious of his whereabouts, never to travel too far away from the sight of land, equipped with a sail onboard the boat. During daylight hours it would be visible for many miles out into the open ocean; besides this, he was given a small torch to light his way at night. This rescue attempt was what they rested all their hopes on.

As the small boat slowly paddled out to sea, they all prayed for Bram's abilities to persuade Captain Beaumont, but truth be told, everyone knew that was nothing more than a fantasy. You don't become a pirate captain over a ship by being foolhardy or naïve; instead, you become a ruthless, untrusting cutthroat in the end.

With enough food and water to last him the fortnight, Bram set off the following day, paddling out to sea toward the last known location he'd seen the smoke. He did not know what to expect upon meeting Captain Beaumont again, but as an added caution, the group of men took to decorating the boat with blood from a wild boar they captured, making it look like a fight had broken out and they had killed one another over some buried treasure Mauricio had known about—being an Iron Born Pirate—leaving only Bram as the only survivor.

Rowing the boat against the current was a struggle that Bram contended with for several hours until at last he had to rest. With his small arms burning from the exertion, he sat there panting for breath. Nevertheless, the island they took as refuge soon began to fade from view. Bram experienced the most breathtaking sunset he had ever seen on the first day's evening.

Alone with no one to talk to, he imagined how his life would've been different if he had stayed home in Holland and become a blacksmith like his father. Instead, he decided to become a sailor, much like his uncle Lucas before him. When the chance came to board a merchant ship sailing to New Guinea, he was more than eager to take the job as a cabin boy.

Being a cabin boy was hard work, but he enjoyed it; he had already traveled around the known world, where he saw things that were only matched by his imagination, with many ports and world markets that provided a wonderland of opportunities. His captain, Ulrik De Vries, was a patient man, willing to teach him skills to become a seaman if it wasn't for those accursed pirates that killed his captain and all others, except for those they could put to service including himself and the good doctor, Tjerk Hiddes.

He looked into the sunset, praying to God that the pirates who killed his crewmates were the ones ablaze, dying in pain, only second to Hell's self-burning flames of fire. There was no love lost for those murdering bastards.

As the sun slowly disappeared into the horizon, there was little to do but lay down to gaze up at the stars, which appeared alive against the dark background. He saw so many stars that he couldn't conceive the beginning of nor the end. Looking up, he marveled at the sight, closed his eyes, and soon fell asleep.

IT WAS STILL DARK WHEN he awoke sometime later; he realized he had forgotten to light the signal torch. Now the benefit of such effort would last only a short time before the sun arose, and the morning light was already appearing just above the horizon. At that time he decided to desist from doing it altogether.

In the light of day, he gazed back at the last known location of the island that he had left behind and could no longer see its silhouette. He guessed he had traveled at least twenty miles from his last location. Perhaps he could still be seen from the high perch on the volcanic peak, but if not, then his comrades had to keep their faith that he would not fail them in his rescue attempt.

It was discussed before he left the previous morning that if he were taken back aboard the *Abraxas*, Tjerk and the others would be on their own to find a way off the island, indeed, now that they were presumed to be dead. Nonetheless, after three days he was to return to the island, and they would devise another plan that would not involve capture by the pirates.

A few passing hours later and feeling hungry, he went about eating a banana and drinking from a coconut that he stored fresh water inside. Slowly, he took a few sips, knowing it would need to last him for the next few days.

The little boat remained afloat, often rocked by the passing waves. Bram, surmising the boat's location, estimated he had only traveled about thirty miles from the island. With no sight of land, he again grabbed ahold of oars to paddle. He rowed for several hours until his aching arms could not roll another minute longer, deciding it was best to take a break.

By guessing the sun's position in the blue sky, it seemed right to him that it was close to noonday. With little to eat to give him nourishment, he felt exhausted. Again, taking another sip of water from the coconut, he reached over to a small sack where they stored some food—taking out a banana and a mango. He quickly devoured them. Gratefully, the sugar-filled fruit brought needed nourishment; it revived him somewhat.

The thought of rowing another mile was depressing, but instead, he was content to take in the warmth from the blazing sun. No longer could he see any sign of smoke coming from the burning ship; in his estimation that could only mean the ship had succumbed to its damages and plunged beneath the waves.

What ship could it be? He had no idea, nor could he guess, but still, he hung on to the hope that it was those cutthroat pirates that had been destroyed. Now he was having second thoughts about the decision to volunteer on a mission that could cost his life. Still, he wanted to look brave among the others. His bravery was never questioned, nor should it have been, because he fought hard against the pirates only to become their prisoner like the others.

Barely holding a sword, he had run to attack the first pirate that appeared. However, the man laughed at him to scorn his feeble attempt at swordplay, knocking the sword from his hand, striking him upon his jaw, and knocking him unconscious. He was the scariest man he'd ever seen. The pirate wore a long black beard with eyes of fire; the man looked huge. Acting like a fool, he screamed a war cry, attacking him headlong.

Thinking about it now, Bram realized he was no match for the man, but in all good conscience, he felt that he could not stand by to watch his shipmates be murdered; he wanted to do something and feel proud in his attempt.

Sitting there, he was somewhat bored, with an unknown future continually eating at him. Time, however, can wash away the worry and doubt. Peace soon shrouded him as he accepted whatever fate God had in store for him. His family were devoted believers in God and hard work. Remembering his family, it was then that he thought of his younger sister, Fenni. It had been many years since he had been home. At least five that he could recollect. The last time he was home, the butcher's son had proposed to her. Indeed, they would have many children running about, with one on the way.

He then laughed aloud, thinking to himself, *Perhaps the man could not stand Fenni complaining, deciding instead to live in the barn*. Although she was the only girl in the family, his other brothers were there to keep her company and examine every suitor that appeared, each one to be approved by every male family member.

His loving mother, Nora, he missed the most. It was the same for all his fellow merchantmen. In the passing years aboard his ship, the *Batavia*, he would listen to stories from the men whom he sailed; they all had something in common: their mothers, some sadly gone and departed, while others sat at home waiting for their return. Sadness then blanketed him as he realized for the first time that most mothers would never know what happened to their beloved sons, who had died a horrible death at the end of a sword from those pirate scum.

Perhaps he would never see his mother again. Today would mark the day of his death. So young to die. Whatever his fate would involve, he didn't see it happening here, floating alone in a boat.

Gripping the oars, he began to paddle further away from the island's safety. Toward dusk, at the end of another day, he became hungry and ate a few bananas. Only a few were left inside his sack; he knew he would have to save what was left for the following days.

Finishing the last of his water, he drank the coconut dry. Tossing it overboard, he saw the remaining two coconuts tucked neatly beneath the adjoining bench.

The sun dipped behind some clouds and soon disappeared, fading from view. The end of another day drew to a close. Bram gazed upward at the stars. The moon slowly rose and took its place among the celestial bodies in the night sky. Its light, partly hidden from the passing cloud cover, would occasionally illuminate the iridescent colors of the water that shone about him. He could make out small images of fish beneath him that flashed suddenly atop the water's surface, which looked primarily dark, absent of life. Again, he looked up at the vastness of space to watch the twinkling stars. He felt utterly alone, with no one to talk to or express his feelings.

Floating upon the water, he allowed the ocean current to carry him further than he ever expected. He felt tired, unable to row any longer. He was warned not to lose sight of the island, but it didn't seem to matter any longer. Still, remembering the last location of the smoke cloud, he turned to gaze back in that general direction, but something caught his eye; what he saw surprised him.

Squinting his eyes, he looked intently into the darkness, catching a glimpse of small light flickering a considerable distance away. It burned bright enough that he could see it from his position. Instantly, being familiar with sailing ships, he knew that a lantern mounted high above the ship's forecastle near the bow was the only plausible answer.

"What ship?" He had no idea, but little did he expect his plan to come to fruition. There it was, traveling in his direction; it was, indeed, a ship. Its high mast soon appeared through the darkness, along with the white sails reflecting off the dim moonlight.

Bram's heart quickly raced within his chest; he became excited and yet nervous, not knowing what to expect. He was given a piece of flint, which he could use to ignite a small torch as a signal just in case such an event did occur.

Undeniably, coming in his direction was a ship of some unknown origin. He knew he had to decide whether to ignite the signal flare or let the vessel pass.

He quickly searched out the small boat and found the torch near the bow; the piece of flint he was to use was also quickly discovered in the darkness. Now taking the torch, he sat it over the side of the boat and tied it in place. Then he remembered Thomas's words, "Take this small amount of gunpowder to lay it upon the torch. Strike the flint with your knife; the sparks will ignite the gunpowder. Soon the torch will be burning brightly, but one must be careful not to set your boat on fire as the fire will appear quickly."

Bram took the piece of flint in his hand and was about to strike the flint when he remembered he had to add the gunpowder. Quickly looking about the boat, he couldn't find it anywhere. Growing upset, Bram cursed his decision to volunteer. Now even if he wanted to there was no way to ignite the torch; it was foolish even to attempt such a rescue.

He sat on the bench, thought of the small powder pouch, and wondered where he had left it. There was very little from a pistol that the doctor gave him as his way of putting up a fight against the pirates. He then remembered how persistent Mauricio was about keeping his powder dry and even gave him a small leather pouch to store it in. *That small leather pouch, damn it,* he cursed. *It still has to be in my pants pocket.*

Quickly, he felt about his person to discover the powder where he last put it. After removing it, he took a long breath and opened it, untying the leather tie that held it closed. Then, after spreading some black powder atop the torch, he tied the pouch again and stored it in his pants.

Looking out to sea at the visible ship, which was still some distance away, the realization of both rescue and capture frightened and delighted him.

He said aloud, "Bram, you fool, what have you gotten yourself into?!"

Chapter 17

MIGUEL SAT SILENTLY IN HIS prison cell for days, refusing to speak to anyone, including his daughter. He had an inkling that his life was ending shortly. Not wanting to be disturbed, he sought peaceful solitude to contemplate his remaining hours of life.

One evening during mealtime he heard a loud commotion outside the prison walls as he sat enjoying his bowl of stew. Heavy boots were pounding upon the stone walkway, with trumpets blowing and drums beating. Such fanfares were usually meant for someone of high importance. Miguel realized at last that the governor had arrived in Puerto de La Guaira.

Nothing to do but wait for the inevitable, Miguel quietly sat in the corner of his cell, finishing his stew. However, Abella and Mariana, upon hearing the pounding drums, arose to their feet to look out the small iron bars of their cell. After seeing the massive military force approaching, Mariana excitedly wondered who had arrived with such importance and fanfare.

After turning away, seemingly disappointed, Abella said aloud, "Never mind; it's that pig, Governor Escobar."

Mariana returned to her seat without any further response, knowing their judge had arrived. She also had heard stories of this Escobar's torture chamber, including the stories of the poor souls who entered his dungeon never to leave alive. Soon the torturous misery would begin.

At that time she felt a deep shame while she contemplated her past, which filled Mariana's soul to overflowing. She wanted more out of life than becoming a harlot working on her back. She was haunted by a regret never experienced. She had always dreamed of having a family—a husband who loved her and children by the dozen—but it wasn't to be. For her, a secret desire for an ordinary life was something that she kept hidden.

Within the hour they heard the entrance to the jail squeak open as soldiers advanced inside. Then, suddenly, dozens of them poured into the small area where they were housed and stood at attention, facing one another.

Amid the army Escobar, the governor, appeared with his new friend, Felipe San Sebastian, the local magistrate, pompously staring at the prisoners inside their cells. A broad smile appeared on his face, knowing that he had finally captured his prey. Escobar looked at him sourly and walked over to Miguel.

"Señor, finally you're all in my grasp; I will soon learn what you've done with Pablo, my trusted servant."

Not frightened by the little man's appearance, Miguel clutched the iron bars tightly; he stared back at Escobar and calmly said, "Pablo, I'm afraid to say, Señor, is no longer with us; you see, he is sleeping with the fishes. I know this because I'm the one who sent him there!"

Escobar's face suddenly changed from a smirk to a frown. "You admit you killed Pablo?"

Miguel softly said, "Yes, I am the one who killed your soldier, Pablo. Spare my daughter, señor, and her friend Mariana. They had nothing to do with this; it was a choice I made before God, and now I must live with my decision. It is his blood that I cannot wash from my hands."

"Oh, yes, you are correct; you shall hang, señor."

Then, turning to Felipe, the city's magistrate, Escobar demanded that Miguel be taken to the gallows at once, without a need for a trial.

"You have heard the man admit to his crime; now he shall pay for it with his life!"

A screaming "No!" was heard from the other cell as Abella screamed for mercy for her father, saying that it wasn't her father that killed Pablo, but she alone killed that pig. "It was my idea!" she pleaded.

Ignoring her pleas for Miguel's life to be spared, Escobar turned back to Felipe, the magistrate, demanding a response. Without hesitation Felipe turned to his prison guards, ordering them to bring Miguel to the gallows to hang for his crime.

"The man must be punished for his murderous ways."

Abella shouted, "Please, let him see a priest, one last time, to confess his sins; I beg you."

Felipe turned to Escobar and said, "Yes, it's true that he has confessed his crime, and he shall die because of it. But it shall take some time to arrange his execution. While we search out a henchman for the task, please allow the prisoner a brief time to confess to the priest."

Escobar seemed upset by the delay but finally agreed.

"Very well, send for a priest."

Then, turning to Miguel, Escobar said, "Hurry, señor, make your confessions for soon you shall have an appointment with God that I would not want you to miss."

Laughing abruptly, Escobar ordered everyone out of the room and said, "You have a task to perform this day; see to it quickly."

Soldiers then escorted the governor and the magistrate out of the tiny prison cell to enjoy a meal, now that their official business was concluded.

Knowing that the end was near and that there was no way of escaping this punishment, Abella cried out to her father to forgive her for all the terrible things she had done to him in the past and how she brought him to the point in which it eventually cost him his life. Her sad tears fell upon the iron bars, trickling down onto the tile floor.

Miguel looked across the way at Abella, who wept bitterly, and said, "Daughter, I have always loved you. I decided to kill the soldier, Pablo, to keep you safe. I wish I had spared his life but saw no way out of it. It's my decision alone. Now I must make my peace with God."

Abella grew silent, except for her sniffling; she simply nodded in response. Mariana, standing by, reached out to hold her friend, consoling her as best as possible. The realization of what was to happen was too much for Abella, whose strength vanished. After collapsing to the floor, she gripped the bars hatefully.

Now knowing that her father was about to die, there was so little time left; she wanted to tell him how sorry she was for living the life of a prostitute. But she chose to allow him his time of peace by himself, to reflect upon the end of his life.

Within the hour the priest arrived to meet with Miguel, who received absolution for his sins. Everything from that point on happened much too quickly, as the minutes of his life were speedily pouring out. When a small group of guards appeared, Miguel was escorted from the prison cell to the waiting gallows.

Abella watched the criminal proceedings from her small window. Sadly, her father was led up the gallows. There to greet him was a hangman's noose. The governor demanded his pound of flesh and was seated above the scaffold in full view of the anxious crowd. They all waited anxiously to see the murderer hang for his crimes—the murderer, not the loving father that no one knew of except the one daughter that loved him most.

Miguel accepted his fate, hoping for a quick end of his life, not to suffer or feel pain. He bravely walked up to the wooden steps to the platform that overlooked the crowd of people below. He spoke no cursing words nor made any threats; he gave no resistance as his hands were tied behind his back. Then the noose was laid around his neck and tightened slightly. With the black hood having been placed over his head, no longer was he able to see his accusers; only the darkness obstructed his view.

He then heard a man's voice announcing the crimes he was charged with, then eerie silence. Heavy footsteps were moving past him; a squeaky device was moving into position. Unexpectedly, Miguel felt weightless as the floor beneath him collapsed, and the weight of his body careened downward in one quick motion. Then a jabbing pain when his neck snapped in two, causing instant death. His hanging body jerked about as a result of the nerves being severed. Then his life was gone.

After seeing her father executed, Abella gasped in disbelief, knowing that her loving father had vanished and would never return. She stared at the theatrical spectacle of nobles sitting in their places of honor. An unknown rage filled her entire being, something horrifying, and she fought against the bars that held her captive, wanting to get at the cruel authorities that killed her father.

"Listen to me, Escobar, and magistrate Felipe San Sebastian," she screamed. "Your time will come to hang on the gallows; I pray I'm there to see you both beg for your lives. You murdered my father, you cowardly sons of bitches!"

Resounding laughter was heard erupting from the place where the nobles sat. Then, after hearing their laughter, other townspeople also began laughing. After some time with nothing left to see, the crowds of people slowly disbursed to return to their houses.

Miguel's body continued to hang lifelessly from the rope around his neck. The squeaking fibers strained at his weight as the gentle breeze passed, turning him in every direction. The sight was more than Abella could stand; she sat down on the small stool and buried her face in her hands, bawling.

The following day the prison doors opened and in walked Escobar, looking much like an egoist in bloom, exposing his bright-colored plumage. He stopped in front of the iron bars and stared directly inside, seeing Abella and Mariana comforting one another from the memory of her father's death upon the gallows.

"No, it is not I who murdered the innocent; your father admitted that he murdered Pablo, my trusted captain of the royal guards. He was truly the innocent one in this game of life. Sadly, he died at your father's hands," Escobar answered.

"We all must die, señor; hopefully, you will suffer when you meet your end!" Abella screamed.

"No, you're wrong. You and your friend are the ones who will suffer before you beg me for a quick death. You see, that is what I wanted to tell you this morning! You and your whore friend next to you are sailing back with me to Trinidad. I shall torture you until you beg me to end your miserable lives."

"We shall ask nothing of you, señor, including our lives!" Mariana shouted.

"That remains to be seen. I have been busy since you escaped, prying information from the whores who used to work for you. I'm sad to say that none of them survived their ordeal and died much too quickly."

"You monster!" Abella screamed, crying.

"It seems that no one knew of your whereabouts, no matter what device I used to torture them to get at the truth. Now it is your turn, Abella Sanchez!"

"Fine, but know this—I will fight you up to my dying breath, you bastard."

"Oh, yes, you will die, this I promise. But I have just one question to ask you before I go: Why not bring me the British uniform as requested? You would have had your reward and been off living your whorish ways. Why not just give it to me as I asked?" Escobar questioned.

"I do not trust you, señor. Besides, why did you need it? Why on earth did it mean so much to you? Was it worth the lives it has cost everyone?"

"You foolish women. What you don't understand is the diplomacy required when dealing with British affairs and how it could affect my standing with Spain. So tell me what you did with the uniform. We tried to find it back at your bordello. We even tore down the building looking for it, but we still couldn't find it."

"Well, señor, I'm happy to tell you that the British captain now has that ridiculous uniform; no doubt he will want an answer from you on what you did with the man it belongs. I wish they bombard your beloved city to the ground and destroy your house with you inside it," Abella shouted.

"This is very unfortunate, Madam. Sadly, no matter, you will not live long enough to see your desire come true."

Then Escobar turned to walk away. However, he had barely taken a step when Abella suddenly spit a large wad of saliva that flew through the air, landing on the governor's face. She laughed aloud as the man whom she hated most in her life was taken by surprise. He took out a silk handkerchief to wipe the liquid clean from his face.

After looking back at her with a wicked grin, he said. "I'm going to enjoy seeing you suffer." Then he left the dungeon.

Mariana suddenly said, "Abella, do you think it wise to anger the man who holds our lives in his hands?"

"You do not understand that it's not that pig who holds my life in his hands but God himself. It is He whom I trust, not that coward."

SEVERAL HOURS LATER A MAN appeared carrying a basket of food. He quickly slid the small basket between the iron bars and said, "Quickly, eat your fill before the other guard returns."

Without hesitation Mariana knelt to quickly grab what she could of the basket and hid the food beneath the straw. After returning the woven basket to the man, she returned to her seat.

Abella looked at the stranger and said, "Whom shall we thank for this precious gift?"

The man cautiously looked about, then replied, "I was sent here by your father's cousin, Ramón Cardenas, the doctor in Caracas."

Then a commotion was heard outside the prison cell window. Glancing outside, Abella saw two men cutting down her father's body; with them was the priest who took her father's confession, Father Basilio Alvarez. He had his Bible in hand, saying a prayer as Miguel's corpse was laid into a cart driven by a donkey.

Instantly, Abella lost her appetite and sat back down on her small stool, weeping.

Mariana stood silently at the bars of their cell, allowing her friend time to grieve for her loss. A moment later she spoke to the stranger.

"Have you heard any news on when they were to set sail for Trinidad?"

The man again looked behind him for any sign of the guard's return and whispered, "Listen to me, come closer; I have some news to tell you both."

Quickly, Mariana appeared at the bars, motioning for Abella to join her. Then, turning to the man, she said, "What is it? Tell us quickly."

"My name is Pablo Salinas; my wife and I have agreed to help you escape. We owe the doctor much; he saved our young daughter, Anita, from death."

"How do you propose we do this?" Mariana asked.

"The doctor has devised a plan of escape for you two women; there isn't much time left. You set sail in two days," the stranger answered.

After regaining her composure at hearing the news, Abella said, "Tell us what we must do."

"Tomorrow night when the guards have dinner at the local cantina my wife will serve them wine that will be drugged. The two of them will sleep like babies within the hour."

"Very nice," Mariana whispered.

"It's a concoction that the good doctor had put together. At that time I will simply walk into the prison to unlock your cell doors. After all, I am a locksmith by trade and will have no difficulty opening the iron gate. Once free, I'll escort you to a waiting boat to take you both to Jamaica."

"Jamaica? That was where we initially intended to escape, but it never came to fruition," Abella announced.

"Well, it is our plan so be ready tomorrow night. Don't forget."

Then the man went down a dark passage in the shadows of the prison. They heard some squeaky doors open and close; a moment later he was gone.

Mariana looked at her friend and remarked, "Abella, it looks as if we're going to be saved, isn't it wonderful?"

Abella looked out the small window, out to the courtyard where her father was executed, and said, "I will not put my faith in any plans of men whose sweet dreams of success quickly sour in your mouth. No, I prefer to watch to see where this leads us; if I find myself on the deck of a ship bound for Jamaica, I will be amazed. But if I'm caught and hanged from a rope, this will come as no surprise."

With nothing else to say, Abella returned to her small stool, looking destitute, having lost everything at this time in her life. Nothing else could bring her happiness, especially after seeing her father executed. No, even the possibility of being set free would not bring joy to her.

CHAPTER 18

THE SHIP HMS *DEFIANCE* SUDDENLY released its heavy anchor into the crystal water bay. Afterward, it fired a single cannon to announce their presence to the men on the island. Captain Edmonton ordered a small boat to pick up the survivors. Bram had drawn out a detailed map of where they would find Thomas and his friends

When they rescued Bram that evening, Edmonton had questioned the young lad in detail concerning whom they would find on the island. To his dismay, when he heard the name Thomas Banish, he came away with mixed emotions. However, with Mr. Blackwood dead from the sword fight against the French pirate Lafayette Beaumont, the man's services would become helpful when it came to making repairs that needed fixing.

After the battle with the pirates, they did receive some damage to their ship, most notably to their main decks and gun ports, plus their mainsails were cut completely through, with giant gaping holes through the fabric.

Edmonton watched from above his perch as the small detachment of soldiers rowed away toward the shore of the mysterious island. They had been directed by Bram, the young castaway who pointed upward to a cave as the place to begin their search.

Looking below at the buzz of activity around the ship, Edmonton watched a group of workers call to one another, asking for a replacement beam of oak for the boat's repairs. This brief stop to the uninhabited island would allow them time to make some needed repairs and nothing else; they would soon sail back toward Port Royal.

The eleven pirates, buccaneers who bent the knee rather than face certain death, would have to be brought to justice for their piracy. Their trial, no doubt, would prove them all to be murdering dogs for the lives they lived.

Unexpectedly, Mr. Ericson, the lead carpenter, appeared. After coming to a halt, he saluted.

"Yes, what is it, Mr. Ericson?" the captain questioned.

"Captain, sir, we don't have enough oak beams to finish the repairs needed for the gun ports and bow. It seems that the pirates were good shots, sir."

"Well, do what you can until we arrive at Port Royal. I wish to be underway as soon as possible; we sit here defenseless, with pirates roaming about."

"Very well, sir." He saluted, then returned to his work.

Edmonton returned to his cabin to plot a new course for Port Royal. From this moment on he wished not to be disturbed so instructed the cabin boy not to allow anyone to bother him further.

Bram led the small group of men back on the shore to where he last left his party. They climbed up the steep hillside where they saw a black column of smoke rising from a nearby fire. When they arrived at the camp, Thomas Banish greeted them. The Dutch doctor, Tjerk Hiddes, was busy cleaning fish, and Mauricio stood opposite the small fire, looking nervous.

Suddenly, the sergeant-at-arms ordered his men to raise their muskets at Mauricio, the known Iron Born Pirate, to place him under arrest. Thomas, however, argued against the incarceration, but his request was ignored. Tjerk stood by, surprised by the show of force and unsure what to do.

The sergeant-at-arms looked at Thomas and ordered him to remain calm; otherwise, he, too, would be placed under arrest. This whole matter seemed ridiculous—having survived the ordeal with the pirates only to be put in chains as a criminal by his fellow sailors.

Regardless, the small group left the camp and boarded the small boat, leaving the island's security behind.

As the small party rowed back to the *Defiance,* Mauricio was the only one fearful of his future. Being a pirate aboard a British man-of-war, he had no future, just a painful death on the gallows.

When Thomas arrived at the ship, he quickly ran to meet up with the captain, with whom he had some choice words to share, ignoring the shipmates that called out to him as he hurried past. Thomas wanted to argue Mauricio's case before the captain. It was evident that Edmonton had pried information from young Bram and no doubt discovered that Mauricio was an Iron Born.

When Thomas reached the captain's quarters, he pounded on the door and yelled out Edmonton's name, wanting to enter.

Edmonton gave a short response, "Enter," knowing the brashness that Thomas possessed and how he would stand at that door pounding upon it for hours until at last he agreed to see him.

When Thomas walked inside, he saw Edmonton seated at his desk, writing something in his ship's log.

"I need to talk to you at once, Captain Edmonton. Your decision to place in chains the very man I owe my life is something I must argue. For now, I'm willing to set aside our differences. No, sir, the fact remains that you have arrested the wrong man."

"What you don't understand, Mr. Banish, is that you have befriended a pirate! An enemy of the British crown. It is you who must answer for these charges. When I discovered your whereabouts from young Bram, I was restrained at placing you in irons. It was my first intention to place you in irons along with your pirate friend, sir, so do not forget who you address here this day!"

"I shall not forget, sir, who I address, nor the fact that there is no love lost between us, but this is another matter altogether. I'm not here to discuss our differences."

Thomas's demeanor changed; he began acting more rational. "Captain Edmonton, I beg you to show mercy upon this matter; please, I beg you to release the man named Mauricio. As I explained, I owe him much; if it weren't for him, I would still be hanging from the yardarm of the pirate ship *Abraxas*."

"Mr. Banish, I'm glad to report that the pirate ship *Abraxas* has been sent to the bottom of the sea, blazing with Hell's fire. All are dead except eleven pirates, which I have in irons. You can rest assured that the French captain Beaumont is dead as well. I saw fit to perform the task, entrusting no other; I have slain that pirate dog."

Thomas stood quietly, then responded, "I'm glad to hear the news, sir. Truly, upon hearing this news, it brings me great joy knowing that Beaumont wanted my hide. But, sir, again, I beg you to let Mauricio free for he has done no wrong in my eyes nor any crime against the crown."

Edmonton looked sternly at Thomas and said, "I made my decision; it's final. Your young pirate friend shall join his pirate brothers down below decks and go on trial for piracy when we reach Port Royal."

Thomas, upset by the news, could do nothing. For now, his options were limited. However, hopeful that he could appear as a witness for the defense, perhaps there was still time to save Mauricio's life. He saluted the captain and left his quarters feeling distraught.

Two days had gone by; finally, they departed the island, having concluded what repairs were needed to set sail on the way to Port Royal. There was always an extra portion of food brought to Mauricio, more than any other pirate held down in the hold. Thomas had not forgotten the friendship that the two shared. He always tried to make Mauricio comfortable as he sat in his cage, held in irons. However, Thomas felt assured that he could present a good defense for his friend, telling him not to worry.

Having two doctors aboard the HMS *Defiance* meant there was no shortage of medical aid to the crew. As they sailed toward Port Royal, Tjerk befriended the ship's doctor, a Mr. Allen; both doctors soon became good friends and shared their medical knowledge. Bram also found work, helping the cabin boy, Mr. Scott, who attended to the captain's needs aboard the ship.

One day while Tjerk was speaking with Mauricio, Thomas appeared and sat across an oak timber that formed the ship's hull. He looked on as Tjerk checked Mauricio's wound for any infection. Gratefully, his injury seemed to be healing well.

While Thomas was sitting there one of the prisoners, a large man chained together with the other pirates, yelled out, "I wonder if ye were able to get that smell of piss out of your nostrils."

Looking back into the dark space, Thomas saw his nemesis, Mr. Stark, seated at the back of the rows of pirates, chained to a large wooden beam with iron anklets and an iron collar around his neck.

Quickly standing to his feet, Thomas began walking forward but was suddenly halted by Tjerk, who grabbed his arm.

"Leave the man alone, Thomas. He'll soon be hanging at the end of a rope for his crimes. He has nothing left him in this life except to bear his scornful hatred toward your British kind."

Thomas looked upon the group, knowing of their impending doom, and said, "I shall be there to testify at your trial; if you're found guilty, then you know the punishment for piracy—hanging! The British crown's stance on piracy is it will not be tolerated in any circumstance."

The men then turned back to look at Mr. Stark as if he could make a difference. In return he simply shook his head, saying nothing else.

Mauricio then spoke aloud, "I'm assuming that would include me as well, for I bear the mark of the Blood Pirates; it's obvious to me that no matter what good I've done, the court will be biased to find me guilty so I, too, will hang from the gallows."

Tjerk, wanting to be optimistic, said, "We do not know this for sure; we just have to put our faith in God above."

Mauricio laughed aloud and said, "You sound like my mother!"

Thomas also laughed, enjoying the chuckle. When the doctor finished Mauricio's examination, he excused himself and went to the other group of prisoners to treat their elements. Thomas stayed behind to talk with Mauricio further, wanting to calm his nerves and not have him worry over his situation.

Mauricio looked at Thomas with concern and said, "I only have one favor to ask you; if it is possible, could you find my sister, Mariana, back in Trinidad and please implore her to return to our mother and quit her wicked ways?"

Thomas quickly answered, "Yes, of course, you need not worry, my friend. Believe me, I will do my best to exonerate you of any wrongful charges and plead your case to the highest court."

"I appreciate that Thomas, but we must be honest. Look where I'm at; I don't see much hope for me now, señor."

"I'm not giving up the fight; neither should you," Thomas announced.

"You must realize that I'm where I'm at because of my choices, for I have taken innocent lives for gold, silver, and precious jewels. I've done things that I should not. No, I'm here because I deserve to be."

"No matter, I still plan on defending you and your actions."

Then Thomas grabbed his friend's shoulder, gripping it tightly, and walked away. After walking up the stairway to the upper deck and out into the sunlight, he tried not to worry about his friend. However, he understood that if Mauricio were found guilty, he would hang like the other pirates.

THE NEXT DAY THOMAS REPORTED to the captain on the ship's condition and supplies, including how much gunpowder and provisions they had in their stores. Edmonton took down his recommendations, reasoning that they would not have enough supplies to last them to Port Royal.

Thomas then suggested traveling to Puerto Cabello, where they could resupply the ship and drop off Tjerk Hiddes with young Bram. According to the doctor, it was a place known to have Dutch smugglers. Perhaps they could obtain passage on a sailing ship bound for their homeland. Edmonton agreed, informing the navigator of the new course.

That evening over dinner Thomas asked the captain to recount the heroic deeds. After making his rounds aboard the ship, Thomas asked crew members about the battle they fought with the pirate ship *Abraxas*. He heard about the damage sustained in that battle and how their captain singlehandedly defeated the French pirate captain. It made the most exciting conversation; Edmonton himself left out no details.

By the time dessert rolled around, all the naval staff seating at the table had their own stories to share. Most notable was Mr. Cornwall, the ship's commander, recounting how they struggled to get across the gangplanks. Jason Jones tossed a grenade at the pirates aboard the *Abraxas*, killing several of them at once and giving his life to save his shipmates.

Edmonton announced that they had lost several good men that day. He seemed saddened by the loss of Mr. Blackwood, the boatswain mate who replaced Thomas.

"The man was a noble sailor and a true spirit that one could not find any guile." Then he admitted that he found writing to his family about his death challenging.

At that moment the officers sitting around the table saw a different side of the man they served. The usual staunch appearance and by-the-book captain, whose orders gave little leniency, seemed humbled as if he had lost a close friend.

This exposure to humility gave Thomas an opportunity that was never offered. He wanted to speak candidly with the man.

"Captain, I'd like to ask you for the truth; what is it you have against me, sir?"

The officers left the dining table, and they were alone.

Edmonton finished his glass of wine and stood to his feet, staring out the glass window into the darkness of the roaring sea. He turned back and said, "Sir, it is your relaxed attitude that I cannot stomach. Aboard this ship there must be regiment and discipline; there is no allowance for relaxation or halfhearted attitude in one's duties. No, when you are captain you must command your crew by the book, regardless of your feelings; there is no room for softness or friendships aboard the ship."

"Captain, I had always carried out your orders to the letter, sir, even when I disagreed with them. Still, I had a job; I did it to the best of my abilities!"

"Did you, sir? Did you do it to the best of your abilities? I believe that you wanted to be liked by all the men under your command; you, sir, allowed certain lawbreakers to have certain freedoms that caused division between the crew and myself."

"Honestly, I've never thought of it that way, sir. I thought you were harsh with judgments, unable to bend or break. I hadn't realized I was putting a wedge between you and the men," Thomas admitted.

"It is getting late; I feel the need to rest. So if you will excuse me, Mr. Banish, I must retire for the evening. I still have letters to write of the men who died in battle."

"Yes, Captain, I understand. Many I have known since I entered the naval academy."

"All the families back home want to know if their loved ones were brave until the end. I'm glad to report that every man fought bravely at their post."

"Of this, I have no doubt," Thomas answered.

"However, there is something that vexes me the most. How was the enemy ship unaware of our approach? Somehow being caught off guard, they had little recourse given them. I cannot understand, sir, that they had their anchor down, as though peaceably at rest in the open sea."

"That is strange, indeed."

"When I questioned several pirates, I discovered that their captain Beaumont was delivering punishment to two of his men. These men had helped you, and this young Mauricio, the Iron Born Pirate, escaped."

"I'm not sure what to say," Thomas answered.

"You see, inadvertently, without knowing it, you helped us defeat the *Abraxas* by your noble escapes."

Thomas was unsure how to respond so he just

saluted the man, thanked him for a pleasant evening, and then left the cabin.

THE FOLLOWING DAY THOMAS AGAIN walked down into the ship's bowels to check on his friend, regardless of the captain's feelings toward Mauricio. When Thomas arrived, he ordered the guard over the prisoners to unshackle his friend from his heavy chains.

Mauricio, ever so grateful, thanked him for his kindness as he rubbed both his sore ankles that looked reddish after being irritated. Thomas still had his duties to perform aboard the ship; he could only stay a short time. Thomas promised again that when Mauricio went to trial, he would speak on his behalf. Regrettably, Thomas had to leave to get back to his duties. Staring at the jailer, he ordered him to give Mauricio another hour before putting the heavy shackles back on. Thomas walked away from the small dungeon, feeling frustrated in seeing his friend in chains.

After he returned to his cabin, Thomas again reviewed the ship's log to review what stores remained on board the vessel. Mr. Blackwood had kept a detailed report of all the supplies, but since the skirmish with the French pirates, the collections seemed to be growing thin. He looked over the manifest containing the ship's stores, deciding to recheck the supplies himself.

When he arrived below decks, he recounted all the musket balls and gunpowder kegs. The food stores were dangerously low as well; inspecting how many barrels of grog were left, he saw only two.

That day he discussed the ship's repairs with the carpenter working on the forecastle's railing. The man complained his supplies of oak timbers were running out, having barely enough to repair the broken gun ports. However, along the hull were large holes where cannonballs burst through the side of the boat, leaving gaping holes.

Later that afternoon three men appeared on the main deck carrying large white sails, which were repaired with patches in the fabric. The men screamed to one another as they climbed up to the mainmast to stretch the fabric over the topgallant sail, including the topsail, then they refastened the lines, holding them in place. Thomas watched as they climbed past the railing to return the sails to the area.

The mizzen topgallant sail and the spanker sail received minor damage, but they had to be repaired again as some holes were visible. The main topgallant yardarm was broken, hanging loosely with all its rigging. This job seemed too large for only these three men so Thomas ordered five more sailors to climb up the mainsail to help them with their job.

Repairing all the sails took the entire day, but by the night watch all the sails had been restored; afterward, the sizable white fabric filled by a passing breeze pushed them along. During dinner Thomas ordered an extra glass of grog for each sailor for service—a job well done.

At the officer's dining table Thomas discussed the shortage of supplies with the captain, who noted his remarks and informed him that he would record the matter in the ship's log. The harshness of the man again seemed softened as they discussed their lives back home in Bristol, England.

Thomas never knew that the captain had a wife still waiting for his return, including three children, the eldest entering the naval academy that fall. Of all things, the captain suddenly withdrew a small portrait of his family with his three children—two boys and a girl—back home, allowing the picture to be passed around the table.

To everyone's surprise, the captain talked of retirement, saying he had been away from home for too long. Every time he returned it was as if he was a stranger, and none of his children recognized him.

Many of the men could relate, remembering their wives back home. Harper Brixworth, the second lieutenant, raised his glass and proposed a toast to the families and friends they left behind.

Hearty cheers all around as the men finished their drinks, slamming their glasses down upon the table.

The captain ceremoniously ordered a second round to be brought immediately.

THE FOLLOWING DAY THOMAS AROSE early, watching the sunrise appear over the body of water; the clouds tried their best to hide the brilliant color of the sun in their attempt to shadow its bright light. The ship seemed to lumber along on its course to Puerto Cabello. According to what the captain had said, they should reach their destination in two days.

After walking over to the navigator, a man who generally spoke little, he unexpectedly shared stories with Thomas of the battle with the pirates, including Mr. Blackwood's death—how it infuriated the captain. After seeing the man dead, Edmonton ran headlong at the French pirate as the two captains met in a clash of swordplay, one against the other. Thomas didn't realize the mastery of swordplay displayed by his commander, having been taught back in England. According to the navigator, he fought brilliantly. The result: Captain Beaumont fell to his accursed death.

After returning to his duties, Thomas suddenly heard shouts from the man in the crow's nest.

"Sails approaching from the southeast."

The captain was immediately informed. Moments later he appeared at the bow of the ship holding his spyglass. He was quickly joined by Thomas and the other staff of officers who could barely see the objects with their naked eyes.

Edmonton turned to Thomas and said, "It looks like a two-masted schooner, probably a merchant ship, but perhaps we should alert the men to their battle stations. What say you, man?"

Thomas grabbed the spyglass from the captain, stared through it intensely, and then said, "Yes, it looks like it's French. I can see the ensign flying off the transom. Still, you're right; we should alert the men, just in case it's a disguise."

"Order the men to their battle stations," the captain announced.

Then, turning to the navigator, he said, "Maintain your course, man."

The man steering the ship grabbed ahold of the wooden wheel to grip it tightly.

Suddenly, there was a beehive of activity aboard the ship as everyone ran to their battle stations, opened the hatchways, and loaded the cannons to fire.

Then the crow's nest lookout yelled, "There be another set of sails behind the first!"

"Two ships, Mr. Banish," the captain said, looking back at Thomas. "I understand it to mean one thing: These two ships are off our port bow."

Thomas remembered Mauricio telling him that it was a tactic of the Iron Born Pirates when they traveled these waters, not in one ship but two. He quickly said, "Mauricio might have some information regarding this scenario, sir."

"Bring this Mauricio to me at once," the captain ordered.

Thomas hurried down below decks to where the pirates were imprisoned and shouted to the jailer, "Release Mauricio at once; the captain wishes to speak to him."

Without hesitation the jailer grabbed ahold of his key ring and fumbled with the rusty lock, holding the small cage closed. Soon the lock fell open, and without hesitation the jailer stepped inside the small jail, releasing Mauricio from the heavy chains. Afterward, both men appeared at the bow.

Edmonton stood gazing through the spyglass and said, "I realize it's a known tactic of your pirate brood to sail these waters with two ships, not one, right?"

Mauricio replied, "Yes, plainly, it is as you say, señor, a common practice, thereby guaranteeing victory for the Iron Born."

"Then we shall give a stern answer to these cutthroats," the captain said plainly. Turning to Thomas, he said, "Looks like a fine day for the men to prove themselves in battle again."

Addressing Mauricio, the captain asked him, "Where does your alliance lie? Is it with these bloodthirsty pirates or do you fight with us? You only have a short time to decide before God, sir. If you do not pledge allegiance to the crown, I shall end your life where you stand."

Mauricio considered the captain's words carefully.

His choices were limited. What would that say of his character if he chose to change his alliance with his pirate brothers before the battle began? What response could he give except the truth, even if it cost him his life? No, he had taken an oath to become an Iron Born Pirate.

Acknowledgments

I want to thank my family, who has contributed to creating this book. I appreciate hearing their suggestions and comments.

Apart from my family, others participated in this book's development through stories they shared with me.

Thank you again.

***

Other Books by Timothy Patrick Means

The Bishops' Sacrifice Series
 (prequel to The Bishops' Resolve Series)
The Demon Shadow
The Family Curse
The Guardian Alliance

The Sterling Chronicles
Dear Someone
The Pirates' Blood Oath

The Bishops' Resolve Series
The Bishops' Struggle

About the Author

Timothy Patrick Means was raised on the sunny beaches of Southern California. As a young boy, his love of pirates began while spending summers swimming and playing in the ocean without care.

After learning that becoming a pirate was not a viable career in the late 20th century, he landed a job in Aerospace, working for McDonnell Douglas. He worked there on military aircraft and, most exciting of all, rockets! He worked on all types of space hardware, including the space station, Space Shuttle, and the Delta rocket.

Timothy is a father to four children and two stepchildren, and a grandfather to fourteen, giving away his heart to all. He has always loved writing and has written in many genres, letting his imaginations soar.

He has published several books and has more in the works. The first three books in *The Bishops' Sacrifice Series* are available on Amazon and other book websites. *The Sterling Chronicles*, currently available through Amazon Vella, further explores the adventures of the mystery's psychic detective. Timothy plans to add more books regularly to his growing list of published works.

Learn more about Timothy and his latest works at:
Timothypatrickmeans.com
Facebook.com/tmaddog38